Falling for the Cowgirl

Books by Jody Hedlund

Colorado Cowboys

A Cowboy for Keeps
The Heart of a Cowboy
To Tame a Cowboy
Falling for the Cowgirl

The Preacher's Bride
The Doctor's Lady
Unending Devotion
A Noble Groom
Rebellious Heart
Captured by Love

Beacons of Hope

Out of the Storm: A Beacons of Hope Novella
Love Unexpected
Hearts Made Whole
Undaunted Hope

Orphan Train

An Awakened Heart: An Orphan Train Novella
With You Always
Together Forever
Searching for You

The Bride Ships

A Reluctant Bride
The Runaway Bride
A Bride of Convenience

FALLING FOR THE COWGIRL

JODY HEDLUND

BETHANYHOUSE
a division of Baker Publishing Group
Minneapolis, Minnesota

© 2022 by Jody Hedlund

Published by Bethany House Publishers
11400 Hampshire Avenue South
Minneapolis, Minnesota 55438
www.bethanyhouse.com

Bethany House Publishers is a division of
Baker Publishing Group, Grand Rapids, Michigan

Printed in the United States of America

Library of Congress Cataloging-in-Publication Data
Names: Hedlund, Jody, author.
Title: Falling for the cowgirl / Jody Hedlund.
Description: Minneapolis, Minnesota : Bethany House Publishers, a division of
    Baker Publishing Group, [2022] | Series: Colorado cowboys ; 4
Identifiers: LCCN 2022015494 | ISBN 9780764236426 (paperback) | ISBN
    9780764240843 (casebound) | ISBN 9781493439065 (ebook)
Subjects: LCGFT: Novels.
Classification: LCC PS3608.E333 F35 2022 | DDC 813/.6—dc23

LC record available at https://lccn.loc.gov/2022015494

Scripture quotations are from the King James Version of the Bible.

Cover design by Kirk DouPonce, DogEared Design

Author is represented by Natasha Kern Literary Agency.

Baker Publishing Group publications use paper produced from sustainable forestry practices and post-consumer waste whenever possible.

22 23 24 25 26 27 28   7 6 5 4 3 2 1

The steps of a good man are ordered by the LORD: and he delighteth in his way. Though he fall, he shall not be utterly cast down: for the LORD upholdeth him with his hand.

Psalm 37:23–24

CHAPTER

1

Ivy McQuaid was gonna win the roping contest. She could feel the victory in her blood.

She flicked her wrist just enough to keep the loop whirling over her head, and she pressed her thighs against her galloping horse, maintaining the perfect pace and distance from the steer.

"C'mon," she whispered. With everything lined up, she cast the rope, aiming in front of the steer's head.

As the lasso soared through the air and landed around the horns, she dug in her heels, leaned back, and held on with all her might while pulling the slack. The rope tightened around the steer's horns even as she wrapped the excess around the pommel in an expert dally. The rope angled across the creature's right side, dragging up its hip. In the same motion, she turned the steer's head, throwing it off-balance.

She could sense the beast going down and dismounted from her horse, landing at a run that brought her to the steer. She grabbed one of the front legs and slipped a hooey knot over it. Then, with practiced skill, she strung the front leg to the two back, circling the rope enough to keep the creature from getting loose.

She hopped up and raised both hands to signal she was done.

The crowd on the outside of the corral fence let out a whole lot of whooping at her record time.

A thrill pulsed through her. Nothing beat the sound of winning. Of course, it'd be better if she could hear the sound of winning while dressed as a woman instead of as a man. But something was better than nothing.

She tried not to grin and give away her disguise. Instead, she shrugged off the praise and sauntered a few steps from the steer like all the cheering didn't matter. That's what a real man would do. And that's what she needed to do now—stay in character as Buster Bliss, the expert roper.

She had to keep up the charade for as long as she could, at least until she had enough for the down payment on the parcel of land Landry Steele was selling south of Fairplay. With today's winnings, she'd be closer to having what she needed. But only a mite.

Her face itched beneath the crusty charcoal she'd smeared over her skin to imitate scruffy facial hair. She'd tightly pinned up her long dark brown hair beneath her battered hat. And she'd wrapped strips of linen around her chest to flatten her womanly figure. While nothing could conceal her curves completely, the baggy flannel shirt and vest helped. So did the trousers and men's boots. So far she'd fooled everyone into thinking she was a skinny runt of a man.

The big, round spectacles she wore made her appear scholarly and only added to the good-natured teasing the cowhands gave her—as Buster Bliss.

As the hooting and hollering came to an end, she tipped the brim of her man's hat in thanks before she returned to the steer. Only then did she allow herself a smile. She'd done it again. And the honest-to-goodness truth was that she loved every single second of the cattle roping and would've competed without any prize money.

She knelt and jerked the rope free from the steer's horns before releasing the binding from its legs. The creature hefted itself up with a bellow. Before it raced off, she slapped its hide affectionately, letting it know of her appreciation for the fun.

Coiling her rope around her arm, she cast her sights to the sun making its way toward the western range. Looked like she'd have time for the last—and best—event before she needed to start home.

Folks all thought Buster Bliss came up from Denver over the Kenosha Pass on the weekends to participate in the cowhand competitions. While friendly contests had always existed in some form on the local ranches, the gatherings were growing in popularity and size, so it wasn't unusual nowadays for fellas to travel from outside of the area to join in, especially as the prize money increased.

Her cover worked well, given that Buster always had to depart early enough in the evenings to travel for a spell. The leaving helped her avoid questions about why she didn't want to go with everyone else to the saloons after the contests were over. It was already hard to keep her cover for the few hours she competed. She'd never be able to last well into the night.

"Bliss!" At the shout of her name from Mack Custer, Elkhorn Ranch foreman, the organizer of the Sunday-afternoon competition, she pivoted as casually as she could while she kept wrapping her rope.

Instead of looking her way, the foreman was clasping hands in greeting with someone else—a man with a strong, lean outline and a determined set to his shoulders. For several heartbeats, Ivy could only stare, trying to make sense of the familiar form.

It couldn't be. . . .

The fella shifted enough that she got a full view of his profile—a chiseled jaw covered in a layer of stubble, firm lips, and light brown hair peeking out from underneath his hat.

Her pulse began to race unsteadily. She didn't have to see him head-on to know he was Jericho Bliss, her girlish infatuation.

As though sensing her attention, he glanced her way.

She spun and faced the opposite direction. Holy Saint Peter. What was Jericho Bliss doing back in South Park?

She hadn't heard a peep from him since the night he'd ridden away with Dylan nearly two years ago. At the time Jericho had been doing her and her brothers a big favor by helping Dylan steer clear of the danger he'd been in from Bat and his gang for the gambling debt he'd owed them. Like everyone else, she'd been grateful to Jericho for saving Dylan's life.

Eventually Dylan had written, letting them know he was fine and had steady work. He hadn't told them where he was or what he was doing. And he hadn't said anything about

Jericho either. They'd guessed Dylan hadn't wanted to give too much away in case Bat and his gang got wind of his letter and decided to come after him.

Ivy had waited impatiently for another letter, for more news, for anything from Dylan. She'd told herself she was just concerned about her brother and wanted assurance he was okay. But deep down, she couldn't deny she'd wanted information about Jericho too.

For a long while, she hadn't been able to resign herself to the fact that he'd walked out of her life, that he hadn't wanted her. She'd clung to the hope that maybe, once he was gone, he'd realize how much he missed her and would return to tell her he couldn't live without her.

But as the weeks had passed into months and the months into years, the hard truth had taken up residence and crowded out any hope that was left—Jericho had never cared about her and wasn't coming back.

"We got Roman-style riding next," Mack Custer said to Jericho. "Saved the hardest for last. Wanna join in for old time's sake?"

Jericho was silent, and she was tempted to turn around and gawk at him.

"Winner gets a whole dollar."

If Jericho raced, what if he ended up beside her? She hadn't changed all that much during his absence. With her luck, he'd recognize her and blab her identity.

As his silence stretched on, her muscles tensed.

"Thanks for the offer." Jericho's voice was low and cautious. "Maybe next time."

She didn't wait around for him to say anything else. And she sure as heaven wasn't waiting for someone to question why she and Jericho shared the same last name. When she'd picked the alias, it'd been the only surname she'd been able to think of quick-like. Clearly she should've tried harder to find a different one.

Now it was time to hightail it on home. As much as she wanted an extra dollar to add to her winnings, she couldn't risk the exposure.

She made her way across the corral toward the barn entrance, hoping to disappear inside before any of the fellas noticed she was gone. Unfortunately, one of the Elkhorn Ranch cowhands saw her coming and slapped her on the back so hard she almost winced. "You nailed it out there, Buster!"

"Yep." She lowered her pitch, trying to make herself sound like a man.

"Got my bets placed on you for the next event too." The cowhand strode alongside her.

Another of the fellas fell into step. "You aimin' to ride with saddles or without?"

One thing was for blamed sure. She wasn't about to get away from the competition unnoticed. Every fella around was itching to watch her race. And why shouldn't she stay? Jericho had no right to come strolling back into South Park and prevent her from earning more money for her new ranch.

Stiffening her shoulders, she veered toward the horses already waiting for the contestants. Six horses meant only three riders. She'd have no trouble winning the contest this time. Maybe she oughta make things fair-like and ride bareback.

"Let's take them off." She eyed the horses, the most docile Elkhorn Ranch had. "Might as well give everyone the show they paid to see."

Her declaration brought a few more whoops.

When she'd hatched her plan to disguise herself as a man, she hadn't realized it'd be so hard. But she hadn't had much choice, not after she'd been banned from entering the competitions as a woman.

The first time she'd tried, everyone had laughed at her. No one had given her the time of day, even though most folk for miles around knew she'd been working with cattle since she'd moved to Colorado when she was twelve.

Fact was, after years of perfecting her cattle roping, she was a heap better than the majority of men. This past spring during branding time, the Healing Springs' foreman had made her the main roper, giving her the job of heeling the calves and dragging them to the iron men. She rode steady, had perfect timing, and could judge distance.

But when it came to the competitions, her skills hadn't mattered a lick. The organizers wouldn't allow her to participate. Not until she'd come riding in as Buster Bliss. Then they'd been more than happy to let a scrawny man like Buster take part, thinking he'd be easy to beat.

Over the past month, she'd shown them Buster wasn't as soft and fluffy as a goose-feather pillow. Buster had some gumption and grit. And he didn't give up easily.

In no time, she was ready to ride with her pair of horses at one end of the open range next to the other two contestants and their horses. The finish line was near the main barn, where the spectators had congregated.

As she situated her boots on the backs of her mounts and adjusted the reins of both, she couldn't keep from scanning the crowds. She didn't care where Jericho was or what he was doing. She really didn't. That wasn't why she was searching for his lean frame. Nope, she was only looking so she knew where not to focus later.

When she didn't catch sight of his stiff, proud shoulders or his handsome face, she released a breath. See, she had nothing to fear. Jericho had already left. That's because he was an expert at leaving.

At the crack of a pistol from the side of the field, she shook the reins and started her horses. Riding while standing up and straddling two horses wasn't an easy feat. Not many could do it. During the Roman-style racing the previous Sunday over at Bear Creek Ranch, one of the men had fallen and broken his shoulder and arm. He'd been real lucky he hadn't cracked open his head with the way he'd landed.

Yep. This race was one of the most dangerous events. But that's why she liked it. She thrived on danger. And the earnings were decent.

Between the fees for the contestants and the charges to the spectators, the winners of each contest always left with a prize. Even if it wasn't grand, at least it was something. The real money was made in the betting. Something she didn't do. Ever. Not after all the trouble Dylan had gotten himself into as a result of gambling.

The horses trotted forward, not too fast or too slow. She used a few paces to get her balance and crouch into the rhythm of the up-and-down sway of first one horse and then the other. The jolting was challenging. But she'd learned that the more she relaxed into the movement, the easier it was.

She kept abreast of the other two riders who clutched at their reins and strained to hold their horses close enough together that the straddling wouldn't get uncomfortable.

As the halfway point neared, she snapped the reins and

clucked to the horses. Time to speed things up and give the crowd the show they were hoping for. The horses took her cue and lengthened their strides. But with the increase in speed, one of the mares veered from the other.

She jerked on the reins to keep the horse in line. But it only continued to pull away. Her boot began to slip. And although she grasped the leather straps as tightly as she could, she was gonna have to let go before she fell and crashed.

CHAPTER

2

Jericho Bliss pushed away from the barn and straightened, his muscles tensing. The little fellow at the front was losing his position on the left flank. In a matter of seconds, the horses would be too far apart for him to race. And he was destined for a terrible tumble, one that would put him in the direct path of the contenders behind him. Not only would he be trampled, but he'd possibly cause the other two riders to lose their footholds too.

Jericho gauged the distance between himself and the approaching disaster. He didn't have time to intervene, not with the onlookers blocking his way. All he could do was watch with a churning gut.

Why had the man in front decided to go bareback? Without the saddle, he had less traction.

Jericho shook his head. The man was an idiot.

The crowd seemed to be holding a collective breath as the fellow fumbled and lost his footing. For several seconds, he rode with one leg hanging in the air.

Jericho cringed and waited for the fall.

Somehow, the man hung on to the reins from the runaway mount and began wrapping them around his wrist, tightening the slack between himself and the uncooperative horse. He had amazing control, drawing in the steady mare, bringing her closer to the other horse.

With a daring that defied death, the man planted his boot back into position and shifted in such a way that the runaway horse was able to read an unspoken request to do his bidding. It calmed and aligned with the other horse, so that within seconds the rider was firmly in place straddling the two.

The crowd let out a cheer.

At the sound, the man flicked his reins and urged the horses even faster.

More whistles and encouraging shouts filled the air.

Jericho released a pent-up breath but couldn't release the tension in his muscles. The fellow was a daring idiot.

As he crossed the finish line, the accolades rose to a deafening level. Only then did the scrap of a man let go of the left horse and shift himself with ease onto the other one. Nimbly, he lowered himself first to a sitting position before he swung both legs over and hopped down even as the horse continued galloping.

The move was effortless. And it reminded him of the way Ivy had practiced and perfected dismounting during their months of trekking west together. He, Dylan, and Ivy had all been just kids and had invented fun ways to pass the time, including trick riding and dismounting.

His chest pinched at the remembrance of those carefree days. What he wouldn't give to have just a fraction of that untroubled life back.

A beefy hand clamped on his shoulder, followed by the sour, sweaty odor of Mack Custer. "Think you could've done better, old man?"

Jericho shrugged and tried to loosen the knot inside. "Probably."

Custer laughed, his rounded middle wobbling beneath a too-tight shirt that outlined the dark sweat spots under his arms and on his chest. "Ain't nobody beat Buster Bliss yet."

Bliss? Jericho returned his attention to the short, slim man.

"You know him?" Custer homed in on the fellow too. "He kin of yours or something?"

"I don't have any relatives left." Aside from his dad. But no one out in the West knew about Elijah Bliss, and it was better if things stayed that way.

Buster Bliss trotted to the other two contestants and shook their hands. "Well, Buster might be puny," Custer continued, "but he sure does bring in the crowds."

And the money.

Custer had always been a gambler, even when Jericho had been the foreman of Elkhorn Ranch. Jericho wouldn't have chosen the man to replace him, but the boss had given Custer the job anyway, even though Jericho had recommended several others.

Buster Bliss finished shaking hands with his competitors. Then he tipped his hat toward the crowd before ambling toward the barn.

Jericho narrowed his eyes on the fellow, taking in the patched trousers with frayed hems. The rear end hung over his frame, clearly too big. His boots were clunky and his shirt baggy, almost as if he were playing dress-up in someone else's clothes.

The brim of his hat shadowed his face, large spectacles shielded his eyes, and a dusty layer of charcoal coated his skin. Was he trying to hide himself, make himself appear older and more manly?

If so, he'd done a terrible job. There was no concealing the youthful, delicate lines of his face. How old was he? Sixteen? Maybe seventeen? No doubt the kid had been teased for looking so feminine.

"Where's this Buster Bliss from?" Jericho asked.

"Denver." Custer stuffed his hands into his pockets and jangled the silver dollars he'd already collected. "A schoolteacher. Been comin' up here on the weekends to compete."

Jericho nodded and kept his expression from revealing anything—something he'd always been good at, just like his dad. The kid wasn't a schoolteacher. That was obvious. He was too young to have gone to teacher's training. And he wasn't from Denver. That was obvious too. A fellow like him wouldn't have the means to ride up into the high country every weekend.

"So what brings you back to the area?" Custer eyed him warily, almost as if he feared Jericho might demand his job as foreman back.

He'd anticipated the questions, had known he needed to have an excuse for being there, like he always did whenever he hunted for a criminal. This time, if he told people he was just visiting, he'd chance stirring up lots of questions, since he didn't have a good reason to *just visit*.

No doubt Rodney James was already expecting a bounty hunter to be coming after him. If the crook got even a whiff that a new lawman was now in the area, he'd take off before Jericho could figure out where he was.

20

There was too much riding on this hunt, and Jericho had to keep it as secret as possible for as long as possible. The only thing to do was tell everyone he'd missed the West—which was true—and then start making efforts to buy land. It was the most believable tale he'd been able to come up with.

He leaned against the barn again and tried for a casual pose. "Always wanted a ranch of my own. Heard Steele's selling land for a fair price and figured it's time to settle down."

"He's sold off the best." Custer spat a glob of tobacco juice into the dirt at their feet. "What's left ain't worth piddle."

Jericho had heard that too. The truth was, it didn't matter what the quality of the land was like. Once he ferreted out his prey, he had no intention of staying. But in the meantime, he needed a way to mingle in the community without drawing suspicion.

"Guess a man's got to start somewhere." Jericho glanced at the distant range and the disappearing sun.

"There's still homesteading land in the western parts of the territory." Custer watched him too intently.

"Won't be long before the railroad is finished up here and runs into Denver. Can't turn down the chance to have easier access to eastern markets."

Custer's eyes widened as though he'd never considered the possibility. "Reckon that makes a whole lot of sense."

Jericho watched from the corner of his eye as Buster Bliss took his silver dollar, tucked it into his pocket, and started toward a horse tied up at a hitching post. With each step, the lingering crowd congratulated Buster, but his movements and greetings in response were stilted and forced.

Something wasn't right. Jericho felt it down to his bones, though he couldn't explain exactly why.

As if sensing the scrutiny, the man paused in unwinding the lead line of his horse and cast a glance at Jericho. The last rays of sunlight illuminated the man's eyes behind his spectacles. Big brown eyes. Beautiful big brown eyes he'd recognize anywhere. They belonged to the one and only Ivy McQuaid.

His pulse took off like a runaway train engine. But he forced himself to glance away nonchalantly, as if she was just another boring ranch hand.

No wonder her dismount had seemed familiar. No wonder she appeared so feminine. No wonder she was out of place in that clothing.

Blazing smoke. What was she doing here dressed up as a man?

His mind couldn't work quickly enough, and before he knew what was happening, Ivy had mounted her horse and was heading away from the ranch to the north toward Fairplay. Why wasn't she heading east, toward Healing Springs? Wasn't she living there anymore?

He could hardly hear what Custer was telling him about the benefits of the railroad. All he could think about was Ivy, the fact that she'd been the idiot on the backs of the horses during the Roman-style race. She'd put herself in grave danger. Didn't she realize that?

His blood turned cold as he pictured her dangling between the two animals, about ready to fall to her death. What had she been thinking? As usual, she probably hadn't been thinking. She was still foolish and impulsive and wild.

And as usual, none of her brothers knew what she was up to. If Flynn had any idea Ivy was running around South Park and entering the cowhand competitions, he'd give her a whupping she wouldn't soon forget.

But the truth was, Ivy had never listened to her brothers, had always been headstrong. And she apparently hadn't changed one bit.

Jericho's body turned rigid with the need to ride after her and hand her a whupping of his own. At the very least, he intended to let her know she wasn't fooling him with her disguise and that if she didn't put a stop to her shenanigans, he'd go directly to Flynn.

By the time he managed to find an excuse to take his leave from Elkhorn Ranch, she had at least a thirty-minute lead. With darkness settling in earnest, it was harder to track her. He trailed her far enough to know she'd taken a circuitous route—to make a show of riding toward Kenosha Pass—but had eventually headed around to Healing Springs Ranch.

As he neared the section of Middle Fork River that ran through Wyatt's land, he dismounted and led his horse along the stretch of riverbank where he'd come that September night almost two years ago.

That had been the night he'd freed Dylan from the mountain shack where Bat and his gang had locked him up after beating him. Getting past the guards hadn't been easy, but Jericho knocked them both out and broke Dylan free from Bat's hangout.

Only then did he learn Bat had placed a death warrant on Dylan. As long as Dylan remained in debt to Bat and stayed in South Park—even in Colorado Territory—someone eventually would turn him over to Bat again.

And the next time, Dylan wouldn't get away, not unless it was in a coffin.

Even though Jericho hadn't been as close to Dylan during

those last couple of years living in South Park, he'd still con-sidered him one of his best friends. At the time of Dylan's run-in with Bat's gang, Jericho had already quit his position as Elkhorn Ranch foreman and had been readying to leave. It'd been an easy decision to move up his departure and take Dylan with him.

The night they'd ridden out, Jericho hadn't known where to go. But his horse took him in the direction of the one place he'd thought he'd never return. To his dad's home in Chicago.

When his dad had sent Jericho and his older brother, Nash, west to Missouri in early '62 to get away from the War of Rebellion, Jericho had been livid. He'd already had a distant relationship with his dad since his mom's murder. And with his dad pushing him away even more, he'd decided he never wanted to see the man again.

When talk of conscription had turned into a reality in the early part of '63, Dad decided to move Nash and him farther west. He telegrammed about the arrangements he'd made for them to drive cattle to Colorado. After gaining experience driving cattle in Missouri, they were just the kind of help Flynn McQuaid had been looking for in moving Wyatt's new herd of Shorthorns to the high country.

Nash had never once questioned their dad's decisions, and Jericho had always thought Nash was weak because of it. But now, in hindsight, he understood why Nash had gone along with their dad's plans. Since their mom's death, his brother had become a father to him and had wanted to keep him safe more than anything, especially from the long reaches of the war.

Jericho guided his mount closer to the river but then froze

at the sight ahead. Ivy. Submerged up to her shoulders in the middle of the river.

The sky wasn't completely black. The moon was full, and the stars were out in abundance. And he had no trouble seeing the shore, which told him everything he needed to know. She'd discarded her men's garments and left them in a pile next to her horse. Now she was washing off her disguise before she put on her everyday garments, because she couldn't very well show up at the ranch dressed like a man.

She splashed more water on her face and scrubbed both hands over her cheeks. With her back facing him, his thoughts turned again to the night he left Colorado, when he discovered her bathing in the stream.

His anger had been swift. Even though she'd only been seventeen at the time, it wasn't lost on him that she'd been turning into an attractive woman. He'd seen the attention she garnered every place she went. He'd heard the comments men were making. And if any one of them had come across her taking a bath, they wouldn't have thought twice about seducing her.

He'd sneaked up on her and proven just how dangerous it was for her to be out alone. But apparently his lesson hadn't taught her anything. Maybe he ought to try to teach her another one. After her stunts at the competition and now this, it was clear she needed someone watching over her better.

Looping his horse's lead line over a nearby branch, he tossed aside his boots and socks before wading in. For June, the water was still icy, containing the runoff of the melting snow in the higher elevations. As he tiptoed toward her over the slippery rocks on the stream bottom, the water numbed his toes and soaked his trousers up to his knees.

He made it within two steps of her when she shifted and twisted around. At the sight of him, she let out a yelp and dropped further under the water to cover herself.

She couldn't have heard him. Had she sensed him?

He halted. Though she was shadowed by the darkness and the river, the creamy white of her skin was as evident as the moon overhead. The smooth expanse of her neck. The delicate arch of her shoulders graced with the straps of her chemise. The slight curve of her chest that wasn't submerged.

Her eyes were large and luminous in the paleness of her face. Her hair had fallen loose from a bun on the top of her head, and strands stuck to her cheeks and neck. A smudge of charcoal remained on her chin.

Blast it all. Her face was the prettiest he'd ever laid eyes on, especially as she peered up at him.

He gave himself a mental slap—just like he'd always done—for letting his thoughts wander to how beautiful she was. Not only did over three years of age difference stand between them, but so did Dylan. He'd promised Dylan from the start of their friendship he'd treat Ivy as a sister and nothing more.

"Jericho." Her tone was mild but contained an edge. She wasn't surprised to see him, had obviously recognized him at the competition.

"Buster Bliss." He might as well let her know he'd figured out what she was up to.

She didn't bat an eye. "What are you doing here, Jericho? You make a habit of spying on women taking their baths?"

Obviously, she remembered the night of their parting too. "Looks like I make a habit of sneaking up on foolish young girls who still need to learn important lessons about safety."

"Young girl?" Her voice rose a notch. "I wasn't a young girl when you left, and you can bet your last dollar I ain't one now."

He waved his hand at her, then at her pile of clothes. "This is childish, dangerous, and irresponsible, Ivy. Thought I warned you last time I caught you out here."

"Childish?" She stirred in the water, lowering her feet.

She wasn't thinking of standing in front of him in her unmentionables, was she?

Lord in heaven help him. Before she could push herself up, he jerked his gaze heavenward and spun as fast as he could, nearly tripping and falling into the cold water. "Ivy McQuaid! What in the name of heaven do you think you're doing?"

"Reckon I oughta give you a gander at a woman, since you don't know what one looks like."

His mouth went dry. "Don't you even think about it." From what he could tell from her stillness behind him, she'd abandoned her plan. Regardless, a part of him wanted to turn around and peek. Thank the Lord he had a willpower of steel, and he stood as stationary and straight as a lamppost. "Get out and get some clothes on. Now."

"I'm not a girl, Jericho. And it's about time you realized it."

From the little bit he'd seen of her above the water, he agreed. She was all woman and even more gorgeous than he remembered.

But it didn't matter. She was still Ivy. And he'd always think of her as Dylan's little sister, a gangly girl in two braids, a fun playmate during the trip across the Santa Fe Trail. That's all.

She expelled a long, drawn-out sigh, one filled with ex-asperation. Then from the splashing he could tell she was making her way toward the shore. She was right there behind him, dripping wet, wearing nothing but her unmentionables and the skin she'd been born in.

His pulse gave a swift and hard surge, sending heat right through him. "It's about time you stopped acting like a wan-ton woman."

"A wanton woman?" Hurt tinged her question.

Maybe in the short term his rebuke would hurt her feel-ings, but if he could keep her safe—even from himself—that's all that mattered. "Yes. And while you're at it, stop pretending to be a man."

At the shuffling of linen, he tried to block out the image of her slipping on her garments, but just the prospect was enough to send more warmth through his gut. He pressed his palms over his eyes, as if that could somehow make the picture disappear. He couldn't let his thoughts about Ivy get carried away, not after all these years of keeping them from wandering.

"You've got no right to be upset with me," she said.

"Why not?"

"You ain't had a part in my life for so long, what makes you think you can tell me what to do now?"

Weren't those nearly the same words he'd spouted at his dad shortly after his return home when his dad had started ordering him around and planning his life? After Dad had abandoned him time after time, Jericho had resented his sud-den interest.

Was that how Ivy felt? Maybe it wasn't his place to start bossing Ivy around. On the other hand, now that he was here, how could he ignore her foolishness? Someone had to talk some sense into her before she got herself hurt or killed.

"I guess I don't have any right to tell you what to do after being gone all this time, but lucky for you, I'm planning to tell you anyway."

CHAPTER

3

Ivy tugged up her split skirt over her drawers. Her wet skin made the process of dressing painfully slow. And her frozen fingers and limbs were sluggish to obey the commands her mind was giving them.

The thrill of seeing Jericho in the river and knowing he'd followed her back from Elkhorn Ranch had vanished the second he called her a young girl and told her she was child-ish. She'd wanted to throw a bucket of icy water in his face and wake him up to the fact that she wasn't a girl anymore and hadn't been even when he'd left Colorado.

Maybe he was right about her threat to stand up in her unmentionables—it *had* been a tad wanton. But Jericho was about as dense as a brick. He'd always talked down to her like she was stupid, had always seen her as more of nuisance than anything else. Even those last couple of years before he left, he'd viewed her as a little girl.

Her face flushed just thinking about what she'd almost done in standing up in the river so brazenly, and her fingers fumbled at the skirt button at her hip. Of course, leave it to Jericho to be too noble to look at her. She shoulda known he wouldn't.

Even now, he remained unmoving in the stream, facing the opposite way, waiting and giving her plenty of time to cover herself. Part of her respected him for treating her so carefully. But another part of her wished he'd finally recognize how grown-up she was.

She shook her head. It didn't matter. She swiped up her blouse, stuffing in first one arm and then the other, the thin material sticking to her skin.

"Why're you here, Jericho?" The question had burned within her during the ride to the ranch.

"After almost killing yourself in that race, what do you expect?"

She wasn't asking about why he was standing there right now. She wanted to know why he'd come back to Colorado—if he was here to stay or just passing through. But asking him those kinds of questions would make it seem like she cared too much and had been thinking about him often. And she didn't anymore—care or think about him. She'd put her infatuation with Jericho Bliss far from her mind a long time ago. "I didn't almost kill myself."

He snuck a glance at her over his shoulder. At seeing her fully clothed, the tension seemed to ease from his stiff spine, and he began to wade out of the water toward her.

"I had a hiccup near the end but caught myself just fine."

"That wasn't a hiccup. That was more like a gut-splitting cough."

"Aw, c'mon. You've seen me ride enough to know I rarely meet my shadow on the ground."

"You not only almost met your shadow, but you almost met your Maker."

She fumbled at the buttons of her blouse, her fingers still numb. As he stepped out onto the bank and drew nearer, she tried not to notice the assured way he held himself and the strength that radiated from him.

But as he stopped only a couple of paces away, it was as if only a day had passed since he'd left. She was just as aware of his rugged good looks, work-roughened body, and no-nonsense blue eyes as she'd always been.

Why couldn't he be as plain as paint? Just wasn't fair for one fella to be so handsome. And just wasn't fair she was drawn to him worse than a bear cub to a bowl full of honey, even after how hard she'd worked to stamp out every little bit of hankering for him. All it had taken was one glimpse of him standing there at Elkhorn Ranch, and earlier tonight all that desire had come flooding back worse than before.

Her fingers shook, and she lost her grip on her button.

"Look at you." Irritation laced his words. "Frozen to the bone."

She'd always had a knack for irritating him to no end. Seemed she still did.

"One more reason you shouldn't take baths in the river."

"I always manage fine."

He reached for her button, as though to help her, and in the process, his fingers brushed against her chemise. A shiver skipped along all her nerve endings, one more powerful than any she'd ever experienced with him. And she'd had plenty of innocent contact with him over the years—hands brushing while roping, shoulders touching while sitting together on a corral fence, feet bumping beneath a table.

But this . . . this was different. His presence powerful and raw and real. Warmth radiated from him. And his touch was somehow more intimate.

His fingers hovered above her as if he'd just noticed her curves and his proximity. She could almost see the realization clicking in his head, could almost hear his mental berating. She couldn't keep from taunting him. "Scared if you help me, you won't be able to let go when you're done?"

He gave a low, scoffing laugh. "Of course not."

"Prove it."

He hesitated, stared at the button, and then dropped his hands and fell back a step. "I don't need to prove anything to you, Ivy."

She was being wanton again, wasn't she? And he was still set on rejecting her. This was the way it had always been. Clearly nothing had changed.

"Reckon I can take care of myself just fine and don't need to prove anything to you either." She bent and swiped up her Buster Bliss outfit and began stuffing it into her saddlebag.

He watched her silently.

When she'd hidden away every last stitch of the clothing and spectacles, she combed her fingers through her hair and wound it into a knot on top of her head, heedless of how messy the bun was. She stuck in a pin to hold it in place, then pressed her hat down.

She tucked her boots under one arm and reached for Poppy's reins. "See you around, Jericho." With that, she started walking along the river path that led to the house.

Jericho didn't respond, and she forced herself to keep going and not glance back at him, even though everything within her wanted to stop and stare at him all night long.

As she reached the low point in the river and started crossing over, she heard him following her and relief weakened her knees. The truth was, she didn't want to part ways with him yet. She wanted the chance to talk with him, find out what he'd been up to, where he'd been, what he'd done.

With his long stride, he easily caught up, guiding his horse next to her. When they sloshed to the opposite side and reached the path that led up to Wyatt's house, Jericho halted.

She paused beside the chokecherry bushes, loaded with clusters of fruit that were still green, although some were beginning to turn red. Wyatt's wife, Greta, used the chokecherries in her jam-making, but it would still be a month or two before they were ripe enough for picking.

"I take it you haven't told Wyatt and Flynn you're competing." Jericho spoke casually, but she'd learned long ago he rarely said or did anything without a purpose.

She swung around, arms stiff, body on edge, ready for a fight. "Nobody knows. And it better stay that way."

"Or else what?" He pulled himself up to his full height so that he towered above her.

She knew as well as he did there wasn't anything she could do if he decided to tell her brothers about her duplicity in entering the cowhand contests. And if they found out, they'd hog-tie her to a hitching post for a month. At the very least, they'd make sure she never competed again.

She crossed to Jericho and poked her finger into his chest. Hard. "Don't you dare say a word to them."

His gaze darted to her finger as if it were nothing more than a pesky fly he could bat away.

"I mean it."

"You can't expect me to sit back and say nothing. If they

found out I knew and didn't alert them, they'd string me up in the nearest tree."

Her mind did a rapid calculation for how much more money she needed until she had enough for the down payment on the land. She might be able to convince Steele to hold it for her with the little she'd saved so far, but she still had at least two months of Sundays left—maybe three—before she'd have the amount Steele wanted.

"I need more time."

"What for?"

"I'm saving up so I can buy my own spread."

He studied her face. And he didn't scoff the way some of the cowhands did when she talked about trying to start her own ranch. That was one thing she appreciated about Jericho. He never discouraged her from roping and riding and all the other duties that came with cattle ranching. He'd let her tag along with Dylan and him and had been a patient teacher, more so than most.

"How much more do you need?"

She dropped her hand from his chest. "Ain't gonna lie. I got a long ways to go."

"How long?"

"Was hoping I'd save up enough by the end of the summer."

He started to shake his head, protest crinkling at the corners of his eyes.

"End of August." She spoke fast before he could give her an ultimatum. "I'll for sure earn enough by the end of August."

He pressed his lips together.

"Please, please, please, Jericho. Try to understand."

"For the love of heaven, Ivy. Why are you so headstrong?"

"This is important to me. I need my own place." As much

as she loved Wyatt and Flynn and Brody, they had their own lives and families. She was still living with Wyatt most of the time but bedded down at Flynn's or Brody's once in a while when they needed an extra hand. She'd even stayed for a couple of months with Brody and Savannah after the birth of their first child, Hartley, who was now a toddling one-year-old with a sibling on the way.

The truth was, the more her brothers' families expanded, the more pressure Ivy felt to give them the room they needed. Besides, she was ready to put an end to the roaming and finally put down roots. It had been too long since she'd been able to call any place home, not since the farm in Pennsylvania before Ma had died.

More than anything, though, she didn't want to end up like her ma, having to rely on a man. She was short on memories of Ma and Pa together. Most of what she remembered came from the years her ma was married to Rusty. She'd had to wed the fella to save the family farm. But in doing so, she lost herself. Ivy couldn't recall her ma being anything other than worn down and wearing Rusty's bruises.

Yep, no how no way was she ever gonna be dependent on a husband. Instead, she aimed to make her own way.

"I'll do it," she said. "You'll see."

In the starlit night, the scruffy layer of unshaven hair made Jericho's face darker and more foreboding.

"I'm gonna raise sheep." Maybe if she expounded on her plans, she'd have a better chance at convincing him. "Already been in touch with a sheepherder in Utah."

"Your brothers know of your plans?"

She released an irritated huff. "I reckon I can live my own life without having to involve them." What was it with her brothers? And now Jericho? Why did they think they had to oversee everything she did? She might be the baby of the family and the only girl, but she was eighteen, soon going on nineteen. They needed to stop holding on to her so tight.

"They're watching out for you because they love you. That's what older brothers do."

She guessed he was thinking of Nash and missing him. "I know." Compassion pushed aside her frustration. Jericho had tormented himself since the day Nash had died. The night Jericho had left South Park, he told her he wanted to get away from the reminders of his brother.

What had brought him back? The question was on the tip of her tongue, but before she could ask it, Jericho spoke. "Alright. I won't say anything about your competing. But . . ."

"But what?"

"But you have to promise you won't do any more Roman-style racing—"

"That's not fair. I'm good at it. The best—"

"No more Roman-style," he stated with as much stubbornness as an ornery bull. "It's too dangerous."

A long string of protests burned for release, but from the set of Jericho's shoulders, she reckoned she had about as much of a chance of getting him to change his mind as she had in getting a cow to climb a tree.

"Fine," she said.

"And only until the end of August."

She started up the path again. "Anyone ever tell you how bossy you are?"

"Only you." His words hinted at the memories of days gone by.

They'd had lots of good times, especially those months on the trail west when they'd been kids with nothing more to do than fish and hunt and learn new riding and roping tricks. Yep, the trip had been dangerous and tiring and long. But she'd loved every minute, mainly because she'd been able to spend as much time as she wanted with Jericho. He'd always been easy to talk to. And since they'd each lost a parent, they'd been able to confide in each other the frustration of having remaining parents abandon them, almost as if they'd died too.

She'd been disappointed when shortly after they arrived at Wyatt's ranch, Nash and Jericho had gone up into the mountains to mine gold like so many other men, lured by the prospect of getting rich.

They'd only lasted a year before they returned to South Park completely broke, hungry, and in need of work. When Nash had taken over running Flynn's place while he'd gone east to track down Brody after the war ended, she made up excuses to visit Jericho and work alongside him.

But by that point, the camaraderie from their trip was long gone. Jericho considered himself too grown-up to associate with her. After he took the foreman job at Elkhorn Ranch shortly after Nash's accident, he snubbed her even more.

As much as her attraction to him was still very much alive and well—even after all she'd done to forget about him— she had to keep those feelings cinched up and on a short rope. She'd already let him trample her heart once. And she couldn't throw her love out there only to have him stomp all over it again.

CHAPTER
4

"Look what the cat dragged in," Ivy called out as she entered through the front door of Wyatt's house.

Jericho hesitated at the threshold. He wasn't sure he'd be welcome among the McQuaids after riding off with Dylan the way he had without a word all this time. But even if they were upset with him for the silence, he owed them an update on their brother—at least as much of an update as he could afford without ruining his cover.

The front room was brightly lit and a hub of activity like it had always been whenever he'd visited. The log walls belonged to the original cabin Wyatt had built, which he'd added to over the years. A table took up the center of the room, the benches on either side filled with Wyatt's family finishing a late supper.

How many children did Wyatt have now? Jericho counted three little heads. From the way Greta's abdomen rounded out beneath her apron, he guessed another child would soon join the household. Greta's sister, Astrid, was also at the table. A few years younger than Ivy, Astrid had become a good friend to her. Yet, it'd always been a sore spot of his that Ivy hadn't made more female friends and instead gravitated toward the men.

From the end of the table, Wyatt's eyes locked on him and filled with recognition. "Jericho Bliss." Wyatt stood. "It's been a long time."

Jericho sized Wyatt up in an instant. The solidly built man not only had the same brown eyes as Ivy, but they shared the same dark hair color. Wyatt's weathered face contained a thick layer of scruff that made him appear more mature. It fit him well. Thankfully, his expression contained only anticipation and not a hint of animosity.

"Wyatt." Jericho reached out for a handshake. "Good to see you."

Wyatt's grip was firm but friendly. The oldest of the McQuaid brothers was even-tempered, which was why Jericho had decided to visit Wyatt first instead of Flynn. More like a father figure to the family, Flynn viewed life seriously and wouldn't be as easy on him as Wyatt. Jericho couldn't put off visiting Flynn for long, but he hoped to give his old friend a little time to get used to the idea he was here—without Dylan.

In no time, Jericho found himself seated at the big table with the family. Astrid insisted on Greta staying put and resting her feet while she went to the big kitchen in the next room and dished Jericho up a plate of beef with vegetables and gravy. The rich roasted scent mixed with the aroma of freshly baked bread, and his mouth watered at the prospect of slathering his bread with some of Greta's famous mountain-berry jam.

As he ate, Wyatt caught him up on the doings around the ranch, including the construction he'd begun on a new house and inn adjacent to the hot spring on his property. Apparently Greta had the idea of developing a resort for people who wanted to experience the fresh mountain air and the healing hot water of the spring. She planned to run the new business as well as continue to sell her wares.

Jericho didn't see how Greta could possibly find the time or the energy for all her endeavors, not with her young ones underfoot. But she was a hard worker and a savvy business-woman. In fact, all the McQuaid brothers had married smart women. Flynn had married Linnea, a botanist. And Brody had married Savannah, a veterinarian.

Jericho doubted Dylan would be as lucky, not with the type of women he spent time with. Dylan might have stopped his gambling, but he was still a heavy drinker and as wild as always.

"If you're needing work," Wyatt said, "I'm looking for a few more reliable fellas to help with the new building projects."

Jericho nodded and scraped the last of the gravy from his plate. Maybe the temporary job would buy him time and give him more opportunities to investigate the newcomers to the community.

Wyatt held his youngest child—a boy named Ryder—on his knee and bounced him up and down. The infant slapped his hands on the table and grinned with glee, revealing a couple of tiny teeth. Jericho didn't have enough experience with children to guess ages, but the baby had to be younger than two since Greta had given birth right before he and Dylan had left.

"Just until you find something steady," Wyatt added. "Reckon you'll be wanting a foreman position like before?"

"Actually, I'm considering getting my own ranch." Jericho didn't like having to lie, but he had no choice with the kind of criminals he hunted, especially his newest. Rodney James was too intelligent and always managed to stay one step ahead of the law. They'd only been able to trace him by linking his victims. He cut out their tongues the same way he'd done during the war. Jericho suspected he did it so that if anyone lived, they wouldn't be able to talk about him.

Maybe now was the time to change the subject and update the family on Dylan. He'd sensed how eager they were to hear about their brother, and he was grateful they'd given him a chance to eat first.

Before Wyatt or Greta could ask him any more about his plans or his reasons for being in the high country, he pushed aside his plate. "Suppose you'd like to know how Dylan is doing."

"Yep." Wyatt stopped bouncing his baby. "Been praying for that kid a whole heap, and I'm hoping you're bringing good news about him buckling down and getting back on the straight and narrow."

Jericho could feel all eyes on him and suddenly noticed Ivy wasn't in the room. Where had she gone off to? Just the thought of her competing in the riding and roping contests needled him with fresh guilt. Not only was he lying about himself, but now he was lying for her too.

He tucked away his guilt and said what he needed to. "Dylan's got a job as a police constable in Chicago."

"Police?" Wyatt and Greta asked the question at the same time.

"He's doing real well for himself." Except for the women and the drinking. Good thing Jericho was already an expert at rescuing and taking care of drunks. The Lord only knew how many times he'd had to step in and drag his dad home from saloons after his mom died.

"Why Chicago?" Wyatt persisted.

"I took him to my home—to my dad." Even though Jericho had told himself he'd never return, he'd gone because he had every confidence Elijah Bliss would keep Dylan safe from Bat and his gang.

"Didn't know you were from Chicago." Wyatt was watching him, as if he was waiting for more enlightenment. He was probably wondering why Jericho hadn't mentioned he was from Illinois, especially since he'd known that was where Greta and Astrid had once lived.

Jericho couldn't say much. Didn't want word leaking out about his dad's identity as a Pinkerton agent, not now that his own was connected so closely. But Wyatt and the family deserved at least the barest of explanations.

"Yes, I . . ." He sat up, trying to think, but before he could formulate his answer, Ivy breezed into the room.

Instead of wearing the disheveled, half-buttoned, and damp garments from before, she'd changed her clothes and had on a light blue dress. It wasn't fancy, but it wasn't like any of the simple girlish outfits she used to wear. This one was tailored to fit. And fit it did. Giving him no excuse to think of her as anything but a woman ever again.

She'd brushed her dark hair, and it hung in long, damp waves over her shoulders and down her back, as thick and luxurious as the finest Arabian horse's mane. Without the night or anything else obscuring her face, he could see that her features had matured—her lips were fuller, her lashes thicker and longer, and her cheeks narrower and more defined.

She wasn't just pretty. She was absolutely breathtaking. Any man who could mistake her for Buster Bliss was either blind or a fool.

He couldn't tear his eyes from her as she crossed to the nearest of Wyatt's children, a little girl who had Greta's fair hair and silvery blue eyes. Ivy bent and hugged the child. "How's my sweet Ellie?"

After a kiss, Ivy wrapped Wyatt's oldest son, Ty, in a hug. If Jericho remembered correctly, the boy was about five, maybe six, years old and growing into a polite little man. He returned Ivy's embrace with more reservation, while the youngest tyke held up his arms to Ivy and babbled, apparently not wanting to miss out on his aunt's affection.

With a tender laugh, Ivy took Ryder from Wyatt and lifted him above her head. He squealed, and she laughed again. The sound of it nearly knocked the wind from Jericho.

"Looks like everyone missed you today, Ivy," Wyatt said with one brow quirked at Jericho.

Jericho jerked his attention away from Ivy and down to his coffee.

"Well, I missed them." With Ryder above her, Ivy blew a noisy kiss onto his belly, earning his giggles.

Jericho tried to focus on the sludge left in the bottom of his mug, but his gaze had a will of its own, and before he could stop himself, he was staring at Ivy once more. With her head bent back, every sweet inch of her womanly figure was right there for the viewing, including all that soft, creamy skin showing from the lace at her bosom to her neck.

He had a sudden vision of her in the river, the moonlight shining down on her. He hadn't seen anything he wasn't supposed to. But son-of-a-gun, his imagination was trying to head in a direction it shouldn't.

Heat shot into his veins as it had earlier. No. That was lust, and the last thing he wanted to do was lust after Ivy McQuaid.

Even so, as she pressed another kiss to her nephew's belly, he couldn't keep from admiring her changes. Gone was the dusty, windswept girl. And in her place stood a tantalizing, almost-dangerous beauty of a woman.

Wyatt blew out a half laugh.

Jericho jerked his sights back to his coffee, trying to keep his expression emotionless even as his insides churned with feelings he couldn't begin to name.

Ivy had always attracted attention wherever she went. During that last summer he'd been home, he'd had to threaten several of his ranch hands to stay away from her. He could only imagine how many fellows were falling over themselves to have the chance to come courting.

At eighteen, she was still a mite young to be thinking about marriage and men, wasn't she?

As Ivy took a place on the bench surrounded by her adoring nephews and niece, she thanked Astrid for the plate of food and began to eat as politely as any grown woman he'd ever met. When had Ivy turned into such a lady?

Astrid used the opportunity to distribute pieces of pie around the table. And as Jericho savored his first bite of sweet berry mixture and perfect flaky crust, he was relieved for the distraction so he could gain his composure.

While he ate the pie, he somehow managed to extinguish

the sparks Ivy had ignited inside him, mainly by keeping his gaze from straying toward her. Afterward, with a fresh mug of coffee in hand, he shared more about Dylan and his new life in Chicago, leaving out all the bad parts about their brother's waywardness and telling everyone instead about all the criminals Dylan had been involved in capturing and how he was gaining a reputation as a fair and decent lawman, especially because his sharpshooting skills were unmatched.

Finally, when Astrid and Greta ushered the little ones up the stairs to bed, leaving him with Wyatt and Ivy, Jericho pulled out his pipe along with a match. "Since Bat still has the death warrant on Dylan's head, I think it's best if everyone keeps quiet about him being in Chicago. And it'd be best if no one mentions that's where I've been holed up."

As Jericho lit the tobacco, he waited for them to ask how he knew about Bat's ongoing death warrant. He wished he could tell them the truth, that as a Pinkterton agent, he had access to more information than most people, but he scrambled to have another excuse ready.

Wyatt scratched his head. "Reckoned that lowlife wouldn't care a lick about Dylan anymore."

Jericho took a puff from his pipe. "Unfortunately, Bat has a good memory and doesn't let go of his grudges."

Ivy sat forward, leaning her elbows on the table. "So you're telling us Dylan ain't gonna be able to come home so long as Bat's here?"

"That's what I'm saying." He allowed himself a glance at her, and this time he worked extra hard not to show any surprise at how beautiful she was. Her big brown eyes were the kind that could suck a fellow in like quicksand and make him forget his next thought. He gave her a curt nod and then cut short his view, switching back to Wyatt and safety.

Wyatt slipped his hand around the back of his neck and kneaded the muscles. "Is there a way to drive Bat out of the area?"

"Even though he brags about the men he's killed, no one can pin any particular murder on him or anyone in his gang." Jericho knew every last detail about Bat, had already ruled him out as a suspect for Rodney James. Bat was a mean, dirty cheater who wouldn't think twice about pounding bullets into anyone who double-crossed him. But he wasn't the war criminal Jericho was seeking.

For a few seconds, the pattering of little feet overhead and the creak of floorboards filled the silence.

Wyatt dropped his hands, his shoulders decidedly more stooped. "At least assure me Dylan's got his life together and made his peace with the Almighty."

Jericho wanted to squirm under the intensity both Wyatt and Ivy directed his way.

"Just spit it out," Ivy said impatiently.

Jericho fingered the pipe's stem. He'd deceived everyone enough for one day, and now the truth pushed for release. "I wish I could tell you he's the old Dylan we all knew and loved, but he's still making some pretty stupid choices."

Wyatt and Ivy were quiet, but their disappointment seemed to pull up a chair and join them as a guest.

"The good thing is that he loves his work and does a decent job at it." When he was sober.

Wyatt opened his mouth to say something, but Ivy stood abruptly, clanking the dishes and silverware remaining on the table. "You should have brought him with you."

The accusation whipped against Jericho. If only she knew how many sacrifices he'd made over the past months for Dylan. The biggest one had been in setting aside his pride and asking his dad for help.

He placed a half-dollar coin over the bowl of his pipe, extinguished it, then stood. "Best be heading out." He reached for his hat where he'd discarded it on the bench and fit it over his head.

"Hold on." Wyatt jumped to his feet.

Jericho paused.

"None of us ever got the chance to thank you." Wyatt slanted a look toward Ivy, who'd begun to gather the pie plates. "Reckon we owe you a real big debt for all you've done for Dylan, including saving his life."

Jericho accepted the thanks with a nod. Sometimes in the giving of gratitude, a man could find a sense of peace. And he hoped that was true for Wyatt. Neither Wyatt nor Flynn were to blame for Dylan's wild living. They'd done the best they could to raise him up right, but Dylan had gone his own way.

Jericho started across the room.

"Where you staying?" Wyatt followed him.

"In town. I'll get a room at one of the hotels—"

"Take Dylan's bed in the cabin with Judd."

Ivy stopped midmotion, a stack of dishes in her hand.

Jericho halted at the door. "I don't want to impose."

"It's been empty all this time." The edge of sadness in Wyatt's tone told Jericho they'd been waiting for Dylan to return, that they'd left his things untouched with the hope he'd come back. And now, Jericho had just crushed their hope.

"I'm sorry—"

Wyatt clamped Jericho on his shoulder. "It'd make us real happy to have you live here as long as you need. Until you get yourself settled into your own place."

Jericho hesitated. Staying in town at the hotel would allow him to listen in on more conversations, spy on the comings and goings of everyone, and poke around for information. But how could he graciously turn down Wyatt's offer?

"Free of charge," Wyatt added quickly. "With your meals here at the house."

"I couldn't—"

"After everything you've done for Dylan, it's the least we can do."

Jericho didn't glance at Ivy, but as her silence stretched out, he guessed she wasn't feeling quite as hospitable as Wyatt.

As though recognizing Ivy's resistance, Wyatt pinned another gaze on his sister, this one with his brows furrowed. Wyatt wasn't a strict disciplinarian like Flynn and always had trouble keeping control of Ivy. Her participation in the competitions today was proof enough of that.

Ivy started to busy herself again. "Jericho might like town, where he won't be tempted to butt into other people's business."

Wyatt palmed the back of his neck again, his expression confused, almost comically so.

"Ain't that right, Jericho?" Ivy didn't pause in her cleanup.

Was she hoping he'd refuse to stay at Healing Springs for fear he might tattle on her for pretending to be Buster Bliss? Or was she sneaking around doing other things she shouldn't be? Things she was afraid he'd discover if he stayed on?

"Actually, I like butting into other people's business, especially when they're involved in deception."

51

Ivy started toward the kitchen and shot him a glare filled with warning.

Jericho forced his gaze to Wyatt. "Thank you, Wyatt. I accept your offer."

Wyatt said something else that Jericho let go in one ear and out the other, his attention too fixed upon Ivy's stiff shoulders and remembering what those shoulders had looked like bare in the moonlight.

As soon as he stepped outside and closed the door behind him, he released a pent-up breath and stared at the starry host. He was as tight as a nail driven high into a horseshoe. What had he been thinking to decide to stay? Such a move had been impulsive and totally out of character for him.

Who was turning into the idiot now?

With a shake of his head, he started toward the ranch-hand cabins.

After starting at the Pinkerton Agency shortly after his return to Chicago, he'd solved several important cases within the first few months. He'd realized what everyone else at the agency had—he was a good detective. And he liked the work. Much more than he'd ever thought possible.

With the Department of Justice possibly offering the Pinkerton Agency a contract for tracking down the hardest federal criminals, the agency had given him this job in Colorado to prove to the DOJ that their detectives were the best. Everyone was counting on him to help the agency get the lucrative and prestigious deal.

He'd stay a night or two at most with the McQuaids, then he'd focus on his mission, one that required all his wits and then some. He didn't need any distractions. And he certainly didn't want to put anyone else in danger on account of his work.

His dad had done that, and look what had happened to his mom. One of the criminals Dad had been tracking had kidnapped and killed her in retaliation. And his dad had been a wreck ever since.

Jericho had ended up following in his dad's footsteps into detective work, but he'd never follow in his dad's footsteps and get married and put a wife in peril. He knew where to draw the line—had already drawn the line—and he had no intention of crossing it. Not now or any time in the future.

CHAPTER

5

"How do I look?" The slant of the ceiling of the dormer room prevented Ivy from straightening all the way. But she managed to twirl around anyway and give Astrid full view of her appearance.

Perched on the edge of the bed they shared, Astrid cocked her head, studying Ivy with narrowed eyes. "If I tell you the truth, do you promise not to be sore at me?"

Ivy paused and swished the green skirt with white pin-stripes, relishing the silkiness against her bare legs. She knew she needed to wear the petticoat that had come with the outfit, but the fancy skirt was progress enough without having all the other stuff underneath.

"Of course I won't be sore." Ivy smoothed a hand over the matching bodice and the tiny velvet-covered buttons that ran up the front, for once wishing their room had a mirror.

Astrid stood and folded her hands. "The bodice is much too tight."

Ivy glanced down at her chest. The buttons did strain a

little, but who would notice? Especially with the lacy collar and identical lace at the cuffs of each sleeve.

"You should take out the seams as Linnea suggested."

"It'll be fine." Ivy swiped up a straw hat with a ribbon of the same pinstripe material and dainty flower on the side. "What do you think?"

"Wear it like this." Astrid tilted it so far, Ivy was afraid it would slip off.

Earlier in the spring, Linnea had given Ivy a trunk full of gowns she no longer wore. They were all much fancier than anything Ivy had ever owned, but for a wealthy eastern lady like Linnea, the clothing had become outdated. Since Linnea's mother sent her new garments from time to time, Linnea had no need to hang on to everything.

At first Ivy had been skeptical of accepting the gift, but with Greta and Astrid encouraging her to, she'd decided it wouldn't hurt anything to wear a nicer outfit now and again.

She took off the hat and smoothed back her hair, which Astrid had already styled for her in a braid wrapped into a knot. "I look like a heifer playing dress-up."

"You look just fine." Astrid fluffed out her own skirt, a fashionable gown she'd sewn herself. Her light brown hair was perfectly coiled in a chignon. With her pale skin and dainty features, she was every inch a lady. And she acted like one too. The fun, precocious Astrid who'd loved adventures was long gone.

At sixteen, Astrid had mostly overcome the consumption that had brought her and Greta to Colorado. She still struggled with shortness of breath occasionally, but she'd learned to manage her breathing, had in fact become quite proficient in all things having to do with health and medicine.

She even talked of going east someday and getting nurses' training.

Ivy released a sigh. She was never gonna be as smart or as pretty or as refined as Astrid. And she wasn't sure why she was trying, except that she liked the attention fellas paid her when she walked around in her new clothing instead of the old, worn stuff.

Of course, Jericho hadn't paid her much attention last night when she'd gone to the effort of changing back into what she'd worn to church. His eyes had widened with surprise when he'd first seen her. But then he'd mostly ignored her the rest of the evening. Just like he'd always done.

She obviously hadn't impressed him none. She never had.

Picking up her shoes and stockings, she started to the door.

Astrid followed. "You really should put your shoes on before you go down. Real ladies don't walk around barefoot."

"I'll put them on right before I get to town." Ivy had always gone barefoot in the summer, and if she had to wear shoes, she preferred her boots over the satiny pointed things that had been in Linnea's trunk.

Astrid just shook her head as they crossed the hallway toward Ellie and Ty's room. They helped the two children dress and finish making their beds before leading them downstairs, the usual scent of bacon and eggs and coffee drawing them.

Wyatt was already at work, up before daybreak with the rest of the ranch hands. Greta, too, had been busy, preparing her butter and eggs for her Monday-morning trip to town. Today, Ivy was going with and intended to visit Mr. Steele and give him everything she'd already saved toward the land.

Once he saw her hard-earned dollars and realized she was serious about purchasing the property, he'd hold it for her.

That was why she'd dressed up. So Mr. Steele would see her as a grown woman, someone respectable, a buyer he could take seriously.

She hadn't taken extra care with her appearance for Jericho. Not in the least.

But all the while she ate her breakfast and helped Ellie and Ty and Ryder with theirs, she kept one eye on the door, waiting for Jericho to come walking through. Wyatt had told him he could take his meals with them in the house instead of with the cowhands, who had their own cook. The cook was decent enough. She'd sampled his vittles during cattle drives, the extended times when he followed along behind the drovers in his wagon.

Didn't matter. Greta was a superior cook. Her and Judd's garden was enormous. And the meals were better by far.

So where was Jericho?

By the time Ivy finished the morning meal and cleaned up, her insides felt half-baked. So during the ride to town, she chawed herself out for letting herself think on him so much.

As Greta directed the team and wagon down Main Street, Ivy finally put on her shoes. The wagon wheels kicked up clouds of dust—adding to the grimy film that covered the front windows of all the businesses. At midmorning, the town was busy, mostly with men loitering about. But more women were moving into the area every year, and new homes were being built.

When the wagon rattled to a halt in front of Simpkins General Store, Ivy hopped down and winced at the tightness against her toes.

"You alright, Miss McQuaid?" asked a tall fella passing by.

She was half-tempted to kick off the shoes, but she haltered the urge and instead offered the man a polite greeting. "I'm doing just fine."

Greta had dismounted and was hobbling toward the end of the wagon with one hand on her back and the other on her rounded belly.

Ivy started after her sister-in-law. "Don't you dare lift a finger with any of those crates."

"They weigh less than Ryder. I'll be fine."

"Don't matter. Wyatt told me to tie you to the wagon seat if you start carrying things."

"That man worries enough for the both of us."

"Reckon he's hoping for some extra smooching time later and doesn't want you too tired for it."

"Ivy!" Greta's rebuke was tempered by a smile and twinkle in her eyes.

Ivy just smirked. She wasn't sure which of her brothers took the prize for the most kissing. They were all pretty-near the same in cornering their women and kissing them every chance they could get.

"You ladies need some help unloading?" asked the tall fella as he followed Ivy.

"If you've got a mind to it." Ivy sized up the man—Hance Payne, the owner of the barbershop that had opened up last summer. With neatly combed blond hair that was slicked back with some sort of musky cream, he was a distinguished-looking gentleman, especially with his spectacles and fine trousers and vest. His trim mustache and sideburns lent him a dashing air.

Recently during her visits to town, he'd made a point

of approaching her, inquiring if she needed assistance, and complimenting her on her outfits. Last time, he'd asked if he could come out to the ranch to visit her.

Since he was a spell older than her and more worldly-wise, his request had flustered her, and she'd told him she was too busy for any visitors. But later, when she'd lain in bed with Astrid and whispered about Hance, Astrid scolded her for refusing. "You're of the proper age to have men come courting," Astrid said. "And Hance Payne is mature and responsible. You should have said yes."

Another fella approached the wagon bed. Otis Profitt, the dentist whose office across the street was connected to Hance's barbershop with a shared waiting room. "I'd be happy to help you ladies too."

Otis was shorter than Hance and twice Ivy's age. But he was always real friendly, even if he had the habit of blushing a bright red every time he talked to her.

As the men unloaded, several other fellas rushed over to help.

"Looks like you draw quite the crowd." Jericho spoke near Ivy's ear, sending her pulse into a full-out gallop. She'd taken up a post at the door, holding it wide for the men as they carried Greta's butter and eggs into the store.

Jericho had come from out of nowhere and was now standing beside her on the plank walkway. Maybe he'd been inside the store and had seen them pull up. "You could have offered to help too."

"You have more than enough men at your beck and call already."

"Maybe because everyone 'round here's real friendly, unlike you." She didn't look at him, but she caught a whiff of his unique scent, a blend of sage and gunpowder.

"Every man around here is friendly because you're flaunting your feminine figure."

She sucked in a sharp breath and spun to face him.

Freshly scrubbed and shaven, he was more handsome than even last night, more grown-up looking, more assured, more determined. But his eyes were a frigid blue, like a cold winter sky. He let his sights drop to her bosom for just an instant before pressing his lips together grimly.

She glanced at her bodice. The velvet buttons were still straining against the material, and the top two had already come loose. Heat spilled into her cheeks. Oh, land sakes. Astrid had been right about making alterations before wearing it.

Quickly, Ivy reached for one of the loose buttons and attempted to close it. But her fingers fumbled. Her mind spun back to her encounter with Jericho at the river, when her hands had been frozen and Jericho had almost buttoned her blouse. His gesture had been innocent enough. But she hadn't been able to forget about the brush of his fingers.

She didn't want to meet his gaze, but her eyes were drawn to his anyway. His pupils widened and darkened. Though his expression remained unreadable, something hot seemed to spark between them. Something she didn't understand but wanted more of.

He gave a curt shake of his head, as though fending her away. "I'd offer to help you with the buttoning. But I'm sure you could get any of the other men to do the job."

At the brazen insult, she lifted a hand and smacked his cheek. It happened before she could think, before she knew what she was doing.

He didn't flinch.

Around them, both inside and outside the store, the commotion came to a halt.

"You're a pig," she ground out, burning with fury but not sure why.

In an instant, Hance Payne was at her side, his face creased with concern. "Miss McQuaid, is everything alright?"

Jericho's cheek darkened with the print of her hand, but she didn't care. He deserved it for being rude. "I'm fine. Thank you for being so kind and polite, Mr. Payne. It's good to know such men still exist in this world."

"You're welcome, Miss McQuaid." Hance's gaze darted between Jericho and her. Of course he wouldn't know who Jericho was since he was fairly new to town. "If I can be of any assistance, just let me know."

The hurt inside Ivy swirled like a dust storm, growing stronger with each passing second. She didn't know the first thing about flirting or playing coy. But she slipped her hand boldly into the crook of Hance's arm and batted her eyelashes up at him. "You still interested in coming for a visit?"

"I'd love to." Hance nodded eagerly but then focused on Jericho's fingers moving to the handle of his pistol. "I, uh . . ."

"Tonight?" she persisted.

"Sure?"

Jericho gripped his gun.

Hance's Adam's apple bobbed.

Ivy reached over and swatted Jericho's hand away, unable to stop the perverse pleasure in knowing she was irritating him. "Quit trying to scare Hance."

Jericho's expression didn't falter. "If he's getting scared already, then he won't stand a chance."

She bristled. "A chance against who? You?"

"No, against you."

Against her? What did that mean?

With eyes narrowed in contempt at Hance, Jericho started on his way, his boots hitting the plank sidewalk with a force-fulness that nailed into Ivy's heart, making it ache with each step he took.

Hance watched Jericho's ramrod straight back before turning to her with wide eyes behind his spectacles.

"Don't worry about him." She wanted to stomp after Jericho, spin him around, and . . . and what? Slap him again?

He made her mad enough to bust. That's what. He was back less than twenty-four hours, acting like her brother, and already scaring off suitors worse than Wyatt or Flynn had ever done. Come to think of it, Jericho had always been worse at that. It was past time to show him he had no sway over the men she chose to court.

CHAPTER

6

"Then you'll sell me the land?" Jericho sat in the chair across the desk from Landry Steele. As longtime mayor of Fairplay, the man had done everything he could to build up the town's businesses and prosperity. He was good and fair, and Jericho had the utmost respect for him. His dark hair, mustache, and sideburns were threaded with more silver than had been there the last time Jericho had seen him, but Steele maintained a powerful and youthful appearance in his tailored black suit.

"I don't know how I can turn down your offer." Steele reclined in his chair and clamped down on his cigar. He inhaled before releasing the spicy-sweet tobacco smoke, adding to the haze that already clouded the room.

"But?" Jericho sensed Steele's reluctance and had ever since he'd stepped into the office and brought up the purchase.

"But . . ."

Steele met his gaze levelly. Did the man see through his ploy? Did he sense something was off?

Jericho didn't blink. Maybe he should have made a show of visiting other parcels that were up for sale. Problem was that most of the rest of them would take him too far from Fairplay.

Besides, he didn't want anyone else purchasing Steele's land before he did. If that happened, then he'd forfeit his reason to stay in the area. Without an excuse, he'd all but announce he was in town for something else. Wouldn't take Rodney James long to get suspicious of him.

Jericho steepled his fingers against his chin and forced himself to remain quiet and unruffled. Even with the self-doubt escalating, he had to wait and let Steele speak his piece.

The middle-aged man took another puff of his cigar. "Listen. Your deal is fair and square. Better than anyone else can come close to." He tapped ashes into a marble bowl. "I'll sell it to you, but then that means I'll have to forgo selling it to—"

"Mr. Steele?" A woman's call echoed in the hallway followed by the closing of the front door.

Steele blanched. "Ivy McQuaid."

Jericho jumped up from his chair, knocking it backward but catching it before it could topple. Ivy had talked about saving for a little place of her own. He hadn't for a single second realized she was aspiring for Steele's land. But in an instant, he knew that's exactly what she was doing. She'd been putting her life at risk week after week in the competitions for the same land he intended to buy.

The footsteps in the hallway drew nearer to Steele's office door, which was open a crack.

Jericho suddenly felt like a bear cornered in a baiting ring. He glanced around, seeking an escape. The window. It was open. He could dive out. But at a firm knock, he knew he'd run out of time. The best he could do was hide in the shadows and pray she wouldn't see him.

As the door opened, he leapt behind it and out of sight—at least he'd be out of sight as long as she kept her attention on Steele and didn't turn around.

Steele glanced in his direction, his brows rising.

Jericho shook his head and made slashing motions across his throat, hoping Steele would read the cue not to say anything about his presence.

Ivy stepped into the room, and Steele rose from his chair. "Well, Ivy McQuaid, how timely that you've decided to stop in just now."

"Timely?" As she crossed to Steele's desk, Jericho's heart thundered in his chest like a dark prairie storm. What was he doing? Why was he hiding?

Blast it all. He was turning into a raving lunatic around her, just like always. He lifted a hand to his cheek, feeling the sting of her handprint from a short while ago.

He'd deserved it. And he deserved being called a pig. He'd behaved worse than an animal.

And why? Why had he gotten so ornery seeing all those men falling over themselves to help her and win her attention? It hadn't really been about the loose buttons on her bodice—although he hadn't liked the idea of anyone getting to see her creamy skin. Anyone but him.

No. He gave himself a rough mental shake. Not even him.

She straightened her shoulders. And all he could think about was how grown-up she was. In that pretty dress and little hat, she was a picture of perfection, the light green contrasting with her dark hair and eyes and tanned skin.

When he'd watched her out the store window, he'd been as overwhelmed as he'd been last night. He hadn't been able to move or speak. Not until she opened the door and bestowed a heart-melting smile on one of the men. Then a strange burn had flamed inside and only raged hotter.

Had he been jealous?

He almost snorted at the thought but caught himself, especially as Ivy finished retrieving something from her pocket and plunked it down on Steele's desk. The clank was none other than the sound of money.

She took a step back. "I wanted to give you that just so you know I'm real serious about buying the land."

Steele stared at the bag.

"It ain't—isn't—the full amount of the down payment. But I guarantee I'll have the rest by summer's end."

Steele kept his focus on the bag and cleared his throat. "I'm sure you will, Ivy."

She crossed her hands behind her back, and it didn't take Jericho but a second to realize why. Because they were shaking.

The raging storm in his chest dwindled to a soft patter. She was nervous. But she was more courageous than any other woman he'd met, working hard to earn the money and going after her dream. Not many women would have the guts to do it. And not many men would give a woman a chance to buy land.

If Ivy wanted the land and Steele was willing to sell it to her, then who was he to stand in the way?

He almost moved out of the shadows but then stopped himself. He needed the land. Or at least needed to project the image that he was planning to buy it. The truth was, once he caught Rodney James, he was returning to Chicago for another assignment, and he intended to sell or lease the land at that point.

But, of course, he couldn't tell Ivy that. He couldn't tell anyone.

Steele released a long sigh. "I know you've been saving to purchase the parcel. But I had another buyer come in and give me a better offer."

Ivy twisted her fingers together to stop the shaking. "Didn't know anyone else was interested."

Jericho was surprised at how calm her voice remained.

"I didn't either."

Ivy was silent for several heartbeats. "I'll match the offer."

Steele picked up a pen, completely ignoring the bag of coins. "As willing as I've been to consider this deal without saying anything to your brothers, I've been up-front with you about my hesitations."

"I know, but—"

"As a woman, you'll soon be married and will have your home and children to take care of. You won't have time for ranching."

Jericho's gut pinched. Soon be married? Was Ivy already serious about someone? She hadn't mentioned a fellow. Neither had anyone else. Then again, she wouldn't have invited the barber to come calling on her tonight if she was engaged, would she?

"My sister-in-law Savannah has a baby and owns the Double L now." Ivy's tone contained a note of desperation.

"She's also got a husband and a ranch manager."

"I don't see what that's got to do with anything."

"It has to do with the fact that once you get married, your

husband will have his own occupation and won't want to be saddled with your ranch."

"He won't be. I'll run it myself."

With each passing second, Jericho's muscles tightened with the need to rise to Ivy's defense. Ivy was as skilled a rancher as any he'd ever met. In fact, she knew more than most about the operations of a ranch. She deserved a chance at making her own way as much as any fellow.

Steele tugged at his collar as if it were strangling him. "Ivy, I'm sorry—"

Jericho pushed the door and stepped out of the shadows. Steele glanced up, and Ivy spun.

Her eyes widened upon him, and she half jumped. "Holy Saint Peter, what are you doing here, Jericho?"

He pressed his lips together, not sure how to inform her of his objectives.

Ivy studied his face, then glanced at Steele before looking back at him. "You? You're the buyer?"

He didn't have to say anything. He guessed she could read the answer in his expression.

She strode to him and lifted her hand as though to slap his cheek again.

Might as well let her take her frustration out on him. He braced himself.

Stopping in front of him, she started to swing but then halted. Her body was rigid, and her beautiful face etched with anger.

"Let me explain."

"You're despicable." Her words came out an anguished whisper.

"It's not what you think—"

"I took you for a good man."

"And I am—"

"But I shoulda known you wouldn't care a lick about what I want." Her hand, poised in the air, trembled. She lowered it and retreated a step, her eyes blazing with contempt.

A strange disquiet pierced his soul. He'd riled up Ivy plenty of times in the past, but her eyes had always retained a measure of admiration. She'd looked up to him the same way she had Dylan.

The contempt was something new. And he didn't like it. Not in the least.

She grabbed the pouch of coins from Steele's desk and shoved it back into her pocket. Positioning her hat, she tossed Jericho a glare. Then she marched across the room and out the door, but not before he caught sight of tears brimming in her eyes.

Blast it all. He didn't want to make her cry. He had to do something to rectify the situation, but he didn't know what.

Her footsteps slapped on the hallway floor. The front door opened and then a second later slammed shut.

He had to go after her and try to clear things up as best he could. "Listen, Mr. Steele. I need a few minutes to talk with her."

Steele shrugged. "You can certainly try. But I've learned it's best to let a woman calm down first. She'll accept the situation better that way."

Steele might have more experience with women since he'd been happily married for years. But Jericho knew Ivy. And he'd rarely seen her near to tears. He couldn't stand back and do nothing when he'd hurt her like this.

He left Steele with the assurance he'd be back. As he

stepped out of the house and onto Main Street, his pulse tapped with the same uneasiness as before. He hadn't meant to cause trouble for Ivy.

He scanned the thoroughfare and caught sight of her rushing down the plank sidewalk, already halfway down the street. He was tempted to yell at her to stop. But he didn't want to call undue attention to her and have half the men in town pour out of their businesses again.

Instead, he started after her. When she swiped at her cheeks and ducked off the walkway between two buildings, he picked up his pace. At the intersection, he veered off but didn't see a sign of her anywhere.

When he reached the alley behind the buildings, he halted and searched both ways. The only person in sight was one of the saloon owners out behind his business relieving himself. Jericho backed up several steps and then scanned the dry-goods store on one side and the church on the other.

His attention snagged on the side door of the church, and he headed toward it. It wasn't locked, and it also wasn't closed tightly, almost as if someone had entered in a hurry and hadn't bothered to secure it all the way.

At the merest tug, the door pushed open. The town's only church wasn't a big place, had only six pews on either side of the aisle, a simple pulpit at the front, a painting of the Lord's Supper on one wall, and a painting of the Transfiguration on another.

As Ivy lowered herself onto the front pew, her attention darted to him. Though the one-room building was dark except for the light coming through the dusty windows on either side of the main door, he had no trouble seeing the tears streaking her cheeks.

"Go away, Jericho."

"We need to talk." He closed the door quietly behind him.

"I don't wanna talk to you ever again." She twisted so he couldn't see her face anymore. But the wobble in her voice told him she was still crying.

"Please let me explain."

"I wish you'd never come back to Colorado."

The harshness of her words barreled into him and sent him reeling. Should he just go away, take Steele's advice, and try to reason with her later? He grabbed the door handle and started to open it.

At her sniffle, he stopped, frustration digging into him. He was being an idiot again by causing her pain.

He released the door and sidled between two pews toward her.

She cast a glance toward him. "I told you to go away."

He crossed to the front pew where she was sitting.

"Don't know why you can't listen." Her statement was hard but edged with pain. "When you left, I told you not to come back."

He didn't have to ask her what she was referring to. The words she'd uttered to him the night he'd snuck away with Dylan had been a burr in his side for the past two years. *Go on now. And don't come back.*

He'd hated that they parted on bad terms. But somehow, he'd said the wrong thing, and she'd gotten upset. He should have tried harder to make things better before leaving, should have gone after her, should have parted ways as friends.

"Please just leave now, Jericho."

Heaviness pressed upon his heart, and he lowered himself to the spot beside her.

She stiffened and wiped rapidly at her cheeks. "I mean it. I don't want to see or talk to you again."

He laid a hand on her arm. "I'm sorry, Ivy."

She jerked away from his hold. "Sorry for what?" Her cheeks were flushed. As her chest heaved up and down, he tried to ignore how womanly she was and kept his focus on her face.

"I didn't know you were buying Steele's land until you walked into his house today."

Vulnerability flashed across her expression.

His mind scrambled to find a solution to the problem. There had to be something he could do, some way he could still pretend he was interested in the land without hurting Ivy's chances at buying it once he left.

"I'll tell you what." He lifted a hand to brush a stray tear from her cheek but then stopped himself. "We'll have a contest." A contest? What was he thinking?

She cocked her head slightly. "What do you mean?"

"It isn't fair of Steele to sell the land to me just because I'm a man."

"You're right about that." A spark came to life in her eyes again, exactly what he wanted to see there. He'd rather have her angry than hurt.

"Then whoever saves up for Steele's asking price first gets the place." The words tumbled out, the best he could think of so quickly.

"That ain't fair and you know it."

"Why?"

"'Cause, for starters, you probably already have a heap more saved than I do. And plus, you'll just go on and work construction for Wyatt. But I won't have any way to earn money except through the cowhand competitions."

"Wyatt and Flynn aren't paying you the same as the other cowhands?"

She released a scoffing laugh. "They tell me at least once a week I'm getting too old to be out working with the cattle and oughta be back at the house with the other womenfolk."

Jericho reckoned he might be doing the same if he were in their shoes. He didn't like the idea of Ivy being out on the range with the men, even if Flynn or Wyatt or Judd was always present. She was naïve to think the fellows would ignore how pretty she was and accept her as just another cowhand.

"That's what I'll do." She fiddled with one of the buttons still open on her bodice. "Greta needs the help, has offered to pay me. I'll tell her I'll do it."

"Alright. Then starting today, whoever saves up the most by the end of the summer has the right to buy the land." He'd gained himself some time, which meant he wouldn't hurt his cover as a would-be rancher, but he also didn't have to hurt Ivy's dream of getting her own place.

Her eyes had rounded, making them more beautiful, especially because her lashes were so long and dark. "You'd do that?"

"Do what?"

"Give me a fair chance at it?" She watched his face carefully as though attempting to see behind his expression into his mind.

He tried to ignore the guilt that nudged him, the guilt that told him he didn't want the land in the first place, that he'd let her have it at the end of the summer no matter how much she earned.

She quirked a brow. "What?"

She'd always been able to read him better than most

people. But this was a situation where he couldn't let her in on the truth. It was simply too dangerous. Rodney James was too dangerous. "I'll tell Steele about our competition, that he can sell the land to whoever wins."

She nodded, then plucked at a loose thread in her skirt. "Thank you—" she started.

"I'm sorry—" he said at the same time.

She met his gaze, the hurt gone, the old admiration back in place.

Some of the tension eased from his muscles. "You go first."

"No, you."

Yes, things were getting back to normal. He almost smiled. "I apologize for what happened at the store. I was out of line. For being such a pig."

She fiddled with the loose thread again. "I'm sorry for telling you I wished you'd never come back."

"And I'm sorry for leaving Colorado without trying to make things right between us."

Her eyes lightened with both warmth and surprise. "You are?"

He nodded. "I've regretted it ever since that night."

She drew in a breath.

He couldn't keep his attention from dropping to those open buttons, to the smooth, long line of her neck, and the gentle curve of her jaw and chin. Desire rippled through him, the desire to brush his knuckles along her cheek, to feel her skin, to graze a path down her neck.

Blazing smoke. What was the matter with him?

He tore his attention away and focused on the podium. Ivy was practically family, and he was a selfish son of a gun for wanting to touch her. Even if she'd turned into a ravishing woman, he had no right to view her the same way the other men did. He had to do a better job of controlling himself and couldn't let loose the manly needs he'd kept locked away.

Sure, he'd met nice-looking ladies in Chicago over the past two years, especially after he'd gotten involved in the church he'd gone to as a child. But he made sure to keep his distance and did his best to discourage any interactions.

He'd told himself that's just the way it needed to be. And he'd done fine at it. Until he'd seen Ivy.

He buried his face in his hands.

"What's wrong?" She was slightly breathless, and the sound stirred warmth in his gut.

This was Ivy. He didn't have to let himself get distracted by her. He just had to think of her the same way he always had—that she was too young for him. And too much like a sister.

She got riled up when he hinted at those things. But maybe it was better for her to be angry with him. It kept the barrier between them nice and high.

Her fingers grazed his shoulder.

The touch sent a hot jolt along his nerves. He jumped up, breaking the connection and getting a safe distance away from her. He reached the pulpit and braced his hands on the front edge.

"Something's bothering you." Her statement was firm, giving him little room to wiggle.

She was bothering him in ways he was too embarrassed to admit. So he pivoted and crossed his arms. "Don't worry. Things will be just fine. We're like family. And family looks after one another."

Her lips stalled around a response, and her brows furrowed.

"I promised Dylan I'd keep an eye on you, and that's what I'm planning to do."

She watched him a moment longer before clamping her lips together and standing. The warmth in her expression dissipated as the ice blew in.

Inwardly he sighed. He didn't like causing these kinds of rows, but he didn't have any other defenses against her.

She lifted her chin. "I don't need you looking after me. I never have, and I never will." She rose and strode away, just as she had in Steele's office, her back rigid and her steps angry.

As she exited, he sagged onto the nearest bench. She was mad at him again, but that was alright. Her frigidness would keep him cooled off, and that's what he needed. That, and a good dose of prayer for resisting temptation.

He bowed his head and prayed hard.

CHAPTER

7

Another gunshot filled the air. The blast, as well as the ring-
ing in Ivy's ears, drowned out Hance's retelling of his efforts
to transport a mirror for his barbershop on the back of his
horse up Kenosha Pass from Denver.

Perched on the bench outside the house, she had half a mind
to cross over to Jericho, rip the Colt from his hands, and topple
the pyramid of cans he'd erected to use as target practice. When
he'd returned from the construction work on the new inn, she
hadn't been sure if he'd noticed her sitting with Hance, who'd
come courting, just as she'd invited him to earlier in the day.

Jericho hadn't glanced her way. In fact, he'd disappeared
into the barn, likely taking care of his horse. He strode out
a short while later with a heap of cans in his arms. When
he started setting up the tins between the house and barn,
she hadn't realized what he was doing, until too late. Until
he'd taken aim at the top can and shot it off on the first try.

She'd realized then that not only had Jericho noticed her
sitting with Hance, but he'd placed the target practice right

next to them so he could keep his promise to Dylan to look after her.

Of course, Jericho's target practice had drawn a crowd—Judd as well as both Ellie and Ty—giving Hance and her even less privacy because now Ellie was sitting on her lap and clapping and cheering at every can Jericho hit.

Hance hadn't seemed to mind the noise or the intrusion. Leastways, it hadn't stopped him from rambling on about himself.

"Yay, Jericho!" Ellie squealed and hopped up. At three and a half, the girl was still petite and hardly weighed more than a June bug.

Jericho rewarded the little girl with a grin—one of his rakish, crooked, heart-stopping grins. One Ivy hadn't seen yet since his return. And now the sight of it unleashed a popping of powder burning in her stomach. His grin was a killer. It was a good thing he didn't show it often.

His apologies were killers too. When he'd left Mr. Steele's house and sat beside her in the church and told her he was sorry for everything, she'd been near to swooning. His apology had been about the sweetest thing she'd ever heard. Too bad he'd had to go and ruin the moment by bringing up his brotherly status in her life.

"We're like family." Just the remembrance of his words pestered her worse than a horde of horseflies.

As his gaze flickered over her, she snatched up Hance's hand, wrapped her fingers securely around his, and settled them on the bench between them.

In the middle of finishing his tale about the mirror, Hance pushed up his spectacles and examined their intertwined hands before smiling and scooting closer.

Jericho's grin fell away. He took rapid aim at the next can and fired. The tin flew into the air. Ty, standing next to Judd and well behind Jericho, gave a whoop, and Ellie started to cheer. But Jericho was already aiming at the next can and shooting. Within seconds, he sent the last half a dozen flying.

When the cans lay scattered about the yard, he holstered his Colt, then turned and faced Hance. "Time's up."

Hance paused midsentence.

Jericho rested his hand on his revolver. Was he trying to scare Hance again?

Ivy stood, hefting Ellie with her, which forced her to release Hance's hand. "Who appointed you my chaperone today?"

"I appointed myself and was giving you until I finished my target practice."

"Do it again, Jericho!" Ty shouted, staying close to Judd.

Ellie wiggled her way free and ran over to join Ty. "Do it again, Jericho."

About everything the girl said was a repeat of her big brother, reminding Ivy of how readily she'd followed after Dylan, how she'd admired him for so many years. If only she'd seen his pain and heartbreak coming, maybe she could have been there for him, been a better listener, helped soften the blow of rejection from Bethina Egleston when she'd turned down his offer of marriage and continued west with her family.

"We're done for today," Jericho said firmly. Both children's shoulders slumped and their smiles disappeared. But with the way Jericho was staring straight at her, his statement had been meant for her, not them.

When his attention dropped to Hance, his brows furrowed in a scowl. Hance burst up from the bench quicker than corn popping in an oiled pot.

"Jericho, you stop being a bully!" Ivy reached for Hance's hand again. She couldn't help it. Something inside was driving her to irritate Jericho. Maybe she wanted to believe he was jealous, wanted to make him realize what he was missing. But she'd learned long ago such efforts were in vain. Even if in the short term he acted concerned, that's as far as his bluster ever went.

"I think Hance was just leaving. Weren't you, Hance?" Jericho's question left little room for argument.

Hance opened his mouth to respond, but she beat him to it. "I reckon Hance is welcome to stay at least until Greta calls us in for supper. In fact, been thinking maybe I'll invite Hance to eat with us." That was a lie. She hadn't considered inviting him for supper even once. But with the way Jericho was bossing her around, she relished making him as prickly as a cactus.

"Come on, Hance." She pulled him toward the path that led behind the house down to the river. "Why don't we go for a walk? Just the two of us."

Jericho spread his feet. "The only place Hance is walking is straight to his horse."

Hance glanced from Jericho to her and back. Then he nodded. "I was planning on heading home soon anyway. Tonight, Otis and I are mapping out our next treasure-hunting route."

At the mention of treasure hunting, Ty's face lit. In an instant, he raced over to Hance and peppered him with questions. Ivy moseyed with Hance to his horse, all the while keeping their hands interlocked and making sure Jericho saw it.

She only half listened to Hance explain to Ty some of the treasure hunting he and Otis had already done. Because most of the easy gold in the Rockies had been mined over the past ten years since the start of the gold rush, more and more tales abounded about miners, thieves, and gangs who'd hidden their gold in mountain hideouts, only to abandon their loot for one reason or another. There were even stories about early Spanish explorers, as well as natives, who'd buried gold, hoping to come back for it, but never returned.

With every passing year, the interest in such treasures escalated. And men like Hance and Otis made a sport of searching for it.

As Hance reached his horse, he halted and peeked at Jericho. Even with Ellie holding up one of the cans and asking him to shoot it again, Jericho's attention was fixed on Hance and her like frost on a field.

Jericho didn't budge, not until Hance was mounted and urging his horse to a trot. Then he picked up the cans, carried them to the barn, and didn't come back out.

Ivy plopped down on the bench and watched the dust rising in the distance from where Hance was riding away. For a second, she tried to conjure up a feeling of some kind for the barber, but as she pictured him, she felt absolutely nothing, not even a smattering of interest.

Why not? He was a fine-looking fella. And he was mighty nice to her.

She released an exasperated sigh. She always hoped that in allowing herself to spend time with other fellas, a spark might develop with one of them. But it never happened. No matter how much time and effort she gave anyone who liked her, she could never reciprocate.

"Land sakes, Jericho," she murmured. "It's all your fault."

"What's all Jericho's fault, Ivy?" Ellie remained near the house while Ty had gone off, probably following after Jericho or Judd or both.

"Jericho's ruined me."

"Ruined?"

"I can't make myself like anyone else, 'cause none of them ever match up to him." Ivy reckoned she was safe enough sharing her thoughts with the little girl.

Ellie climbed up on the bench and patted Ivy's hand. Her blond hair was still plaited neatly after the long day, and her calico skirt and blouse as spotless as when she'd first put them on. With having three women—Greta, Astrid, and Ivy—to fuss over her, Ellie was much more conscious of particulars than Ivy had ever been.

Ivy had always been more interested in climbing trees, chasing frogs, and catching bugs than in her appearance. And though she'd tried to heed Astrid's advice the past two years on becoming more womanly and ladylike, she always seemed to fall short.

She glanced down to the buttons straining at the seams of her bodice. Even when she was wearing Linnea's pretty clothes, she still couldn't do it right.

If only Ma had been there for her. But her brothers had been more involved in her life than Ma had been, so that by the time Ma passed away, Ivy—at eleven—hadn't really grieved the loss or missed her.

During their long trip to the West, Linnea had been the

first woman to take a real interest in her. Greta had been a good influence on her too. But that hadn't stopped Ivy from feeling motherless all these years. And it hadn't stopped her from turning out to be a failure as a woman.

She hadn't really cared a whole lot about behaving and dressing properly until after Jericho left. She supposed that, in some ways, she'd blamed his lack of interest on her not being pretty enough or womanly enough to attract him. And she'd tried ever since to do a better job of being the woman everyone expected her to be.

Of course, she was bound to catch the attention of other men in the high country simply because a single woman was about as scarce as a daisy in a dung heap. But apparently she hadn't changed enough for Jericho. He wasn't interested in her now any more than he'd been before.

If only she could finally figure out how to put him from her mind once and for all.

～ゆ～

"Clear as a boil on a bulldog's nose that you care about her." Judd's voice cut through the silence.

With two beds instead of the usual bunks, the place was more private than the other cowhand cabins. Even so, it was cramped and musty, with hardly enough room to turn around. With the door propped wide and the window open, a night breeze blew inside, cooling them after the hot summer day.

Lying on his bed propped on his elbow with his journal before him, Jericho puffed at his pipe and slanted a glance at Healing Springs' overseer.

In the room's lone chair positioned by the oil lantern and

the unheated stove, Judd had his Bible open on his lap. Somewhere in his middle years, Judd had the coloring of an old man, a head full of thick white hair, a white beard, fluffy white eyebrows, and a long handlebar mustache.

Apparently, Judd had been with Wyatt from the start of the ranch. He didn't ride with the cowhands often anymore. Instead he kept watch over the goings-on closer to home. He'd always spent more time with Greta and the children than he did anyone else. While he wasn't much of a talker, he was a beloved father and grandfather figure to everyone who lived there.

Judd met Jericho's gaze levelly. "You always were sufferin' with Cupid's cramp around her."

Jericho wanted to pretend he didn't know who Judd was referring to. But it wasn't worth the effort. "She's like a sister to me. That's all."

Judd released a low *harrumph*, one that told Jericho just how little he believed him. The older man turned the page in his Bible and dropped his attention back to his reading, but not before Jericho saw the twinkle in the man's eyes.

Jericho pulled in another puff, rolled the cherry tobacco smoke around in his mouth, then exhaled it while dragging his focus back to the notes in front of him, ignoring the flush creeping up his neck. He wasn't about to let himself dwell on Ivy. He'd done enough of that for one day.

He picked up his pencil and jotted another note about Hance before comparing him to the small black-and-white photograph he had of Rodney James. Taken at the start of the War of Succession, it showed Rodney with a scraggly beard and mustache. He wore his bowler hat low over long hair, shielding his eyes. He was of medium height without any other features that set him apart.

The lack of identifying qualities made the tracking down difficult, especially because Rodney had likely done all he could to change his appearance, no doubt giving himself a clean-cut look without all the facial hair.

After only two days back, Jericho had listed at least a dozen men who could fit Rodney's vague physical profile. And after a few more days of digging around, he'd be able to list a dozen more.

Of course, he had a short list of other indicators. He knew the man had asthma, had a traumatic childhood of abuse from his father, had eventually lived with his elderly grandmother before joining the war efforts, and had never been married.

But still, it wasn't much to go on.

Judd cleared his throat. "You can pull your hat down and ride blind 'round a swamp. But that's a surefire way to get stuck."

Again, Jericho was tempted to pretend ignorance. But he was too adept at picking up clues to miss what Judd was telling him. He closed his journal, making sure to tuck the picture of Rodney well out of sight. Then he pushed himself up until he was sitting, his bare feet planted on the plank floor.

"Do you want me to admit I'm attracted to Ivy?"

"Reckon it's about time."

Jericho had always fought against such an admission. Even now he didn't want to acknowledge that maybe—just maybe—he'd been drawn to Ivy all along. Whatever the case, he couldn't give in to the craving.

"Admitting to it won't do her or me any good." That was an understatement of a lifetime.

"Snubbing it ain't doin' you a lick of good either."

Was Judd referring to the interaction with Hance earlier that evening? Jericho hadn't intended to get carried away with the target shooting and the bullying. Watching Ivy sitting on the bench with Hance had been hard enough. But seeing them holding hands and cozying up together had been more than he could stand.

"He was moving too fast with her." Jericho's words came out defensive and sounded weak, even to his own ears.

"Reckon he could have been movin' as slow as a half-baked turtle in the desert, and it still would have been too fast in your book."

Jericho rubbed a hand across his forehead and kneaded his temples. The bald, plain-faced truth was that he'd been jealous. He didn't like seeing Ivy with any other men, not any more now than he had in the past.

"Blast it all." He blew out a tense breath. "What should I do?"

Maybe he needed to get a bed at the hotel in town after all. He'd told himself he was only staying for a couple of days, but now that he was situated, he hadn't wanted to leave.

"Instead of skirtin' a swamp, best thing is to slog through it."

Judd insinuated that walking around the issue of his attraction to Ivy would cause him to get stuck. But he was already stuck. Stuck in Fairplay. Stuck at Healing Springs Ranch. And stuck with seeing Ivy every time he walked two steps in any direction. "I can't."

The pages of Judd's Bible rustled as he flipped through them. "Good thing for us, we ain't alone in the slogging. The Lord says in Psalm 37, 'The steps of a good man are ordered by the LORD: and he delighteth in his way. Though he fall, he shall not be utterly cast down: for the LORD upholdeth him with his hand.'"

Jericho wanted to let God direct him. And he prayed that if the time came when he took a tumble, the Lord would be right beside him holding him up. But that didn't mean he was dragging a woman into trouble beside him. His dad had done that, and look where it had led him. When his mom's body had been found strangled and lifeless, Dad had fallen hard, had been utterly cast down, and hadn't ever pulled himself back up.

"The best thing I can do for Ivy is make sure she finds happiness, but that won't happen with me."

Judd gently closed the Good Book and brushed a hand over its worn cover. "If you take the time to get to know Ivy the way I do, you'll see it don't take much to make her happy."

Before Jericho could think of a response, Judd stood, blew out the lantern, then headed out the door, leaving him alone in darkness.

For the briefest of moments, Jericho entertained the idea of getting to know Ivy better. What would it be like to openly court her, to sit on the bench next to the house, hold her hand, and pass the time doing nothing but talking?

He couldn't think of a nicer way to spend an evening.

No. An inner protest jolted him upright. He hadn't ever and wasn't about to start letting himself become infatuated with Ivy McQuaid. She'd always been off-limits. She still was. And that's all there was to it.

CHAPTER

8

The dust blew against Ivy's face, stinging her eyes. The late June heat combined with the lack of rain over recent weeks had caused the ground to dry up worse than the sun-bleached bones of a cattle carcass.

She tugged the bandana up higher over her nose to keep from breathing the dust particles, and she tipped the brim of her hat lower to shield her face as best she could. But her eyes burned, and her throat was scratchy anyway. The open rangeland, with nothing more than sagebrush, shrubs, and shortgrass, offered little protection from the flying dirt that now coated every inch of her from hat to boots.

Regardless, she loved the wide-open sky, the freedom of the vast prairies, and the view of the mountains no matter which way she rode. And she didn't want to be anywhere else. Though the hour was growing late and the shadows were lengthening, she wasn't ready to head home.

She'd made it three whole days cooped up in Greta's hot kitchen. But somehow she was always causing problems.

Yesterday, she'd left the ax out, only to have a porcupine chew the handle off overnight. Early this morning, she'd forgotten to close the garden gate, and the rabbits had slipped inside and eaten half the new beanstalks. When she'd accidentally dropped a pot of hot pie filling, Greta had graciously suggested she take the afternoon off.

Ivy hadn't needed a second prodding, had rushed outside and begged Judd for something to do. He'd sent her out with salt for each of the pastures. The long ride across the land, the hot sunshine, and the blowing wind had reminded her why she wanted her own place.

The problem was, while she was out riding around, she wasn't making a single penny, and Jericho was still at the inn's construction site. Even if Jericho had tried to make their challenge fair, things between men and women weren't fair, not in work, not in the cowhand competitions, not in landowning, not in wages, and not in a whole heap of other things.

She supposed in some ways Linnea's views on women's rights had rubbed off on her over the years. Linnea was always up on the latest in the women's suffrage movement, since her mother and sister were involved in it. Recently, Linnea had been excited to get the news from her mother that Susan B. Anthony and Elizabeth Cady Stanton had formed the National Woman Suffrage Association the previous month. Linnea didn't think it would be long before women gained the right to vote. Places like Wyoming Territory were already considering it.

Too bad none of those women's rights were available to Ivy this summer. And Jericho's interest in buying land had only made things more complicated.

"Oh, Jericho," she muttered under her bandana. "Why'd you have to come back?"

She didn't see hide nor hair of him during the days. But he took his meals with the family in the evenings and lingered afterward, talking with Wyatt and catching up on all the news. She'd wanted to ignore him but somehow couldn't. With each passing day, her attraction kept burning, despite the fact she was doing her best to douse every spark that flared to life.

Even though she'd been sorely tempted to stay with Flynn so she wouldn't have to see Jericho, she'd decided she had to follow through with helping Greta. Lending her sister-in-law a hand was the right thing to do. In fact, she should have offered earlier. With being in the family way and due real soon, Greta was always tired and ached in places Ivy hadn't known existed.

Astrid did most of the child watching and cooking and cleaning. But Greta needed help with her jam and baking business, at least until after the baby was born. And whether Ivy wanted to or not, she'd resolved to stick it out for Greta's sake.

As Ivy dropped the last of the salt blocks to the ground, a distressed bleating wafted her way. She hadn't realized any cattle were out in the eastern pasture today, had seen the cowhands heading to the south at sunrise. But it was possible a few steers had wandered off, especially with how big the herd was these days.

She urged Poppy up an incline so she could get a better view of the surrounding pastureland. The swirl of dust obscured the view for a moment, but as it passed, she saw that several cattle were down a short way, close to the river. One of them appeared to be trapped in a bog.

The bogs were pesky areas that had to be checked almost daily. For this very reason.

Ivy started toward the strays. As she drew nearer, she could tell the bog was nearly dried up, but a calf had wandered in—probably to get away from biting flies, gnats, and mosquitoes. And the poor baby had gotten itself stuck almost near to its belly.

She breathed out a prayer of thankfulness that it was just a little critter instead of one of the heavy steers. Getting the big cattle out of the bogs was a difficult process with the need for chains and a team of horses. Even then, with all the pulling and hauling, the suction of the mud was so great that sometimes the cows died during the extraction.

Eyeing the situation, she grabbed her rope. She'd try digging him out on her own, but she might have to ride back to the ranch and get some help.

The calf cried out again, a pitiful sound.

"I'm a-comin'," she called out to let the other cattle know she was there. Wouldn't do any good to spook the rest of them into the bog. One trapped creature was enough.

She cinched the end of her rope to the pommel. Then making sure her horse was on firm footing, she hopped down and started toward the calf, loosening the rope as she went. At the edge of the bog, she paused, pulled off her boots, stockings, trousers, and split skirt, leaving herself attired in her underdrawers.

No sense in dirtying up more than she had to. She'd already made everyone mad enough the past couple of days with her bumbling efforts around the house. She didn't need the womenfolk even madder for dragging in half the bog on her clothing.

She stepped in, and the mud oozed between her toes, warm and sticky. If the rain held off much longer, the mud would turn as hard as bricks. Even now, it stuck heavily to her skin.

As she sank in up to her ankles, she murmured words of comfort to the calf. He shifted his head toward her and bleated out his distress. The thickness of the mire had prevented the calf from wandering in too far. But still, the poor thing had no idea why he was trapped.

"I've got you." She reached the calf's back end, rapidly finding herself up to her knees. She brushed her hand across his flank, then went to work wrapping the rope around the hindquarters in a sling-like fashion, securing him as best she could.

"Let's see if we can dig away some of this mud before we give Poppy the howdy-do to tug you out." Using her hands as shovels, she tried to free the calf's legs from the mud as much as possible. But the trouble was that with each scoop, more of the slimy mixture slid back into its place.

She worked faster and dug harder but made little headway. Finally, she called a command to Poppy, and the horse began hauling. Ivy worked steadily, rolling the calf back and forth, hoping to break the suction. But Poppy wasn't strong enough.

Releasing a growl of frustration, Ivy straightened. She and Poppy wouldn't be able to do the job on their own. She'd have to head home for help.

"Don't worry." She rubbed the calf. "We'll get you out."

Dusk was creeping out fast. She'd already taken more time than she should have—probably shoulda gone for assistance sooner. She turned to go, but her feet wouldn't move, and she tumbled into the mud. She sank in up to her elbows but caught herself before she flopped onto her belly.

She freed her arms and tried to move her feet again, but she was solidly stuck. Just like the calf. She spewed out a few words that would have prodded a stubborn mule into action. Not cuss words. She hadn't gotten into the habit of cursing like some of the ranch hands. But she knew how to invent a string of words when she needed to let out her frustration.

She struggled and shoveled and tugged some more, but by the time darkness fell, she'd resigned herself to a long night in the bog. Wyatt and Greta wouldn't worry when she didn't return. They'd just assume she'd gone over to Flynn's and decided to stay there. Best she could hope for was being found by the cowhands sometime tomorrow when they rode out to round up strays.

༻✦༺

From his spot at the table, Jericho watched the door. The evening was nearly spent, and Ivy still wasn't home. All around came the usual noises: the clank of silverware against plates, the chatter of the children, and the occasional rattle of the house frame from the wind.

No one else seemed to notice or care about her absence. If the family wasn't concerned, then why was he?

He pushed the last of the potatoes and gravy around on his plate, took a final bite, then washed it down with a gulp of coffee.

"Yep, the fire cleaned out the whole area, not a building left." Wyatt gave a nod of thanks to Astrid as she finished pouring him another cup of coffee.

At some point during the last part of the meal, Jericho

had lost track of Wyatt's conversation about the forest fires burning to the north. There wasn't anything unusual about summer fires. The Utes had the custom of setting fire to areas overgrown with brush in order to clear out the land and make room for more grazing. And there were always prospectors and settlers accidentally starting blazes from unattended campfires or flyaway sparks.

With the lack of rain, however, they'd been getting reports that the fires in the mountains to the north of Fairplay had been burning for longer than a week and the flames were spreading with growing intensity.

As Astrid rounded the table and tipped the coffeepot toward Jericho's mug, he placed his hand over the top. "Thank you kindly. But I'm done."

The petite girl gave him a shy smile and then turned away to return to the kitchen. If anyone would know where Ivy was, Astrid would.

He watched her retreat, his anxiety mounting until he couldn't contain it. "Astrid?"

She spun so fast she would have sloshed the coffee out of the pot if it had been full. "Yes?"

"You wouldn't happen to know where Ivy is, would you?"

At his query, her expression fell.

Jericho replayed the question in his mind. What about it bothered her?

"I'm sorry, Jericho. Ivy's much too wild and independent for me to keep track of."

Astrid's emphasis on *wild* and *independent* held a note of frustration. Or derision. Jericho wasn't sure. But he did know the girl wasn't about to be of much help.

"She's probably over at Flynn's," Greta cut in from where

she sat in a rocker by the open window with Ryder on her lap—or at least the portion of lap not taken up by her protruding abdomen. A breeze fluttered the curtains and brushed against Greta's flushed face. "She often stays with him for days at a time. We never know when she's coming or going."

Ivy always had been restless, never settling down at either one of her brother's houses. Nevertheless, something in his gut told him she wouldn't have run off to Flynn's. Not at the start of their contest, not when she was desperate to earn money.

Jericho excused himself, saddled up, and started on his way to Flynn's. Of course, Flynn had already tracked him down at the construction site and plied him for every iota of information he had about Dylan. Although Flynn's interrogation had been more intense than Wyatt's, in the end Flynn had extended the hand of friendship to him just like he always had.

Flynn's place was only a mile or so to the north, and as Jericho rode the well-worn path, his gut churned with the memories that came to life the closer he drew. Memories of Nash. Memories of their last year together.

It had been a good year, better than the year spent up in the mining camps when they'd lived out of a tent and cooked their meals over an open campfire. When Flynn had gotten a telegram about Brody being in the hospital at the end of the war, he'd asked Nash to live in his house and take care of the place while he traveled east to be with Brody.

They'd given up on the gold mining, and the ranching job had been perfect for the interim. With the war over, Nash had been in contact with their dad and had been awaiting word on whether he wanted them to return to Chicago.

If only Dad had responded sooner and called them home before they'd taken over running Flynn's ranch. Maybe then Nash would still be alive and working in Chicago for the Pinkerton Agency alongside him.

As it was, Nash had died a terrible death when they'd been out rounding up cattle in the Kenosha Range by Windy Peak. Nearly three years ago.

Jericho's chest pinched as he visualized that day all too clearly. Rain had kept up a steady pace all morning, and in the higher elevations, it felt like ice pellets against his face. Dead, yellowed pine needles already made the way slippery, as did the few piles of leftover winter snow.

"Come on now," Nash had said to his mare, leaning in and rubbing a gloved hand along her neck. The horse had been agitated throughout the morning, and Nash claimed it was because Hades was in the area. The tough old mustang and his band ran wild in the mountains and had before the settlers had come to the territory.

Jericho nudged his mount onward, his eagerness to reach the caves driving him. Rounding up the strays was just an excuse to do more exploring in the high mountain caverns believed to have been a hideout to the Kingston Gang during the war. Most of the gang had eventually been caught and had served justice at the end of the hangman's noose. But rumors abounded regarding the loot the thieves had buried in the mountains—gold that might still be there.

"Maybe we better head back down," Nash's voice beckoned to Jericho.

"Just a little farther." Jericho pulled his slicker over his boots. The raincoat was split up the back so that each half lay across the saddle, the long, lightweight canvas falling to his ankles. He was still plenty warm and dry. Now that they were nearing their destination, Jericho had every intention of getting there. "We can warm up and dry out once we reach the caves."

He waited for Nash's protest. When it didn't come, Jericho continued on, guiding his mount carefully over the dangerous terrain.

Behind him, Nash's mare gave another whinny, which was followed by more of Nash's gentle reassurance. If anyone could manage a horse, Nash could. He was a kind soul, and every horse knew it.

"She's growing more agitated by the second." This time Nash's call was urgent. "We must be getting too near to Hades."

The wild mustang was known for stirring up tamed horses and even drawing some mares away from their owners.

"I'm heading back down!" Nash shouted.

Jericho shifted around in his saddle, intending to bargain with his brother again. But Nash was too busy reining the mare and trying to keep her from rearing up. "Whoa, now! Calm down!"

The mare shied near the edge of the trail, sending a cascade of rocks rolling down the steep side of the mountain.

Jericho's muscles tensed and he halted. What was Nash doing? Why wasn't he controlling his horse better? Jericho's mount snorted, clearly sensing the growing turmoil.

As he bent in to rub and reassure his horse, Nash's mare tossed her head. In the next instant, the creature lost her footing, slipped over the trail, and started sliding down the mountain.

Jericho could only watch in horror as the momentum sent

the horse toppling end over end until she became airborne. Nash yelled, tried to grab on to shrubs, but he was flying too fast.

When they landed at the bottom of the steep gorge, Jericho had been sick to his stomach, emptying everything inside.

Even now, Jericho swallowed the bile that rose into his throat every time he thought about all that had happened. How he'd had to backtrack carefully down the mountain, how it had taken what seemed like hours to he reach Nash, how he'd found his brother with a broken neck, lifeless.

For a long while after that day, he'd attributed Nash's death to the wild horses that roamed South Park, mainly Hades, and he'd done his best to rid the area of the creatures. In fact, he'd quit working for Flynn at Healing Springs Ranch and had taken the position as foreman of Elkhorn Ranch because the owner there hated the mustangs and wanted to eliminate them too.

In hindsight, Jericho knew he hadn't blamed the wild horses as much as he blamed himself. But at the time he needed to avenge Nash's death, and killing mustangs had been the only way he'd known how.

Jericho breathed in deeply of the night air, catching the hint of smoke and ash from the wildfires to the north. He still held himself responsible for the loss. If only he hadn't pushed on, had turned back sooner, had paid better attention to the treacherous conditions.

"I'm sorry, Nash," he whispered harshly to the star-studded sky. "I was a selfish fool. I realize that now, and I'm trying to be a better man the way you wanted me to be."

Although Nash had never spoken ill of their dad, he'd made it clear Jericho was to leave alcohol well enough alone.

After watching the way it had destroyed their dad's life, Jericho hadn't argued with his brother. He'd resisted the urge to drown his problems in a bottle, knowing the drowning out of one problem only created a dozen more. He'd seen that truth play out in Dylan's life as well. And Jericho would much rather do the rescuing than struggle with having to be rescued.

As he rode up to Flynn's white-painted two-story farmhouse set amidst a sprawling yard with a large barn and other outbuildings, he shook off the angst of the past and forced himself to think on Ivy. Her well-being was the most important thing right now. All he had to know was that she was safe, and he'd ride away satisfied.

He hopped down and didn't bother looping his horse to the hitching post before bounding up the steps and pounding his fist against the door.

Flynn answered, his limp hurried, his green-blue eyes rounded with worry. He was still attired in his dusty work clothes—dark wool trousers and a loose cotton shirt under his vest. His hat ring was visible in his brown hair, which was a shade lighter than Ivy's. "What's wrong?"

"Is Ivy here?" Jericho peered past Flynn into the hallway and front parlor. Linnea and five-year-old Flora with their curly red hair were close on Flynn's heels, clearly sensing from his urgent knock that something wasn't right.

"Haven't seen her all week," Flynn replied. "Think she's in trouble?"

"Is she with Savannah and Brody?" Jericho had passed another house on his way in and guessed it was Brody's place. Even if he and Brody had clashed over the wild horses last time Jericho was in the high country, he still respected

Brody and was relieved the fellow had found a way to help control the mustang population so they weren't competing with the cattle for grassland.

"Savannah and Brody are still down on the Front Range."

Jericho glanced around the quiet ranch yard. "Then she's not here?"

"Nope." Flynn followed his gaze, the furrows in his forehead deepening. "I take it she's not at Wyatt's either?"

Jericho shook his head. "No one's seen her since early afternoon."

"Maybe she went to town."

"Don't know why she would."

"Don't know why that girl does half the stuff she does." Flynn's tone was loaded part with affection and part with exasperation.

Jericho's pulse hammered harder with a worry that had been growing with each passing hour of her absence.

Ivy was in trouble. And he needed to find her.

CHAPTER

9

Nothing and no one. Jericho held his lantern high and scanned the rangeland that lay before him.

"Ivy!" he called.

In the distance, the night breeze brought the echo of the others shouting her name. With him, Flynn, Wyatt, Judd, and several cowhands out searching for her in all directions, Jericho figured they would've found her by now. Unless she was lying unconscious. Or even dead.

A chill shot through his blood as it had every time he considered what might have happened to her, especially that she'd been kidnapped. Although he didn't want to let his mind go there, he couldn't release the nagging prospect someone had captured her in order to get to him. It wasn't possible anyone had figured out his connection with Pinkerton, was it? Certainly Rodney James didn't know he was working as a bounty hunter. Not yet.

"Ivy!" he shouted again.

Judd had indicated Ivy had been out delivering rock salt, something the cattle needed in order to gain sufficient weight as well as keep them from developing certain diseases. Carrying and distributing the salt was a standard job throughout the summer. Ivy had likely done it dozens of times over the years. So what had happened today?

Had she headed up into the foothills? Gone farther than usual? Maybe she'd raced after a band of wild horses. She had a tender heart for the creatures. Or maybe she'd roamed into a fire zone and been trapped.

Even though Jericho's thoughts galloped at full speed, he tried to rein them in and think rationally. "Ivy, what were you doing?" She would have been going about her job, putting out the salt. And then, no doubt, she'd gotten caught up rescuing one of the cattle. But from what? And where?

Whatever it was had prevented her from returning. Had she gotten stuck?

The only way to get stuck was in a bog. But most were dried up by now, or nearly so. He didn't want to waste valuable time checking them. Yet he was running out of other options.

He veered toward the river and began a slow and steady hunt, the same way he'd rounded up strays when he'd been foreman at Elkhorn Ranch. As he checked first one bog and then another with no sight of her, his fear ran deeper.

Of course, he'd always worried about Ivy. But why was he reacting so strongly to her disappearance this time? The question sifted through him, and though he wanted to ignore it, he couldn't push it away. Not after the conversation earlier in the week with Judd. He was attracted to Ivy. Maybe he'd denied it all these years, but that didn't change the truth. He'd liked her when they'd been just kids. And he still did.

If Judd could see his feelings, could everyone else? Including Ivy? He shook his head. He doubted she saw anything except his aggravation.

He nudged his mount up a short hill and held up his lantern, peering down into the bog that was on the eastern edge of the river and property.

"Over here!" came a cry from the direction of the bog. "Help!"

It was Ivy. "What are you doing out here?" His relief was so staggering it turned his question harsh.

"Thought I'd sit for a bit and let the mosquitos chaw down on me since they're hungry." She paused a moment. "What in the blazes do you think I'm doing? I'm stuck in the bog."

"Hold on. I'm coming." He took out his revolver, pointed it into the air, and fired a shot, letting the others know he'd found her. Then he urged his horse toward the bog.

With his lantern casting tendrils of light over the tall grass and shrubs, he caught sight of her horse first, then a rope attached to her saddle leading to a calf stuck up to its belly in mud. She stood behind the creature up to her thighs, hardly distinguishable with the mud caking her arms, torso, and even face. Most had dried to her skin, which told him she'd been there a while.

From what he could tell, she'd gone in to rescue the calf, thinking she could pull it loose with her horse. But she hadn't been able to work the creature free, and in the process, she'd gotten stuck herself.

"I can't believe you're here." Her wide eyes peered at him from a mud-darkened face.

"You shouldn't have gone after the calf by yourself."

"Mighty fine advice. I appreciate it."

He grabbed his rope and began knotting it around the pommel. "Just once do you ever stop and think?"

"I always figure it's a heap more fun to get into trouble."

"You should try thinking before you act. It's what grown-ups do."

"Why should I when I have you thinking for me?"

He bit back the rest of the frustrated words he wanted to say. He'd only rile her even more and make himself angrier in the process.

"Listen." He tried gentling his tone. "We've been worried. That's all. Let's just get you out."

"That'd be real nice." The defensiveness dropped away, and she sounded weary.

"Form a second sling around the calf with my rope." He tossed the line out to her.

She caught it and wrapped it around the calf, her movements stiff from the mud. When she finished securing the animal, she shoveled away the sticky mixture as best she could. Then she straightened, grabbed on to the calf and the two slings, and gave him a nod.

He flicked the ropes and clicked at the horses. Both moved forward a step. The calf slid only a little, but it was enough.

"Rock it back and forth, and we'll go slow." Even before the words left his mouth, she was digging and pushing. She didn't need his instructions, already knew what to do and was good at it. They inched the calf toward the edge of the bog, using the muscle power of the team of horses along with her shoveling and wiggling.

As the creature reached the shallow mud and pulled free, it gave an almost angry bellow. Once clear of the bog, it charged up the hill like it was under attack from a swarm of hornets, but it was only able to go so far with the ropes still attached to it.

Ivy followed after the calf more slowly, her shoulders sagging, her feet dragging. He could see exhaustion in her every movement. And no wonder. She'd probably been working to free herself and the calf for hours.

Heedless of the mud, he waded in and met her. Without asking for her permission, he scooped her off her feet and carried her like a baby.

"I'm fine, Jericho." Her protest was weak, and she wrapped her arms around his neck to hang on.

He trudged through the sludge. Even though he'd only gone in up to his ankles, the mud was thick and tugged at his boots, trying to rip them from his feet. When they reached solid ground, he stumbled and sank to his knees. He sat back and brought her with him, positioning her on his lap.

For a moment, he couldn't move, and her labored breathing mingled with his.

"You alright?" he whispered.

"I'll be fine in a minute." She laid her head against his shoulder.

The slime of mud coated him too, but he didn't care. All he cared about was that he'd found her, that the mishap had been nothing more than poor judgment on her part, and that now she was safe in his arms.

The rest of the search party would be riding up at any

second, but he needed this brief respite with her, needed to hold her just a fraction longer to reassure himself everything was okay.

Her warm exhalations brushed his neck. And she clung to him as if she never planned to let go.

He liked it. Liked holding her. Liked being near her. He rested his cheek against her head. Stiff mud coated her hair, but he closed his eyes and relished the sweet feel of her pressed against him.

"Didn't reckon anyone would come searching for me tonight." Her breathing was calmer.

"Guess you didn't count on me wondering where you were."

"Were you worried?" Her tone contained a note of teasing.

"Maybe a little."

"Or maybe a whole lot?"

"I didn't think you'd give up on earning that land by going to Flynn's."

"You're right about that."

At the fire returning to her voice, he smiled.

"Appreciate you a-comin' after me. Would've been a long night standing there in the mud."

"You're welcome."

As she relaxed into him, he grew suddenly conscious that one of his arms was still wrapped underneath her at the bend of her legs and was pressing into her backside . . . a scantily clad backside.

He glanced down to find her bare lower legs and feet tucked up against him. Even covered in mud, there was no disguising the beauty of her endlessly long legs. Where was her skirt? It took another second before his mind registered the fact that she wasn't fully dressed.

"Blast it all, Ivy."

"What's wrong?" Her face pressed into the crook of his neck, her mouth so close he could almost imagine her lips brushing his skin.

For a second he held his breath, his body keenly aware of each of her curves, his eyes drawn again to her thin legs, slender ankles, and pretty feet. He'd seen her feet plenty of times in the past since she'd always gone barefoot. But somehow seeing her like this was entirely different. She was different. Maybe he was. Or both.

At a nearby shout, he sat up straighter. The others were coming, having heard his gunshot and narrowing down where it came from.

A strange jealousy prodded him. He didn't want anyone else to see Ivy in her underdrawers. "Everyone will be here soon. You need to get your skirt back on. Now." He started to set her onto the ground beside him, but she didn't release her hold around his neck.

"I'm covered in mud. They ain't gonna see much." She kept her head on his shoulder.

He reached for her arms and began prying them loose. "I can see plenty. Now get dressed."

She stretched her legs out. "Didn't think you were looking at me that way, Jericho."

"I'm not." He finished unhitching her arms and jumped to his feet, trying to find something to focus on besides her beautiful legs. His gaze landed upon the pile of her discarded garments and shoes. He grabbed them and then thrust them at her, keeping his face averted.

She didn't move.

"Take them." He dropped them onto her lap.

"Why are you always stumbling upon me when I'm indecent?" Her question held a note of humor.

"Oh, I don't know." He spoke irritably to keep his longing at bay. "Maybe it has something to do with the fact that you can't keep your clothes on."

She laughed lightly and ignored the clothing. Instead, she wiggled one of her feet as though to tempt him.

And tempt him she did. He couldn't keep himself from taking his fill of the length of her leg to the very tips of her toes.

She laughed again, and this time the sound was sultrier, as if she realized the effect she had on him and liked it.

"Blazing smoke, Ivy. Quit teasing me."

"So you *are* looking at me that way."

"What way?"

"Like maybe you think I'm pretty."

"Of course I think you're pretty."

"You do?" Her eyes darted to his and rounded. In the flicker of lantern light, the brown was rich and dark and her lashes seemed even longer. If he waded in, he was liable to get stuck there every bit as much as in the bog.

In fact, he had to backtrack. Fast. "All the McQuaid women are sweet and pretty."

She stuck her bottom lip out in a pout, one that only drew his attention to her mouth. What would it be like to kiss her?

Before he could reprimand himself for the wayward thought, voices came from behind them. The jealousy needled him again. "Hurry up and get dressed."

As horses and riders appeared over the hill, Jericho stepped in front of Ivy with his back facing her and braced his feet apart to shield her indecency.

"She alright?" Flynn was at the forefront, his lantern held high, illuminating the anxiety in his face.

"I'm fine." Ivy was standing now directly behind Jericho, peeking out and so close he could almost feel her pressing into his back. "Just got stuck in the bog is all."

Flynn reined in and hopped down. Wyatt was right behind him. Several others halted a short distance away but didn't dismount. Thankfully. Since Ivy still wasn't dressed.

Flynn strode right toward Ivy. As he took in her state of undress, his expression went from worried to irate in an instant. "Thunderation, Ivy! What's going on?"

"I just wanted to save Greta and Astrid a heap of laundry by not dirtying up my clothes."

"I don't care if you wanted to save them a month of washings. You oughta know better than to strip down."

"You would've done the same thing—"

"I'm a man!"

"What difference does that make?"

Flynn spun and returned to his mount, grabbed a blanket from the saddle, and tossed it at Ivy. "Hurry and wrap up in this."

As Ivy unfolded the blanket, Flynn reached out and smacked Jericho in the shoulder. "And why you are just standing there? Why didn't you get her a blanket?"

"Reckon Jericho was a little busy," Ivy piped up from behind him, "pulling me and the calf out of the bog."

And he'd been busy ogling her. But he couldn't admit that to Flynn.

Within no time, she was covered, on her horse, and riding toward the ranch house with Judd.

As Jericho freed the calf from the rope slings, Flynn came

to stand beside him. "Listen, I'm sorry about before. You found and saved Ivy. I reckon I owe you a thank-you and not a scolding."

"No, you were right." Jericho started coiling the rope. "I should have given her a blanket."

Flynn watched him silently for several heartbeats. "Got any intentions toward her?"

"No."

"Good."

Jericho paused. Good? Did that mean Flynn thought he was unworthy? Not that he was thinking of pursuing anything. But Flynn's immediate dismissal didn't sit well.

"She's too young, and you know it." Flynn tipped up the brim of his hat, revealing his serious eyes.

Jericho was tempted to agree. But after seeing Ivy over the past week, he was trying to accept that she was growing up. Clearly, that was hard for her brothers to do. No wonder she hadn't told them about her plans to buy Steele's land. They'd say she wasn't ready to be out on her own and running her own place, especially as a woman.

He had the strange urge to defend her to Flynn. "She invited the barber to come courting a few days ago."

"She doesn't have a hankerin' for Hance Payne." Something in Flynn's statement was almost accusatory. Why?

"So you're fine with her courting men, so long as she doesn't like them?"

"I'm not fine with her courting anyone yet." Flynn stared at him pointedly.

Did Flynn think *he* wanted to court Ivy? "I already told you I don't have any intentions toward her. I never have, and I never will."

He could feel Flynn studying him while he finished coiling the rope, as if testing the sincerity of his declaration.

Jericho hung his rope back on his saddle. "You don't have to worry about me, Flynn. I guarantee it."

Flynn released a sigh. "It's not you I'm worried about."

Jericho faced Flynn and crossed his arms over his chest. "Then why don't you stop running me around in circles and tell me what this is really about?"

"I'm worried about Ivy," Flynn said hesitantly. "She's always had a hankerin' for you."

"No—"

"Yep."

"She can't stand me most of the time. All we do is fight—"

"You can deny it all the livelong day. But it won't change things."

Wyatt and the other men had already started driving the strays back toward the ranch, and Jericho was relieved no one else was around to hear Flynn spouting off about Ivy.

Jericho cast his sights on the stars overhead. Maybe he and Ivy'd had a few fleeting moments of attraction over the years. But that's all it had been. Fleeting. Even now, the feelings that sprang to life around her were fleeting too. He was leaving just as soon as he caught Rodney James. He had no future in South Park. Certainly not with Ivy.

Flynn let the silence settle between them.

Jericho wanted to tell Flynn the truth about why he was there and put an end to any concerns. But he couldn't say anything to Flynn any more than he could to Ivy. "I won't let anything happen between Ivy and me, Flynn."

"I don't want her getting hurt. That's all."

"And I don't either." The last thing he wanted to do was hurt Ivy.

"Then keep it friend-like with her and nothin' more."

"I will. I promise."

❧

In the dark, Ivy tossed her dripping-wet garments onto the bedroom floor and unhooked her nightgown from the back of the door.

"W-e-l-l, it looks like you got what you were going for." Astrid's whisper from the bed was filled with censure.

"Don't know what you're jawing about." Ivy slipped the nightgown over her head. After returning from the bog and scrubbing up good in the river and doing her best to get the mud off her body and her clothing, the hour had grown late. She'd been quiet as a daddy longlegs, creeping around and trying not to wake Astrid. But apparently it hadn't done any good.

Astrid propped up on her elbow. "You wanted to get alone with Jericho and figured out a way to do it."

"Did not." Was Astrid jealous? "I wasn't thinking about him at all and was just doing my job."

"You've been doing nothing but thinking on that man since he returned."

Ivy rubbed her arms to ward off a chill before she climbed into bed, bumped Astrid, and forced her to scoot over. She gathered up the quilt, the one her ma had made long ago, and brought it up to her chin. The quilt was about the only thing she had left of Ma's.

It wasn't like the quilt was all that special. In fact, Ivy had almost left it behind in Pennsylvania at the old farm. But she grabbed it up on a whim before leaving because it had always brought her comfort. Maybe because she'd hidden underneath it whenever her stepfather had gotten angry with Ma or Flynn.

During those difficult times, she'd huddled behind the thick blanket and pretended she was someplace else, where everyone was happy. Nowadays, the quilt only made her sad for everything she'd lost and wistful for all she wanted for her own future.

"Jericho's the type of man who will want to marry a real lady." Astrid lay on her side, facing Ivy. The darkness obscured Astrid's face, but Ivy could hear the jealousy again in her voice.

"He's not gonna be interested in you, if that's what you're thinking." Ivy stifled a yawn. "You're too young."

"Sixteen isn't that young."

Ivy always hated when others commented on her age, and here she was now doing the same to Astrid. Shame on her. "Reckon you're old enough to know what you want and make your own way."

So long as it didn't involve Jericho.

"That's right."

"I see the way Logan Steele's been admiring you lately." The mayor's son had shot up over the past year and was turning into a fine-looking man.

"Logan Steele?" Astrid released a scoffing laugh. "He's just an annoying child."

"He's a year older than you."

"He acts like he's Ty's age. Besides, he's leaving Fairplay and going back East just as soon as he can. He hates the West."

"What about Holt?" Ivy threw out the name of another boy, hoping to distract Astrid from Jericho. "He can't keep his eyes off you."

For a few minutes they whispered in the dark like they used to do before they'd gotten all grown-up. Ivy relished such times, when Astrid didn't put on airs and she was simple and fun again. If only those times weren't so far apart and so short.

"Compared with a man like Jericho," Astrid said with a sigh, "they're just boys."

"Yep. Jericho is all man." Ivy wanted to add, *"And he's all mine,"* but she refrained.

"You've never liked Jericho. I don't know why you'd care if he's interested in me now."

Ivy stared through the darkness at the slanted ceiling. How could she explain her complicated relationship with Jericho? Of course, she'd never disliked him. But she sure acted like it for a whole lot of years in order to keep from humiliating herself, especially when Jericho made it so abundantly clear he didn't reciprocate her feelings.

Ivy shrugged. "Just don't go fooling yourself into thinking he likes you, or you're gonna get hurt." She oughta know.

Astrid huffed. "Maybe *you* should be the one not to fool yourself so *you* don't get hurt." With that, Astrid flipped over and faced the wall, her body rigid.

Ivy reckoned they both needed to take each other's advice, but they were too stubborn to do it.

CHAPTER
10

A strange prickling on Jericho's neck told him he wasn't alone. He slowed the team and wagon and casually glanced around the gulch while stroking the trigger of the rifle on his lap. The gulch widened out just ahead, and the sawmill sat at the base of a cleared area less than half a mile away.

When Wyatt had started running short on lumber for the new building projects, Jericho had offered to go after the supplies. He wanted to help Wyatt. But more than that, he'd gotten wind of a couple of men working up at the sawmill who'd fought for the South. Apparently they were a rough breed, and he figured it wouldn't hurt to talk to them. At the very least, they might be able to direct him to others in the area who'd taken sides with the Confederates.

The fresh mountain air, the scent of pine, the rushing of the river next to the trail—it'd all made the long, bumpy ride worthwhile. And it would be even more worthwhile if he could dig up additional information.

He was finding that the fellows who worked construction

with him were talented gossipers and an invaluable source of information on most people in South Park. He'd even gone out on a couple of evenings after work to chase down leads. They hadn't amounted to anything, but he was quickly crossing names off his suspect list.

It always took time to narrow down and identify criminals. Rodney James would take even more effort than usual, based on how sneaky he was. He wasn't the typical gun-slinging, table-turning, glass-shattering kind of man. Instead, from all the reports, he worked much more subtly and was a brilliant con artist.

Most notoriously he was wanted for his role in the slaughter of a regiment of black soldiers who were shot in cold blood rather than taken as prisoners of war.

One of the paragraphs described how Rodney infiltrated a Union regiment and pretended to be a surgeon. He killed at least a dozen injured soldiers before leaving with all the rations and ammunition.

Another incident told of his posing as a friend of a wounded Union soldier and taking news home to the man's family. Apparently, the family had welcomed him into their home only to have him murder them in their sleep before leaving with everything of value.

Jericho wasn't discouraged yet by how slow his progress was. And his lack of discouragement had nothing to do with his getting to see Ivy every day. Even though he'd told himself he'd only stay a few days at Healing Springs, he decided he wasn't in a hurry to move to town. After the bog incident two days ago, he was less inclined, especially with the realization that if he hadn't been around to notice Ivy's absence, she would have been stuck out in the mud all night.

He'd mulled over Flynn's revelation that Ivy'd had a hankering for him for a long while. It was still hard to believe. Especially because she'd always been with one fellow or another at socials and dances.

Even though it'd been difficult to get the image of her long legs out of his head, he was determined to keep his vow to Flynn and keep things with her *friend-like*.

The hairs at the back of his neck stood on end again, and this time he drew the team to a halt. He might as well confront whoever was watching him. It would be better than sitting out in the open.

He slowly descended while scanning the thick pines that grew alongside the sloping gulch. Among the cover of branches and amidst the trunks, he counted three fellows on their mounts, and one of them was wearing a long black cloak.

Bat and his gang.

Even if Bat was a dangerous gambler and wouldn't hesitate to kill anyone who double-crossed him, he wasn't stupid enough to murder a law-abiding citizen like Jericho in broad daylight, especially within sight of the sawmill—at least Jericho hoped so.

"What do you want, Bat?" he called.

"Jericho Bliss. Heard you was back in the area." Bat stayed hidden within the shadows of the pine. "I know it was you who freed Dylan McQuaid from my men."

Jericho tensed, but he feigned nonchalance. He'd long since learned it was best to keep his opponent from sensing any emotion. "That was close to two years ago. Time to let bygones be bygones."

"He owes me two thousand dollars plus interest." Bat

conferred with one of his men before speaking to Jericho again. "That amounts to three thousand dollars now."

"Guess that's your problem. You shouldn't have let Dylan join in your gaming since you already knew he was low on money."

"He vowed he was good for it."

Jericho shrugged. "Anyone with half a brain knows Dylan's a drunk and can't be trusted."

Bat and his men didn't respond.

Jericho made a point of gazing down the wagon path at the sawmill. A few men loitered around the river that generated power for the saws. A couple of wagons were parked near the loading dock awaiting lumber, their drivers watching him, likely wondering why he'd stopped.

"I oughta make you pay in Dylan's place since you're the one who let him go."

"Nobody around here will let you get away with that, and you know it." South Park didn't have a resident lawman, but that didn't mean justice wasn't served when needed.

Bat leaned again toward one of his men. They exchanged terse words before Bat straightened, holstered his gun, and gathered his reins. "You tell Dylan he's a dead man if he so much as steps one toe in South Park without my money."

"I suspect Dylan already knows that."

"And you better watch your back, Bliss. You mess with me again, I'll make sure you pay." With the final taunt lingering in the air, Bat and his men spurred their horses away, climbing up a gradual incline.

Jericho watched until they were out of sight before he hoisted himself up onto the wagon bench. As he clucked the team forward, a strange sadness sifted through him for

Dylan. The fellow didn't complain about living in Chicago and never mentioned that he missed his family, but when Jericho had left, he'd seen the desire on Dylan's face to come with.

The truth was, Dylan needed his family in a bad way— needed their love, stability, and guidance. But after Bat's threats, Dylan wouldn't be able to return for a long time—if ever.

～ꝫ⌇～

Ivy took the outstretched letter from Judd and stuffed it into her pocket before Greta or Astrid could see the Utah address on the front.

Then she resumed stirring the large ladle through the thick jam bubbling in the pot.

The older man cocked one of his fluffy white eyebrows at her.

She was relieved that Greta and Astrid had their attention on Ty and Ellie fighting with each other over a game they'd been playing at the table.

Judd reached for a mug from the shelf above the stove and then the coffeepot on a back burner.

While he poured the steaming liquid, Ivy avoided his gaze, her pulse speeding at the thought of anyone figuring out what she was up to. It was the same excited and yet frightened feeling she'd had the day she'd gone to Steele's house for the first time to let him know she was interested in his land.

Of course, she hadn't left Steele's house the second time with any excitement, not after he'd all but told her she wouldn't need a place of her own when she got married and had children. Thankfully, Jericho was an understanding man. Maybe she hadn't exactly spelled out to him her need to have the land because of everything that had happened to her ma. But he knew how she felt about not wanting to be weak and dependent like her ma had been with Rusty.

"Sheep?" Judd's question was low and meant for just the two of them.

Nevertheless, it made Ivy jump so that she splattered some of the jam onto the stovetop. How had he figured out what her letter from Utah was about?

She frowned at Judd and gave a curt nod toward Greta and Astrid and the children.

He just took a slurp of his coffee and watched her with his wise eyes.

She inwardly sighed. She'd seen that look enough over the years to know Judd wasn't gonna let her get away with any avoidance tactics. Truth was, she'd never been able to get much past him. That man could see a flea on a hairy dog even if the flea disguised himself with fur and whiskers.

"C'mon." She left the stove and headed toward the back door that led to the garden.

As they stepped out into the late-afternoon sunshine, Ivy lifted her face to the rays, not caring one tiny ounce that the sun was darkening her face. In fact, most summers her skin turned a warm brown by the end, same as all the men. If men could let the sun tan their skin, why couldn't a woman?

She wound past the garden, now lush with all of the vegetable plants that could grow well in the higher elevation. She kept to the picket fence until she was good and far from the door. Even then, she made sure nobody had followed them out before she met Judd's knowing gaze. "What?"

"Might as well shoot straight with me."

She slipped her hand into her pocket and felt for the letter. "Maybe there's some things I wanna keep private."

"Reckon you got plenty of secrets already."

Apparently Judd knew more about her than he'd let on to anyone. How did he always figure things out?

"I got two eyes, and I use 'em real well," he said in answer to her unspoken question.

If he did know about her competing as Buster Bliss, he hadn't said anything to Wyatt or Flynn yet, and she needed to make sure he kept it that way. "If I tell you about the sheep, promise you won't go yammering to my brothers?"

"Can't promise you anything except that I'll always do the right and loving thing."

"Fine." She cast another glance toward the back door. Seeing no one else around, she lowered her voice. "I'm aiming to buy a few sheep so I can breed and raise them for the wool."

They'd never had sheep on the ranch. In fact, even back on the Pennsylvania farm, they'd had goats but no sheep. Most farmers and ranchers thought sheep were a nuisance— same as the wild mustangs—competing for the open-range grassland the cattle grazed on.

As far as Ivy knew, there weren't any sheep farmers in Colorado, at least not with large herds. But the Mormon settlers had brought sheep with them, and eastern Utah was now thriving with sheep farms. She'd heard that raising sheep was even more profitable than cattle. In the spring when a ewe was sheared, the sale of the wool covered the upkeep of the ewe for an entire year.

Judd took another sip of his coffee, his eyes never leaving her face.

"Well? You gonna tell me what a blamed fool I am for

considering it?" She wasn't sharing a peep about the land she was gunning for. He'd think she was even a bigger fool.

"Ain't gonna say much at all about it, except that you can call on me if you need help with the critters."

She eyed him suspiciously. "That's all?"

"That's all."

"You sure you ain't gonna blabber to Wyatt about my plans?" If Judd told her brothers about the sheep, that would pop open a whole keg of questions she didn't want to answer—like how she'd be able to pay for them and where she intended to graze them.

"Truth has a way of comin' out in its own time no matter what we do to keep it locked away."

Another Judd proverb, as Linnea called his wise words. Usually Ivy took his proverbs to heart. But she had too many things she was hiding. And this time, she hoped Judd was wrong.

CHAPTER

11

Sweat trickled down Ivy's soot-covered face, and she prayed her disguise would hold out until the end of the competition, until she had her winnings in her pocket. But with the crowds surrounding the wide fence that had been erected to form a contest ring, her stomach twisted as she kept waiting for someone—especially one of her family members—to recognize her and call out.

Judd's warning from earlier in the week still haunted her, that truth had a way of coming out in its own time.

Maybe she'd been too hasty in donning her disguise today of all days, Independence Day, when every family and cowhand for miles around congregated in Fairplay to celebrate with picnics, games, music, dancing, and competitions.

But so far over the past couple of hours, no one had made any comments. Except Jericho. Even now as she perched on the rail near the other contestants, he leaned in beside her, watching the final round of the bronc riding.

"Gordo's good." Jericho spoke low, keeping his conversation with her private. He didn't take his gaze from the tough, muscular cowhand doing his best to stay on the wild horse, even as the mustang bucked to dislodge him.

"Yep. He sure can chase the clouds. And he's never been grassed, at least that I've seen." She kept her tone low too. "But with that bronc doing a circle buck, he's gonna get dizzy mighty fast."

Riding bareback and hanging on to nothing but the gelding's mane, Gordo raised his free arm to keep his balance during the twisting, bone-jarring ride.

"How long has he been competing in these parts?"

"He's been in every competition I've seen." Ivy had been watching the contests long before she'd gotten up the nerve to enter them as Buster Bliss. "That devil sure is bucking the whiskers off Gordo."

"If the fellow is from the East like he says, how'd he learn to ride like that?"

Ivy twisted at the long piece of grass in her mouth. "Heard he lived down in Texas for a spell. Maybe he was a rough-string rider there."

Gordo hung on for several more seconds, an eternity in bronc riding, before a gun went off, signaling he'd lasted longer than anyone else. A cheer went up from the crowd. Gordo's pickup man rode over to help him dismount and get out of the way of the wild horse.

The scent of roasting meat and freshly popped kettle corn permeated the air and made Ivy's stomach growl. Across the field, the children raced in sacks, their laughter a sweet sound rising above the chatter of the bystanders.

Ivy started to climb down. The cattle-roping contest was

next, and Buster Bliss was last on the list of entrants. The best for last. She'd worked her way to that coveted position, and she aimed to hold it the rest of the summer.

If only Wyatt and Flynn and everyone else in the family didn't have to watch. Jericho had recognized her—what if they figured out her identity too? Trouble was, they wouldn't be as understanding as Jericho had been. In fact, he would seem like a holy saint next to Wyatt and Flynn if they discovered her disguise.

She'd ridden with them to town but made up excuses about needing to go off and tend to a few things, telling them she'd meet up with them later for the evening activities. Only Astrid had raised her brows, but no one questioned her, since they were already well acquainted with her independent ways.

"You sure you want to do this today?" Jericho straightened but didn't look at her.

How could he read her so well? She wanted to turn and study him but forced herself to stare straight ahead as a couple of busters roped Gordo's bronc and brought him 'round. The past week since getting stuck in the bog, something had shifted in her relationship with Jericho. She couldn't put her finger on what it was. They'd had normal conversations, talked about ordinary things, and she hadn't wanted to strangle him once.

"I need the money." She half raised her arm to swipe at the sweat trickling down her temples but then lowered it, afraid if she touched her face, she'd wipe away the soot.

Jericho's attention was still riveted on Gordo.

"I'm surprised you ain't wanting to win a quick dollar." There were times, like today, when she didn't think he was all that interested in their contest for the land. If he cared, wouldn't he be seeking out more ways to increase his earnings? "You might be the only one who'd give me a fair challenge in the roping."

"Fair challenge?" He scoffed. "I'd beat you in no time."

"Doubt that. This ain't a knitting bee."

"Last one sure seemed like it."

She tucked a grin out of sight. She loved bantering with Jericho. It reminded her of the way things used to be between them long ago. If only she knew how to keep things simple and friendly without heading back down a path of frustration.

She sensed he was doing his part to keep their conversations from veering in that direction too. Like now. He hadn't once tried to stop her from participating in the competitions, even though he'd hinted that he didn't want her to.

"Maybe you can distract Wyatt and Flynn during my ride."

"What do you want me to do? Dress up like a clown?"

"That might work. Except you won't need to dress up."

This time his grin kicked up.

The sight of it sent her heart bucking against her ribs. Her lips twitched with the need to smile back, but she reckoned no one was gonna take Buster Bliss seriously if he was fawning over Jericho.

She pushed away from the fence before she ruined her disguise. "Wish me luck."

His grin hit the dust faster than a greenhorn getting unloaded from a bronc. "Be careful."

"Ain't I always?"

"No."

"I'll be fine." She ambled away, wishing she wasn't attired in the men's garments, that she was in one of her fancy outfits earning his admiration. That night at the bog, he'd admitted she was pretty. He'd never said anything like that to her before. Even if he'd finished out the compliment by saying something about all the McQuaid women being pretty, he'd singled her out first.

He hadn't hinted at the exchange since. But she'd brought along another change of clothing for later. And she fully intended to dress her best so that maybe he'd take notice. Maybe he'd even dance with her. Something he'd never done either, though she'd sure tried over the years to get him to ask.

She shook off the thought. She had to stay focused for now, remember who she was, and play the part of Buster Bliss to perfection. Her future depended on it.

The air got lost in Jericho's lungs as he watched Ivy dismount at a run from the mare. She was beside the downed steer in an instant, had the rope knotted around one of its front legs, and was completing the three-legged cross tie before the steer knew what was happening.

As she hopped up and raised her hands, the crowd erupted into cheers.

Jericho allowed himself the first breath since she'd started the chase. She was good. No. She was better than good. She was the best roper for miles around. Too bad she couldn't compete as herself. She deserved it the same way she deserved a fair shot at Steele's land.

"You're takin' a heap of interest in that little fella." Mack Custer leaned on the rail beside Jericho. The sour body odor of Elkhorn Ranch's foreman should have warned Jericho of his approach—if he hadn't been so focused on Ivy.

"He's a decent kid." Jericho rapidly composed himself, hiding his emotions away where they should have been all along.

"Said he ain't Roman-style ridin' today." Custer's eyes narrowed on Ivy. "Said he's heading home soon as he's done with the ropin'."

Thank the Lord Ivy was following through on her promise not to compete in the dangerous race. If she'd entered, he would have slung her over his shoulder and carried her off. No doubt she would have been kicking and screaming the whole time.

"You wanna ride?" Custer's question was casual, but Jericho could sense the anticipation in each of the three words. "You were the best. Reckon you still are."

Jericho shouldn't even consider it. But something inside longed for the thrill of competing. It was the same craving that grew inside him every time he closed in on his prey.

"No, I really shouldn't—"

"Can tell you're itchin' to do it." Custer scratched his protruding abdomen with both hands.

Jericho had already told Ivy not to ride because it was too dangerous. Besides, he'd only be putting himself at risk, something he wasn't willing to do when he needed to keep his wits about him.

"Or maybe you've changed too much." Custer eyed him with suspicion.

Jericho met the man's gaze and tried to read what was left unsaid. Was he wondering why Jericho was really back?

Jericho had met with Steele again about the land and let him know he and Ivy were having a little competition for the purchasing rights. He'd asked Steele to respect Ivy's need for anonymity. If anyone asked, Steele agreed to let people know he had a couple interested buyers, including Jericho.

Meanwhile Jericho had spread the word he was doing the construction work for Wyatt to finish saving up to buy Steele's parcel. So far, everyone had believed him—or at least no one questioned him. Except Custer . . .

Custer's eyes were hard and mean in a way Jericho had never liked. Jericho had considered adding Custer to his list of suspects but hadn't yet. The foreman's long history and experience as a cowhand from Texas didn't line up with Rodney James being from Virginia. And he didn't resemble the photo of Rodney either. Custer might be a scallywag and a crook—especially with the betting profits—but he was too forthright to be a con artist like Rodney.

Custer let a stream of tobacco juice fly. "You hidin' something from us, Jericho?"

"You hiding something from me?" Unblinking, Jericho held the man's gaze, needing to prove no amount of pushing or prodding would scare him.

Finally, Custer grinned, dispelling the tension. "Reckon I can drive the stakes high if you ride. How 'bout if I give you a cut of the profit?"

Maybe he was acting too much like an outsider and not playing his role well enough. If he wanted to be accepted without question, he had to do a better job of proving he was still a regular cowhand. And a regular cowhand didn't mind showing off once in a while, especially when he had the skills.

He straightened his shoulders. He should have figured he'd need to compete. "Alright. I'll race."

"Thata boy." Custer's grin widened. "I'll give you—"

"The prize money from winning is enough for me."

"Sounds like something you'd say." Custer grabbed his arm and led him toward the teams of horses awaiting the Roman-style racing. "Guarantee you won't regret it."

Hopefully, Custer was right. At the very least, if he won, the other competitors from the day would welcome him as one of their own. Later, when the liquor started loosening their tongues, he'd be in the perfect position to pry for information.

Thankfully, Ivy was already gathering up her things and readying to leave. Even though she wasn't planning to stick around for the Roman-style race, it was too much to hope that she wouldn't find out later. The community was small, and she brushed shoulders with too many cowhands not to hear mention of it eventually.

She'd be hopping mad. And she wouldn't speak to him the rest of the day. That would probably be for the best. He could admit he hadn't been looking forward to the dance and watching her with Hance and the rest of the men in town who'd be lining up to take a turn with her.

Maybe another argument with her would do him good and stamp out the interest that lingered even after doing his best to treat her as a friend and nothing more. Over the past week during the evenings he'd been home, they'd had a good-natured shooting contest, gone fishing, and trapped a couple of pesky raccoons. He loved that Ivy could do just about anything and make the experience interesting and enjoyable.

Yet somehow, all of the interacting had only made him want to be around her more. She was still just as easy to talk to as she'd always been, and he'd found himself opening up to her about his time in Chicago as much as he could, about missing his mother, and about the continued difficulty he had with his dad's drunkenness.

It had gotten harder and harder as the week went on not to tell her everything about his job for Pinkerton, letting her believe instead that he worked with Dylan in the police department.

He hated the duplicity and feared that if he kept up the friendship, he would end up revealing the real reason he was in South Park. And that would be disastrous for both of them.

Yes, an argument was in order. All the more reason to join in the race.

CHAPTER

12

Ivy was gonna blister Jericho's hide once she got a hold of him.

The whistles and cheers escalated as his horses thundered toward the finish line. Straddling the two, his strong, lean body radiated with determination. She'd always loved watching him race Roman-style. He made it seem effortless—riding as smoothly as if he'd been sitting in the saddle instead of standing and spanning two mounts.

But she knew from personal experience just how difficult the race was, keeping the bouncing rhythm of both horses, drawing them close enough together, maintaining a grip with each foot, holding two sets of reins, and guiding each creature separately while thinking on everything else.

She'd fallen a time or two in her early days, almost been trampled, nearly broken bones, and gotten plenty of bruises. The risk of injury was high. The possibility of death was ever present.

One of Jericho's feet slipped, and her heart leapt into

her throat. In the next instant, he righted himself, as self-assured as usual. With his loose grip on the reins, he shifted and gave more lean into the horse on his left, which was another good move.

An instant later, he crossed the line at least a dozen paces ahead of the closest contender. Jericho was still the best and unbeatable. By anyone except Buster Bliss.

She kicked at the fence post from the far corner where she'd returned to watch the race after hearing his name shouted out from the sideline. The anger boiled again. He'd told her not to ride Roman-style. Why? So that he could go out and show her up? He had always treated her fairly as a woman—almost like an equal.

But this time? He was a hypocrite. Telling her one thing but doing another. If Roman-style wasn't dangerous for him, then it sure as heaven above wasn't gonna hurt her. Apparently, he was more interested in the prize money than he'd let on.

As he dismounted to the backslapping and congratulations of other cowhands, one of his rare grins lit up his face. She had half a mind to stride right over and knock that smile into next week.

Of course, she couldn't do it. She was still wearing her Buster Bliss getup. And if she went over and socked him, everyone would start questioning what was going on and figure out she knew Jericho a lot better than Buster Bliss should.

She was gonna have to wait until she got him away from the crowds. Then she would give him a piece of her mind.

"Hey, Buster!" Mack Custer shouted above the crowd.

She was tempted to duck and slink away. But the Elkhorn Ranch foreman, the organizer of the holiday competitions, was already weaving through the onlookers toward her.

"You and Jericho! Race right now and see who's the best!" Custer's voice boomed loud enough to draw attention, including Jericho's.

His intense gaze picked her out. He gave a curt shake of his head, as though to warn her against racing.

She stiffened. How dare he?

Spitting out the grass she was chewing, she climbed onto the fence rail and dropped down inside the makeshift competition ring. Jericho shook his head again, his eyes flashing— with worry or anger or both?

He had no right to be upset with her. He'd gone behind her back and raced. How long had he been planning to do it? Maybe he'd reckoned he would race all along?

"Fine." Ivy responded in her fake man's voice. "Let's see who's the better man."

Ignoring Jericho, she made her way toward one of the pairs of horses that had just competed. The racing distance was short enough that the horses weren't winded or tired. They could easily go another round.

"No, I'm not doing it again." Jericho's hard statement broke through the commotion. "And no, it's not because I'm afraid I'll lose."

"You're scared Buster's gonna whup the pants off you." Good-natured teasing rose into the air.

"Doesn't matter. I'm not racing a second time." Jericho spoke firmly—and loudly enough for her to hear his decision.

Inwardly she released a frustrated groan as she began to lead her horses to the starting line. Behind her Jericho continued to argue with Custer and others with barely concealed anger.

When she reached the end of the field, she brushed a hand

over each of the horses to get the feel of them and to allow them to get to know her. From the corner of her eye, she could see Jericho stalk away, shaking his head.

"Find me someone else to race," she called out in her manly tone. "Someone who ain't afraid of me."

Jericho stopped abruptly. When he turned slowly, his body was stiff and his jaw clamped tightly, the sure sign she'd pushed him to the edge of frustration. He stared her down, then he started back toward his team, his bootsteps slapping the dirt hard.

By the time Jericho reached the starting line with his horses, the crowds along both sides of the field had increased. She had no doubt Wyatt and Flynn and the rest of her family would be among the spectators. Would they recognize her true identity? If so, what would they think when they realized she was racing? Against Jericho?

He fiddled around with his pair of horses without speaking to her. But he didn't need to say a word. From his jerking movements, she reckoned he was mad enough to burn the field to cinders.

As she began to mount, he spoke in a low growl. "Can't believe you're going through with this. It's too dangerous."

"You've got no right to lecture me."

"Blast it all. Why do you have to be so danged stubborn?"

"You're the stubborn one, keeping me from racing so you could win."

"I wasn't planning on riding, but Custer twisted my arm."

She glanced to where Custer was making his way through a crowd of cowhands. No doubt he was cashing in on the race. The burly man could be persuasive when he wanted to be. "Don't matter. You started this. Now you need to see it through."

"No!" His whisper was harsh, almost desperate.

"Yep." She hefted herself on top of the first horse.

"Son of a gun, Ivy—"

She cut him off with a dark look. She certainly didn't need him revealing who she was right here and now. He wouldn't do that, would he?

For a second, he remained motionless, almost as if he was contemplating doing that very thing. He finally blew out a long, noisy exhale. "You'll be the death of me."

"You're already the death of me." She took the first set of reins in hand and then reached for the second horse. As she rose onto the saddle and balanced herself, she perched her other foot on the opposite horse's saddle, trying not to watch Jericho but unable to stop.

When they were both situated, having tested their mounts, he muttered, "Don't do anything stupid."

She wanted to tell him it was too late, that the stupidest thing she'd ever done was allow herself to care about him. But she focused on the opposite end of the field. "I'll be fine. I've been doing this for weeks. You're the one who needs to watch out for yourself."

The gun went off with a resounding echo, and she wasted no time in urging her horses forward with the controlled speed she'd perfected. She glanced sideways at Jericho to find that he was riding neck and neck with her. His tempestuous blue eyes collided with hers. His dark fury only added to his devastatingly handsome appeal, and she couldn't keep at bay the thrill of knowing she was competing against him.

From a distance, she could hear the calls and cheers from

the crowd, but she was too aware of Jericho and the race. She wanted to beat him so badly and show him she was every bit as talented as he was. At the same time, she didn't want him sore at her. Maybe she ought to slow down and let him take the lead.

Before she could wrap her mind around her shifting emotions, Jericho pushed ahead of her. He guided his horses fluidly, almost as if he could communicate with them the same way Brody could.

In the next instant, however, Jericho's foot slipped from the horse on his right. Rather than acting quickly and correcting himself, Jericho fumbled with the reins. The horses veered apart, leaving him hanging perilously in midair. Even as fear for his well-being gripped her, she pulled ahead and charged the last of the distance toward the finish line. As she crossed over, she glanced back in time to see Jericho easily right himself.

Surely he hadn't. But from the way he avoided making eye contact with her, she had no doubt he'd purposefully thrown the race.

She hopped down even before the horses had come to a complete halt. She stomped the ground, the heat of her temper rising swiftly. He'd let her win. The Gila monster. The Mexican dog. The desert varmint. A dozen more heated words pressed for release. She started toward him, her fists balled, her body taut with the need to haul into him.

Before she could reach him, Mack Custer and the other cowhands surrounded her, bumping and congratulating her. The manhandling was the part about competing she liked the least. But she took the praise and teasing as best she could, even though inside she was furious.

After pocketing her earnings and making her way toward the fence where she'd dropped her bag, someone shouted her real name, almost drawing her gaze. She resisted the urge and instead swiped up her haversack.

"Ivy!" The call came louder and belonged to Astrid.

Of course, Astrid would be the one to recognize her through the disguise. And Astrid would also be the one who wouldn't care about revealing her identity.

Ivy picked up her pace. She couldn't let it happen. Not in front of the entire community. Not when it would mean the end to her competing.

Elbowing her way through the crowds, she pushed until she was free. With the main thoroughfare of town swarming with people, she dodged among them, praying she'd get lost in the throngs and that Astrid wouldn't draw any further attention to her.

At another shout of her name, her heart sped, and she started to jog. She had to find a place to hide and change out of her men's clothing. If she showed up in public wearing one of Linnea's elegant gowns and hats, no one would be the wiser for her deceitfulness.

The church spire seemed to beckon her. She'd found refuge in the church before, and she knew it wouldn't be in use today. If she entered through the side door, no one would guess that's where she was hiding.

Dodging several more people, she ducked off the street to the pathway between the buildings. When she reached the side entrance, she glanced over her shoulder. Her spectacles were sweaty and falling down her nose. But from what she could tell, no one was paying attention to her. If anyone was on her trail, hopefully she'd lost them.

She opened the door and slipped inside. Sunshine from the front windows lit the chapel, showing it to be as deserted as she'd hoped. Only dust wafted in the air, along with silence. Blessed silence.

She lowered herself to the nearest pew, her frustration still keen at winning against Jericho because he'd thrown the race. Of course, she couldn't complain about the extra winnings. But she'd wanted to beat him fairly or not at all.

At the rattle of the front door, she flattened herself on the hard bench and hardly dared to breathe. The door opened and the sounds from the street filtered through the room—women's laughter, children squealing, men joking, horses clomping, and loud calling from the pig-wrestling arena.

Ivy remained motionless. A few seconds later, the door closed, and the footsteps on the plank walkway drifted from the building.

She waited another minute before taking off the spectacles and wiping her sleeve across her face, using the perspiration to clean off the charcoal dust. Finally, she sat up and shed the men's clothing. Smoothing out all the wrinkles, she donned first the skirt and then her chemise. She wanted to unwrap the tight binding around her bosom since it was chafing her skin, but she hesitated. She had to get back to her family before they investigated her connection to Buster Bliss—if they hadn't already.

If Astrid pushed her to admit anything, what would she say?

Her attention strayed to the pulpit where Father Zieber preached most Sundays. Here she was standing in a church and wondering if she oughta lie. What kind of lowlife had she turned into?

144

With a huff, she plopped onto the bench and picked up the bodice that matched the skirt. But the tight linen across her chest constricted her, and without another moment of hesitation, she hoisted up her chemise and began unwinding the long strip. The chemise over the top made the process cumbersome, but she couldn't imagine going the rest of the day and into the night wearing the binding.

She unwound it as fast as she could, but somehow it tangled in the back so that she couldn't pull the last section free. She considered taking off her chemise, but with the way the linen was wrapped, she was afraid she'd get the undergarment halfway up her head and find herself stuck.

"Holy Saint Peter." Her skin was overheating from the exertion in the stuffy room. She'd rushed herself, and now she'd gotten into a predicament. Maybe she was gonna have to wind the strip back up and wear it for the rest of the day after all.

The side door creaked, and she gasped, grabbing her bodice and using it to shield her chemise. This time she couldn't duck down and hide. She couldn't even run away, not in her state of undress.

As a man slipped silently inside, she immediately recognized the lean frame and muscular body.

"Go away, Jericho," she hissed. "I'm mad at you and don't wanna talk to you right now."

"You're mad at me?" His voice was tight as he closed the door. "I'm the one with the right to be mad. Not you."

"You threw the race and let me win."

"You shouldn't have been racing to begin with—" As he turned and caught sight of her, his words fell away. In a sweeping glance he took in her state of undress, and his eyes widened.

She spread her bodice farther over her chemise to act like a shield, although it did nothing to cover her very bare arms. Her mind returned to the night she was caught in the bog, when he'd seen her in underdrawers. And the time before that when he'd caught her bathing in the creek. The same question she'd asked the night at the bog taunted her: Why was he always coming across her when she was indecent?

Of course he'd had no way of knowing those other times or now that she was scantily clad.

"I'm changing." The words came out stiffly. And the second she spoke, she wanted to hit herself over the head for stating so obvious a statement. She tugged on the stuck piece of linen, wishing now that she'd left it in place. "You should go."

"Couldn't you find someplace more private? What if I'd been another man?"

"I'm fine. Or I was until you showed up." She refrained from revealing that someone had already come in the front door.

"You're not fine, Ivy. You have no sense of decency." He waved at her and then rapidly looked away.

"I'm decent enough." She lifted her chin. "At least I didn't go behind your back to race Roman-style."

"I knew you wouldn't like it, but I had to do it."

"Had to?"

He palmed the back of his neck. "Yes. And I wish I could explain why, but I can't."

"Well, explain to me why you have a double standard, why it's fine and dandy for you to race but you have a fit when I do."

"Because it's dangerous."

She stood and glared. "It ain't any more dangerous for me than you."

"If you fell, you'd get hurt easier."

"And how do you know that?"

"You're smaller." He glanced at her but then pressed his lips together.

"Smaller?" She snorted. "What difference does that make?"

"Just finish getting dressed," he snapped, staring at the simple wooden cross hanging at the front of the church, clearly uncomfortable with her state of immodesty.

She reached behind her back and tugged at the linen strip hanging out from her chemise, but it wouldn't dislodge.

"Are you almost done?"

"Something's tangled."

"Hurry and untangle it."

She jerked at it but had the feeling all the tugging was only tightening the knot she'd somehow made. "I need your help." The words were out before she realized what she was asking.

He let out a snort. "You're not serious."

"Serious as a preacher at a funeral." Why not get his help? Things'd go a whole lot faster if he untwisted the knot.

He hesitated at the door, holding the handle, almost as if he was considering exiting the building.

"Don't be a fraidy cat." She shifted and showed him the strip of linen peeking out from underneath her chemise. "It won't bite."

"Blast it all, Ivy." He scowled at her something fierce before he pushed away from the door and stalked toward her.

CHAPTER
13

This was a bad idea. A *very* bad idea.

Jericho's hand was poised above Ivy's chemise. A warning rumbled in his head like an approaching herd of cattle. He couldn't lift her undergarment. It wasn't proper.

"Just do it, Jericho."

He touched her chemise, but his hand trembled. His sights shifted to her slender arms and the smooth bare skin from her shoulder down to the tips of her fingers. The skin practically begged him for a touch.

He closed his eyes for a second, trying to clear his head. She was just a friend. He could do this.

"Am I gonna have to walk around with this thing hanging out the rest of the day?"

"You should have thought of this problem before deciding to compete today."

"I had it all worked out until you joined the race."

"So this is my fault?"

She released an exasperated huff and jerked up her chemise. "There."

At the sight of her lower back, he sucked in a stuttering breath. She was so beautiful.

"Go on now."

"Fine." He forced himself to reach for the dangling cloth and followed it up to where it had knotted. Though his fingers shook, he plucked at the twisted linen and tried to keep his gaze averted.

"You gonna be able to get it?" She peeked over her shoulder. Her face still had smudges of black in places around the rim, but her features were as pretty as always, her eyes curious and her brows drawn.

What he wouldn't give to have those luscious eyes watching him with admiration instead of fury. Why had he wanted to rile her up? He could no longer think of any reason that made sense. Now all he wanted to do was be close to her.

As if sensing the shift in his mood, she twisted back around and stared straight ahead.

He worked at the knot again, trying to keep his fingers from brushing her back. As he finally loosened it and started unraveling the linen, his fingers accidentally skimmed a line near her spine.

She drew in a breath, one large enough for her shoulders to rise and fall.

He paused, the silence between them strangely charged. Something told him he'd done what she asked and that she could take over and finish on her own. But another something drove him onward, so that he continued to unwind the linen, spinning her around until she was facing him.

Her chemise fell over the linen and covered her. But still,

the entire situation was indecent. He needed to walk out of the building and get away from the heat that was undeniable between them—especially at this moment.

He loosened his hold. And as he started to take a step back, she grabbed his hand. "Reckon you should finish what you started." She lifted her long lashes and met his gaze with a dare, her brown eyes a dark melted molasses, hot and sticky.

His stomach flipped. And when she started to turn again to continue unwinding the linen, he gently guided her, unable to do anything else. She moved slowly, pausing when she faced the opposite direction.

He had a perfect view of her neck and part of her back, and he knew he'd never seen anything in his entire life more elegant. He couldn't keep from reaching up and skimming the lacey top hem of her chemise and brushing away a few tendrils of her dark hair that had come loose from the knot at the top of her head.

She stilled. But didn't protest.

He spun her around again. This time, the unraveled linen fell away altogether, completely undone. Just like him.

Her breathing was rapid and shallow. And when she looked up at him again, her eyes were even darker. Welcoming. Even beckoning him.

Did she want him to kiss her?

Her attention shifted to his mouth, almost as if she'd heard his question.

Oh, blazing smoke. He almost closed his eyes to block her out so he could regain his sanity. But her fingers lifted to graze the arm still holding the linen strip. At the caress, heat sparked along his nerve endings so that he dropped the long cloth and reached for her.

He only meant to touch her arm in return, but somehow his hand slipped behind her to the small of her back. As soon as his hand landed there, he guided her closer. The touch was light. A part of him was giving her the opportunity to put an end to this sudden madness between them.

But she came to him all too willingly, which only fanned the growing need inside him—the need to taste her, kiss her, have her.

When he bent closer and angled in, he paused, giving her another chance to break free. But she tilted her head as though readying herself. The slight movement was a summons he couldn't ignore.

He swooped down and captured her mouth with all the power and decisiveness of a cowhand roping a steer. He knotted them together, tightly, tautly, with no room to breathe.

When her arms slipped around his shoulders and she pressed into him, a dangerous jolt rocked him, warning him to let go, not to take this any further. But her mouth moved against his with a passion and fervor that rivaled his. And it only tied the knot more firmly, wedging them together so that he couldn't let go of her.

As his mouth tangled with hers, he knew this was where he'd wanted to be for a long time. Maybe even before he'd come back to South Park. The Lord knew he'd tried for years to deny his feelings for her. He'd done everything within his strength and power to resist the pull. But somehow, inevitably, he'd ended up here.

Did she feel the same way? Had she been waiting for this moment forever? Or was she toying with him like she did the other men in her life?

At the opening of a door and sunlight spilling over them, Ivy broke the kiss with a startled gasp, and her eyes rounded on someone behind them.

The haze of desire clouded Jericho's mind, and he couldn't tear his attention from those lips that had been meshed with his. As she released him and tried to step away, he couldn't let go, didn't want to lose the pressure of her exquisite body against his.

But the thudding of heavy footsteps pounded a warning.

"Stop, Flynn." Ivy's voice wavered.

Before Jericho could make sense of what was happening, a hand clamped on his shoulder, ripped him away from Ivy, and spun him around. Then a fist smashed against his nose, and blinding pain filled his head.

Ivy screamed.

Warmth gushed from Jericho's nose and over his lips. The metallic taste of blood touched his tongue at the same instant a second fist pummeled into his stomach and doubled him over.

"Flynn, you old goat. You stop it right now, do y'hear?" Ivy jumped onto Flynn's back, causing him to stumble backward, giving Jericho a glimpse of the cold fury in his expression and the murder in his eyes.

Flynn was going to kill him. Even with Ivy hanging on, her arms tightening around his neck, he lunged after Jericho again.

A part of Jericho hardened with the need to defend himself. He'd learned to fight long ago and could hold his own. But another part of him knew he deserved every blow Flynn gave him.

"C'mon, Flynn!" Ivy's shout was laced with desperation as

Flynn pried her loose and then turned and barreled toward Jericho, his fist raised.

Jericho braced his shoulders for another punch.

"Hold on now, Flynn!" Wyatt's call came as Flynn threw a fist against Jericho's cheek.

"Stop! Please! Stop!" Ivy rounded Flynn.

Jericho could hardly see, the pain in his face making the room spin.

Wyatt's thundering steps neared the front, and he grabbed on to Flynn before he could slam into Jericho and take him down. Flynn strained against his older brother, but Wyatt wrestled him back, his arms bulging and his shirt straining.

"What in the name of all that's holy do you think you're doing?" Wyatt's yell filled the small chapel, which was quickly filling with other family members.

Flynn shook his hand, his knuckles red and no doubt smarting. "Caught Jericho taking advantage of Ivy."

"He wasn't takin' advantage of me!" Ivy stood in front of Jericho still wearing only her chemise, her bodice discarded and on the floor next to the linen band he'd helped her untangle.

Jericho almost groaned. This looked bad. No wonder Flynn seemed angry enough to commit murder.

"Jericho's an honorable man." Ivy lifted her chin and stared at Flynn and Wyatt, ignoring the rest of her family.

Jericho swiped up her bodice from the floor and draped it across her shoulders. Her eyes widened, and she grasped the item around her, trying to shield herself from the onlookers, pink staining her cheeks.

Wyatt gave a long, meaningful look at Greta, who nodded and ushered the children and others from the chapel.

When the door closed, leaving only Wyatt and Flynn, Ivy's shoulders deflated.

"If he's so honorable," Flynn spat the words, "why's he in here taking off your clothes?"

"He's not!" Ivy clutched the bodice tighter. "This ain't what it looks like. Jericho was helping me get dressed. It's the honest truth—"

"Hush up, Ivy!" Flynn shot her a glare. "You're in a heap of trouble."

"She's not to blame." Jericho couldn't stand back and let Ivy take Flynn's censure. He's the one who deserved it, not her.

"I don't want to hear it from you." Flynn's voice could have frozen a washbasin full of water in the high heat of summer. "You lied to me. Straight-out lied."

Was Flynn referring to the night at the bog when he'd said he wasn't interested in Ivy? He hadn't exactly lied. He just hadn't expected the interest he'd been fighting would flare up so quickly and so passionately.

"Listen, Flynn—"

"Nope, you listen, Jericho. You told me you didn't have any intentions toward Ivy. In fact, you looked me in the eyes and said you wouldn't let anything happen between the two of you."

Ivy shifted and glared at him. "You said that?"

Flynn nodded. "He guaranteed it."

Wyatt had released his hold on Flynn and now crossed his arms and stared bullets into Jericho too. With all three McQuaids mad at him, things were bound to go from bad to worse.

"I didn't mean for this to happen." Jericho glanced from one brother to the other. "It was a mistake—"

"Mistake?" Ivy's question contained a hint of hurt and anger.

"I shouldn't have—" Jericho lowered his voice. "I shouldn't have kissed you, Ivy. Not here. Not like this."

"Not like ever," Flynn said.

Ivy squared up with her brother as though preparing to go to war. "Don't you start tellin' me who I can and can't kiss."

"No one." Flynn's tone was hard. "Never."

"I'll kiss who I want and when I want."

"Absolutely not."

"You did." Ivy clutched at her bodice, but not before Jericho caught sight of the tremble in her fingers. "I saw you smooching with Helen Fairchild plenty of times in the haymow—"

"That was a mistake—"

"Was smooching with Linnea a mistake too?"

Flynn released a string of mutters.

Wyatt glanced between his siblings, his brow furrowing. "Let's quit yammering on about Flynn and focus on the problems right here smacking us in the face."

"From where I stand, there ain't any problems." Ivy lifted her chin. "I'm a grown woman and can kiss anyone I want, including Jericho."

Protest rose within Jericho. He didn't want Ivy kissing anyone she wanted—anyone, that is, except for him.

Before he could figure out what to say, Wyatt responded. "You wanna drag your reputation through the mud, Ivy?"

"I don't care a lick what people think."

"Rumors are gonna start flying about you being in here kissing Jericho, unshucked and half-naked—"

"I'm not half-naked!"

"You've got your top off!" Flynn's roar silenced Ivy. "And last time you were alone with Jericho, you weren't wearing your skirt."

"I told you why—"

"It's indecent," Wyatt cut in.

Ivy heaved a sigh.

The tension in Jericho's body tightened, his cheek hurt from where Flynn had socked him, and one of his eyes was beginning to swell up.

Jericho glanced at Ivy. Should they tell Wyatt and Flynn about her disguise as Buster Bliss? It would be the best way to explain why she hadn't been wearing her bodice.

Her eyes silently pleaded with him not to spill the truth. The rich, dark brown sucked him back in, right where he'd been when he wanted to kiss her—powerless to resist her.

Besides, with how hard it was for her as a woman to have the same privileges as a man, she trusted that he was on her side, that he wanted to help her. And he couldn't disappoint her.

Flynn shook his head. "Heaven help me, Ivy. I thought I raised you better than this. But looks like I failed somewhere along the way."

Hurt flashed across Ivy's face before anger rolled in to replace it. "This ain't the first time you've told me what a failure I am. Reckon it won't be the last."

"Don't get all fired up," Wyatt interjected. "That's not what we're saying."

"Then what?"

"Suppose we're saying it's time to buckle down and act proper-like."

Flynn pinned a hard glare on Jericho. "Or maybe it's time for Jericho to buckle down and marry Ivy."

CHAPTER

14

Flynn wanted Jericho to marry her? Ivy's heart slammed hard against her chest. She couldn't deny she'd dreamed a time or two—or a few hundred—about marrying Jericho. But she hadn't considered it anytime recently. Not since he'd left and never looked back.

But here he was. Here they were. And after sharing that kiss with him? Howdy-doody, she was ready for a repeat. Real soon. Just the thought of his fingers pressing against her lower back, his hard chest radiating heat, and his mouth taking possession of hers made her weak in the knees.

No doubt about it. Jericho Bliss was a mighty fine kisser. Mighty fine indeed. She'd shared a kiss with a cowhand now and again over the past few years. But after kissing Jericho, no one and nothing else compared. Not even a little.

She slid a glance his direction. Even with his bruised face and bloody nose, no other man could compare to his ruggedly handsome looks either. Not only that, but he was a good and decent man right down to his bones. He was considerate, conscientious, determined, and hardworking. He had a strong sense of integrity and justice.

Of course, that didn't mean he was without faults. She'd known him long enough to see every one of his flaws, and he could be headstrong and hard on himself and others.

Even if marriage hadn't been in her short-term plans with buying Steele's land and raising sheep, she wouldn't complain about starting a life with Jericho. Maybe they could eventually buy up more land. But until then, they could make use of the spread together.

Jericho pulled a neckerchief from his pocket and held it against his bloody nose. "You told me at the bog you didn't want Ivy even courting, that she's too young. Now you're wanting to marry her off?"

"Ivy is too young," Flynn said. Ivy started to protest, but he talked over her. "But you're responsible, and you'll keep her safe and out of trouble."

"Reckon Flynn's got a real good idea." Wyatt held Flynn's gaze as an unspoken message passed between them. "Best thing for you to do is accept blame for this here incident and do the right thing by Ivy and marry her."

"I'd do the right thing by Ivy if I'd wronged her—"

"Taking off her clothes is wronging her." Flynn pulled himself up as though he might take another swing at Jericho.

Ivy tensed. So Jericho didn't want to marry her? Why didn't that surprise her?

"You've sullied her reputation," Wyatt said. "The least you can do is give her your name."

"I can't." Jericho glanced at the door as if gauging how far he had to go before he could escape.

"You need to consider it," Flynn insisted.

Jericho shook his head. "It's not possible."

Shards of disappointment pricked at Ivy's heart. After sharing such a passionate kiss, why wouldn't he consider marriage—if not now, then maybe down the road? But he was flat-out rejecting her. Same as always.

"I'm sorry." Jericho didn't look at her, but she had the feeling his words were more for her than Wyatt and Flynn. "It has nothing to do with Ivy. It's me. I'm not planning to get married."

"Well, that's just fine with me." Ivy had the sudden need to storm away, but she couldn't go anywhere without first putting on her bodice. "I don't wanna marry you either. Not now or anytime."

"Hey there, Ivy." Wyatt took off his hat and wiped the perspiration gathering on his forehead. His eyes were gentle and understanding but only made her heart pinch tighter. "We ain't blind to the fact that you've been sweet on Jericho."

"You might not be blind, but you sure do got your head stuck in a gopher hole if you think I'd consider marrying Jericho." They could string her up and whup her hide, and she still wouldn't admit to liking Jericho, not after he'd refused to consider marrying her.

Flynn's lips pursed like he was chewing on chokecherries.

Wyatt spoke again before Flynn could. "Jericho can't keep his eyes off you since he got back to town, and it's clear he's got a big hankering for you."

The anger marching around inside her paused its steps. Was Wyatt right?

Jericho looped his thumbs through his belt buckle and stared at his boots.

He wasn't denying Wyatt's statement. But his face gave

nothing away and was harder to read than bleeding ink on a wet letter. Was it possible he'd taken a liking to her? Why else would he kiss her?

Flynn cocked his head at Jericho. "If you're half the man you used to be, you'd put a ring on Ivy's finger today."

Jericho readjusted the rag against his nose and met Flynn's gaze.

Was he considering the option of marriage after all? If he said yes, she didn't know how she'd say no, or if she'd even want to.

"What do you say?" Wyatt stood next to Flynn in the aisle, both imposing men who had protected and loved her for years, but whose care had been overbearing at times. Like now.

"Stop with the badgering." She glared at her brothers.

"I'd do it if I could." Jericho's voice rose over hers.

Flynn studied Jericho's face. "Then why won't you?"

"Like I said before, I can't." When Jericho met her gaze, the apology in his eyes did nothing but regroup the pain and anger and send it rampaging back through her heart.

"Like I said before"—she fisted her hands on her hips—"I don't wanna marry you. In fact, I wouldn't marry you if you were the last man alive."

Jericho's blue eyes swirled with frustration. But she ignored it and twisted at her bodice still hugging her shoulders where he'd draped it.

Flynn and Wyatt were both quiet for several heartbeats. Wyatt finally broke the silence. "You best think long and hard about what you're saying, Jericho. If you ain't willing to—can't—do the right thing for you and Ivy, then it's best for you to move on out and get a job someplace else where you won't be near Ivy and tempted again to use her."

Protest rose swiftly within Ivy. She might be mad at Jericho, but she didn't want him getting into trouble on account of her.

Jericho released a tense breath. "You're right. I'll move out tonight."

Wyatt nodded. "Reckon that'd be for the best—"

"Nope." Flynn took a menacing step toward Jericho, his fingers resting on his revolver. "Reckon the best thing is if we hog-tie Jericho, track down Father Zieber, and have us a wedding right now."

"Hush up, Flynn." Ivy stepped in front of Jericho. No matter how he'd hurt her, she wasn't letting her brother punch him again. "You really think I'm aimin' to get hitched to a man who has to be forced to the altar at gunpoint?"

As Flynn took her in, he had the decency to look chagrinned. "We're just trying to watch out for you, Ivy. That's all."

"You've watched out for me real well, Flynn." She swallowed the sudden lump that clogged her throat. "But now I gotta figure out my future for myself."

Flynn's expression remained stormy. And Ivy guessed she wasn't gonna be able to convince him of his need to cut her loose, at least not today.

"Now if you all will excuse me, I'll get myself decent." She cocked her head toward the door. Jericho was the first to aim for it. His footsteps echoed heavily, and he didn't glance back at her as he opened it and walked out. Somehow that single act of negligence pierced her more than his words had.

Left alone with Flynn and Wyatt, she was suddenly overcome by the need to weep. Hot tears stung the backs of her eyes, and she was afraid that at any second she'd break down and bawl.

"Ivy," Wyatt started.

She shook her head. "Please, I need a few minutes by myself."

Wyatt nodded, grabbed Flynn's arm, and the two started toward the door. Once there, they both glanced at her over their shoulders as if she were a different breed of animal they'd never come across.

As the door shut behind them, she sank onto the closest bench and buried her face in her hands. An instant later, her palms were damp with her silent tears. How had things gone bad so rapidly?

One minute she was on the brink of heaven in Jericho's arms, kissing him and basking in the attention she'd only dreamed about him giving her. In the next, he was telling everyone he didn't like her enough to consider marriage—not now or anytime soon.

Why had he dismissed her so easily? What was wrong with her?

No doubt she was a mess-up. Even Flynn had said so. He'd tried mighty hard to raise her up to be a good and decent woman. But somehow she was always falling short.

A better woman wouldn't have been caught smooching with a man in a church. A better woman wouldn't have been half-dressed with a man she wasn't married to. A better woman wouldn't have let someone else take the blame for her problems.

None of this was Jericho's fault. He hadn't used her. In fact, he hadn't done anything to harm her. He'd simply been in the wrong place at the wrong time. But by her silence, she was letting her brothers think the worst about him.

They'd fired him and kicked him off the ranch because of her.

"Oh, Lord Almighty, what have I done?" She'd driven a wedge between Jericho and her family because of her selfishness, because she hadn't wanted him to tell anyone about her competitions so she could keep saving up for her own ranch.

The main door of the church opened, then closed softly. Footsteps padded down the aisle toward the front pew where she sat. The steps were too light to belong to Jericho. After their parting, she doubted she'd see him again anyway. Not after how selfish she'd been.

If only everything inside wasn't aching for the need to be with him. Holy Saint Peter. What she wouldn't have given to marry him today. But never in her dreaming had she imagined forcing him into marriage.

Someone sat beside her and laid a gentle hand on her arm.

Ivy didn't have to look to know who it was. The protruding belly and the extra huff of breathing told her Greta had been the one Flynn and Wyatt had designated to come inside and talk some sense into her. From the voices filtering in, she knew everyone else—even all the young'uns—were waiting close-by.

Greta patted Ivy's arm and sat quietly with her. She appreciated Greta's patience. The sweet woman had always made her feel welcome, like she was wanted and loved and accepted.

But it hadn't mattered how widely Greta and Wyatt had opened their home—a piece of Ivy had been missing that they hadn't been able to replace. It was a piece she wasn't sure she'd ever be able to replace, but she'd hoped having her own home would give her a measure of satisfaction that she'd missed all these years.

Yet, how could she move forward with earning money from any more competitions knowing her dishonesty and duplicity had hurt Jericho? She didn't want him to take the blame for everything that had happened. She had to come clean, no matter the consequences for herself and her future.

"Greta?"

"Hmm?"

Ivy squeezed her eyes closed. Even working the rest of the summer for Greta, she'd never save up enough for the land, not without the winnings from the cowhand contests. But she had to do it for Jericho. To clear his name so her brothers wouldn't be mad at him and would hire him back.

"I've been joining in the contests as Buster Bliss." She spoke the words in a rush, waiting for Greta's gasp.

But Greta only shifted and wrapped an arm around Ivy's shoulder. "I know."

Ivy peeked sideways.

Greta's silvery blue eyes were filled with understanding and love.

"How'd you figure it out?"

"Astrid recognized you during the Roman-style race. She chased you down and then came and told us all about it and that you were hiding out in the church."

"Astrid's got a mouth bigger than a canyon." A burst of betrayal stung Ivy. Even though she was tempted to give Astrid a piece of her mind, Ivy had more important things to do. "Flynn and Wyatt are accusing Jericho of using me."

Greta squeezed her shoulder. "You can't blame them, can

you? Finding their baby sister here like this is pretty hard on them."

"Jericho's not at fault, though. I was getting changed back into my womanly clothes, and he was just helping me get unstuck from—" She nodded at the linen strip still lying discarded on the floor.

Greta was silent for several heartbeats as if trying to figure out how to proceed.

"I know we shouldn't have been kissing," Ivy added. "But it was the first time, and it'll be the last."

"So you haven't been—well, you haven't shared other intimacies with him yet?"

A flush hit Ivy in the face. "No how, no way. I'm not a loose woman, and he ain't that kind of fella."

Greta's face was beginning to flush now too. "Of course you're not. And of course he's a fine man. But even two God-fearing and very well-meaning people can get carried away, especially if they're not careful about setting limits on the displays of their affection for one another before marriage."

"Did you and Wyatt get carried away?"

"Ours was an unusual situation. We did things backward— got married first and then let our love develop later."

Ivy had always thought their marriage of convenience was strange, not anything she'd want to do. But thankfully for them it had worked out. "Flynn and Linnea kissed and didn't get carried away."

"True." Greta rubbed her free hand over her abdomen, something she did often, as if she were already caressing her babe and assuring it of her love. "And I know you and Jericho can keep from getting carried away too—"

"There's no me and Jericho."

She shrugged. "If . . . if you're ever tempted to kiss him again, just remember that it's best if you refrain from pouring fuel on the passion."

Ivy had the sudden image of Jericho reaching for her, his eyes radiating with a blazing blue heat like the hottest embers. When he'd circled his hand around her and touched her, it set something ablaze inside her. Even now, just thinking about it sent warmth spiraling low within her belly.

Yep. She could see how the heat would spread and grow if they kept on fueling the fire.

"And, Ivy?" Greta ducked her head.

"What?"

"Next time, stay fully clothed."

Ivy barked out a laugh. "Who told you to say that? Wyatt or Flynn?"

Greta smiled sheepishly. "Both."

Ivy glanced to the closed door. Though the two weren't in sight, she had no doubt they'd been listening. "Lucky for them, there won't be a next time." Though she tried to keep the despair from her voice, it hung there anyway.

Greta's arm tightened. "You're a beautiful and enchanting young woman."

Ivy shook her head. "Nope, that's Astrid—"

"You too, Ivy. You're beautiful inside and out. And some man will be blessed to have you as his wife."

"You're just saying that."

"It's the truth."

Ivy wished she could believe Greta, but all she could think about was Jericho striding out the door and leaving her behind. If she was beautiful enough inside and out, then why didn't he want her? And why did he always walk away?

CHAPTER
15

Blast it all, why did Ivy have to be the prettiest woman at the dance?

Jericho stood with the other single cowhands on the sideline and pretended not to notice Ivy dancing with every man but him. The last rays of the long summer day had faded into darkness, and the night was now lit by lanterns placed strategically along the perimeter of the mayor's spacious yard. The stars glittered especially bright, as if deciding to add to the festivity of the holiday.

On a makeshift stage, the musicians played a lively mixture of fiddles, a banjo, and a concertina. The caller stood near them, his deep voice rising above the music and clapping and stomping.

Ivy twirled with her partner in a circle before switching directions and latching elbows with someone else. She'd shed every trace of the skinny Buster Bliss disguise. In her blue skirt and the matching bodice—which was now in place—

she was fancy and ladylike. And heaven help him, all he wanted to do was kiss her again.

Even now as she turned her face up and smiled at the man leading her in the circle, he watched her lips. She'd been soft and pliable, but their connection had been as explosive as fireworks. The leftover sparkles still tingled inside him.

Jericho's bones ached with the effort of holding himself back from stalking over to her and dragging her away from the other men. He'd stuffed his hands deep in his pockets to keep himself in place. Though he tried to focus on the conversations around him, he could think of nothing and no one but her.

In fact, he'd thought of little else in the hours since he'd walked out of the church and left her behind. He'd given himself a mental lashing at least a dozen times for the whole confrontation and how he'd handled it. Even if she hadn't wanted to marry him any more than he had her, his refusal to consider the suggestion had brought a shadow to her face and into her eyes.

Had he done the right thing by turning down Flynn and Wyatt's proposal? He could only imagine what it would be like to be married to Ivy, the most beautiful woman God had ever created. Life with her would be intensely pleasurable, with never a dull moment.

What if he'd made a mistake in not claiming her for his bride while he still could?

His attention trailed her again. No, he couldn't have her. He refused to drag her into the dangerous life he was carving out for himself. Even if plenty of Pinkerton agents were happily married and had no problems, he knew all too well what could happen, how the situation could change in the blink of an eye, how it could rip the ones you loved away from you.

He wouldn't do that to Ivy. He wasn't willing to risk her life.

The fact was, she'd be happier with someone else. And he had to let her find a man who could love her the way she deserved.

Tearing his sights from her, he spun and started toward the line of tables near Steele's house. They were laden with the pies and cakes and cookies that had been a part of the baking contests earlier in the day and had now been set out by the women who'd made them.

Those who weren't dancing lingered around the food tables, talking and eating. As he stepped up and helped himself to a piece of carrot cake, he half-considered calling it a night. He'd already made arrangements for a room at Hotel Windsor and planned to stay there for the time being.

Of course, he'd have to ride back to Healing Springs Ranch and gather his belongings. But he'd do it at a time when he wouldn't have to face Wyatt again.

"Jericho?"

Speaking of Wyatt. Jericho could feel the man's presence behind him and hesitated to turn. Was there a way he could slip away and pretend he hadn't heard the oldest McQuaid?

As much as he wanted to escape Wyatt and the dance and images of Ivy, he had to stick around until the end. The late hours when people were the most tired and drunk provided him with the best opportunities to hear things he might not otherwise. He'd already gleaned plenty of details over the past few hours, but his work for the day was far from over. And he couldn't forget it.

He was aiming to rub shoulders with Gordon Rathburn and see if he could get the man to slip up and share more about his past. From everything Jericho had heard about the bronc rider, Gordo fit the profile for Rodney James. Nobody knew for sure what part of the East Gordo was from, but in the four years since the end of the war, he'd roamed the West. Ivy had been right about him spending some time in Texas. But beyond that, his past was much too mysterious. And Gordo was too tight-lipped, fitting the profile of a man with something to hide.

Slowly Jericho pivoted. He wouldn't relish another battering, since his cheek and eye still smarted from Flynn's punches. But he was willing to take whatever punishment Ivy's brothers wanted to lay on him.

Wyatt stood alone—thankfully, without Flynn.

Jericho braced himself. He didn't plan to fight back now any more than he had earlier. As much as he'd loved the kiss with Ivy, he shouldn't have done it, especially not under the circumstances with their being alone and her without her bodice on.

"Wyatt." Jericho eyed the cake on the brown paper that served as a plate. Should he put it down or let Wyatt stuff it into his face?

Wyatt lifted his hat, scratched his head, then set his hat back in place before he tugged on his neckerchief. "Listen. I wanted to apologize for Flynn and me getting all fired up earlier."

Wyatt was apologizing? Jericho almost allowed his shoulders to sag with relief. He didn't deserve the kindness, was pretty sure he wouldn't have been able to extend it if the situation had been reversed.

Wyatt glanced over to a nearby wagon where his wife sat on the bench, holding the reins to the team. She was watching them, and from the back of the wagon in the bed, Astrid was holding one of the children and peering his way too.

"You and Flynn had every right to get riled up. I shouldn't have been with Ivy—"

"Reckon it's natural enough for a man to wanna kiss the woman he loves." Wyatt's statement came out soft, but the power of it hit Jericho in his chest hard enough to stop his lungs from expanding. Wyatt's eyes were filled with a certainty and knowing that Jericho wanted to argue against, but he couldn't get his airways to work.

Did he love Ivy?

He shook his head. Impossible.

Wyatt spread his feet slightly. "Flynn and I, we did some jawing since the, uh, incident. And we've both seen it, plain as daylight, you caring for Ivy something fierce."

Jericho might be able to deny that he loved her, but he couldn't disagree with Wyatt about caring for Ivy something fierce. That much was becoming clear with each passing day he was with her.

"Flynn and I agree we couldn't ask for anyone better for Ivy than you. Not a man for miles around can compare with what a good and decent fella you are."

"Thank you, Wyatt. That means a lot—"

"Ivy came clean about competing as Buster Bliss."

Jericho's gaze shot to Ivy in the dance area, twirling away like she'd been before, being passed around among the men like she was the prize of the night. She was a prize. Any man would be lucky to have her.

After how hard she'd tried to keep her secret about being

Buster Bliss, why had she admitted to it? In doing so, she'd lost her chances of competing and making money. She'd never be able to save up enough for Steele's land now. Not on the pittance she'd make working for Greta.

Wyatt took his hat off and scratched his head again. "She said you're not to blame for the indecency at the church."

So she'd made the admission to protect him? "I take full responsibility for everything that happened. I could have walked away, but I didn't."

"Yep. Mighty hard to walk away from a pretty woman you got a hankering for."

Jericho had learned just how true that was.

"That's why I'm standing by my decision that you move on out. Ain't no good gonna come from you living so near Ivy. Reckon you best keep your distance until you marry her."

Until he married her? Wyatt seemed awfully confident, almost as if his being with Ivy was a foregone conclusion.

"Flynn said you could live with him until the wedding. And I'm agreeing to keep you on at the construction site as long as you need the work."

Jericho had to set the McQuaid men straight, and fast. "I appreciate the offer to stay with Flynn as well as the offer of work. But I was serious about not being able to marry Ivy. I can't do it."

Wyatt folded his bulky, muscular arms. The fellow could hit as hard as Flynn, if not more so. Regardless, Jericho couldn't lie to this man about his future with Ivy. "What's stopping you? Another woman?"

"No. Of course not. I'm not interested in anyone else and never have been." That didn't come out right. It sounded an awful lot like an admission that Ivy was his one and only. Was she?

Wyatt cocked a brow.

Jericho shook his head, his frustration mounting. "I'm sorry, Wyatt. I'm not in a position in my life where I can think about marriage."

"Why not?"

"It's complicated."

"Sometimes love is complicated, but you've gotta work through it."

"In this case, I can't work through it."

Wyatt stared at Jericho as if trying to see down inside to help him figure out the problem. If Wyatt knew the danger that came with being a bounty hunter, he'd ride away with Ivy so fast, all Jericho would see would be the dust from their trail.

"Whether you're willing to admit it or not, you love her." Wyatt tilted his hat, as though readying to be on his way. "Reckon every cowhand this side of the Divide knows it but you. Best you untangle whatever's holding you back before you end up losing her."

Without giving Jericho a chance to respond, Wyatt turned and wove through the milling crowd toward his wagon and family. Not that Jericho could have responded. The whole conversation had taken him completely by surprise. From Ivy's admission of guilt to Wyatt's offer of his job back. Most jolting of all was Wyatt's insistence that he loved Ivy.

Surely Wyatt wasn't right. Did everyone else know it but him?

He tried to get his lungs working again. He was supposed to be proficient at hiding his emotions. But in the case of

Ivy, apparently the only one he'd hidden his feelings from was himself.

⚜

Jericho clamped his jaws together to bite back a slew of harsh words for Hance Payne. With the dancing long over and most families having dispersed, the younger crowd remained—mainly cowhands and miners and single businessmen. Men like Hance Payne laying the charm on Ivy with way too much persistence.

Standing at a central bonfire, Jericho had used the opportunity to learn as much as he could about the men on his list. But with Ivy hanging on to every word of Hance's tales of long-forgotten treasures buried in the mountains, Jericho had only grown more irritated and distracted, so that now he wanted to walk over to the fellow, kick him in the pants, and send him to his home at the back of the barbershop.

It had nothing to do with his feelings for Ivy and more to do with the fact that Hance was filling Ivy's head with thoughts of gold. With the way her eyes were brightening in the firelight, Jericho had no doubt she was thinking on how she might be able to get her hands on a treasure.

"Otis and I are going out treasure hunting again on Sunday." Hance was standing next to Ivy. As he stretched his hands out toward the flames, he brushed his shoulder against hers.

Jericho took a puff on his pipe, unable to stop the low burn of anger inside from fanning hotter.

A fist bumped into Jericho's arm. "If looks could kill, Hance Payne'd be a dead man." Gordo guffawed beside him and drew the laughter of several other cowhands.

Jericho had finally worked his way into Gordo's loyal band of friends. And the longer he'd talked with them, the freer they'd been in telling him stories about their pasts.

From piecing together various details, he'd come to the conclusion that Gordo and two of his friends had fought for the South. They'd boasted about some of the guerilla war tactics Rodney James was known for. They'd even admitted to deserting near the end of the war and running off to Texas.

Gordo leaned in, his breath sour from whiskey. "Reckon it's time for you to teach Hance he can't have what ain't his."

"Maybe so."

"If it were me, I wouldn't be letting my girl flirt with every man around. I'd be makin' sure she was plenty satisfied with me. If you know what I mean." Gordo ended with a lewd kissing motion.

His friends burst into raucous laughter.

Jericho opened his mouth to clear up the confusion that Ivy wasn't his girl, then clamped it shut. He hadn't danced with her once. Hadn't even spoken with her. But maybe it was better if everyone believed she was his. Maybe he could frighten them off that way.

His dark glares certainly weren't keeping Hance away. The man hadn't even seemed to notice him.

Hance was caught up in regaling Ivy with another tale of treasures. "In the early 1800s, Spanish prospectors were returning to Mexico City with eight mules laden with gold. Not long after they started out on their journey, Ute warriors chased after them. In order to outrun the Utes, the Spanish had to lighten their caravan. Even though they quickly hid their gold, only three men escaped the Utes and made it to Santa Fe. Later, they tried to return for the gold but never could find it."

Ivy watched Hance with rapt attention.

"Some say the Utes took it all away," Gordo interjected.

"Exactly." Hance didn't break his attention from Ivy. "They say the Utes moved it up here into Pike's Forest and marked the spot with a pile of rocks in the form of a rattle-snake."

"A rattlesnake?" Ivy's face conveyed her growing excitement.

"That's what me and Otis have been looking for." Hance directed a nod toward the hefty dentist standing on his other side, as quiet and shy as always, but who was having another coughing fit from the smoke. "We've found rock piles near Snyder Creek. And some near Rock Creek. But nothing in the form of a rattlesnake."

"Reckon you'll be searchin' awhile." Gordo spoke derisively. "Lookin' for a pile of rocks in Pike's Forest is like lookin' for a piece of hay in an alfalfa field."

Several others chortled, while a couple of the men offered suggestions to Hance and Otis on where they'd seen snake-like rock patterns in the towering mountains to the east that made up part of Pike's Forest.

Once upon a time, the hunt for treasure might have lured Jericho. But that lure had died right alongside Nash the day he'd fallen to his death. In fact, the lure was long gone, replaced by the cold, hard reality of life. He was too practical to waste time chasing after whimsical dreams when he could chase after crooks who needed to face the consequences of their crimes.

Gordo took a swig from his bottle of whiskey and then stared at Hance as if trying to place him. "I swear I've seen Hance before when I was living in Texas."

178

With a neat mustache and sideburns, Hance's unassuming appearance was like that of most of the businessmen in the area. Even so, Jericho hadn't ruled him out as a suspect yet. "Heard he's originally from Virginia," Jericho said casually, "but lived in California during the war."

"Lived? More like hightailed to avoid the fighting." Men like Gordo who'd seen action during the war didn't hold much respect for those who'd chosen to get away from the conflict, even when they admitted to running off themselves at the end.

While Hance rambled on about several of the creeks he and Otis had explored, Jericho attempted to lead Gordo into sharing more about his time in Texas—where he'd lived and who he'd worked for. Gordo didn't come right out and say it, but he hinted at having been an Irregular for the Confederates and having known some of the worst of the war criminals, one of whom was apparently now mining down by Buckskin Joe. A man who went by the name of Tippy Simons.

At the revelation, Jericho mentally rehearsed all the excuses he could find for making a trip to Buckskin Joe. He doubted Tippy Simons was Rodney James. With a big bounty on his head, Rodney wouldn't flaunt his whereabouts so openly. At least Jericho didn't think he would. But he had to investigate the lead, and maybe Tippy would spill more information.

"I know of a couple areas that have rock formations." Ivy's declaration drew Jericho's attention. "I could show them to you if you want."

"We would enjoy the pleasure of your company on Sunday, Miss McQuaid," Hance replied. "We leave at dawn if you're up for the challenge."

"No." The word slipped out before Jericho could stop it. "She's not going."

In the process of nodding her agreement, Ivy fisted her hands on her hips and glared at him. "Stay out of this, Jericho. This ain't none of your concern."

How many times had he heard that from her over the years? Was it because he'd always interfered in her business? Because he'd cared about her something fierce, just like Wyatt had declared?

He shook his head, dumped out the remains of tobacco from his pipe, and pocketed it. He didn't want to admit Wyatt was right and that he'd had a longtime hankering for Ivy. No. He'd interfered because she was reckless and impulsive and needed someone to keep her from doing something stupid.

Like now.

"You're not going." He stalked around the bonfire toward her.

Ivy turned her back toward him and faced Hance. "Where should I meet you, Mr. Payne?"

Hance's eyes widened upon Jericho, and he took a step away from Ivy. Good thing. Or Jericho might have shoved him a mile.

"Let's go." Jericho took hold of her arm and began to tug her away from the gathering, but she dug in her heels.

"Give her a reason to go with you!" Gordo laughed. "Show her you mean it."

Chortles and vulgar suggestions burned Jericho's ears on one side, and Ivy struggled against him on the other. With mounting frustration, he swung her up, giving her no choice but to grab his neck and hang on.

He tromped away toward her horse, whistles and raunchier calls following after them.

Ivy held herself stiffly but didn't persist in fighting him. "What do you think you're doing?"

"Getting you away from the men." He didn't slow his stride. "You should have gone home with Wyatt."

"Just 'cause you don't like being with me doesn't mean other men won't."

Was that what she thought? That he didn't like spending time with her? He just shook his head, frustration twisting at his insides. Why was he always saying or doing the wrong things with Ivy? Why couldn't he ever get things right?

By the time he reached the hitching post and her horse, his jaw ached from clamping it together so tightly. He stopped but couldn't make himself put her down. What could he say to reassure her that whatever reservations he had weren't because of her?

He breathed her in, and in the process his nose brushed against her hair.

She held herself motionless.

"Nothing's wrong with you, Ivy." His words came out low and raw. "I like being with you."

"You do?"

He nodded, her hair tickling his chin and making him want to bury his face against its silkiness. "Don't ever think I don't."

"I can't help it. You're always getting angry with me."

He closed his eyes at the hurt in her voice, hurt he was putting there, and he hated himself for it. "I'm sorry."

Her grip loosened, and she melted against him.

Other revelers lingered nearby in the open doors of saloons, some in the streets. No one seemed to be paying them any attention, and he used the opportunity to hold her longer than he should. He might not be able to have her. But he could savor these tiny moments once in a while, couldn't he?

"You told Wyatt and Flynn about being Buster?" he whispered against her hair.

She nodded. "I wanted to. It wasn't fair for them to think you were at fault for my indecency and to hate you for it."

"I didn't mind."

"I couldn't let you take the blame." She lifted her head and gently touched his bruised cheek.

He winced.

"I didn't want Flynn to hit you again."

"Thank you. I'd prefer not to run into his fist again either."

Her lips curved into a smile, one that stole the breath from his lungs. She was always beautiful, but her smile . . . it made her stunning. "You could've defended yourself, you know."

"Not when I deserved the thrashing."

"You didn't do nothin' wrong."

What about kissing her? It had been a mistake. Hadn't it?

Her attention dropped to his mouth. Was she thinking about the kiss they'd shared too? *"I'll kiss who I want and when I want."* Her words reverberated through him. She was bold enough to kiss him again if she wanted to. It was exactly the kind of thing she'd do. Her aggression, her passion, her forcefulness had never scared him. He liked those qualities about her.

In fact, the thought of her reaching up and pressing her mouth to his sent a ripple of delicious desire along his nerve endings, tightening his muscles. If she chose that moment to kiss him, he'd be powerless to say no.

Swiftly, before she decided to initiate something, he lowered her to the ground and steadied her before he took a step back. "I'll get my horse from the livery and see you back to the ranch." Even though she'd probably made the ride home dozens of times alone, he didn't like the idea of her riding by herself. Besides, he could use the opportunity to get his things.

She studied his face, her gaze flitting over his lips.

Another wave of wanting shot through him, this one just as intense as the last.

Blazing smoke. Was this what he had to live with from now on, remembering their kiss every time he was with her and craving it again? Was that why Wyatt and Flynn wanted him to get married to Ivy, because they knew the temptation firsthand?

He had to resist. He spun toward the hitching post and began to untie the horse's line. "Wyatt offered me my job back but said I have to live with Flynn."

She was silent another heartbeat before he heard the *thunk* of her shoe in the stirrup and the swish of her skirt as she situated herself in the saddle. "And you won't do either?"

He allowed himself to get his fill of her now that she sat a safe distance away. "It's best if I stay in town until I get another job."

She looped the reins through her fingers, twisting the leather. "You don't have to move."

What was she insinuating? That she wanted to be with him? All the more reason he needed to make his escape from Healing Springs Ranch while he still had his sanity about him. "I booked a room at the hotel."

"Are you still planning to work for Wyatt?"

He wasn't sure what he'd do. He had to keep on acting like he was interested in Steele's land, but at the thought of her not being able to buy it anymore, he hated to move forward with the purchase, knowing how much it would bother her. "I'll be checking into a couple of other options tomorrow."

"Then you won't be around at all?" Her question hinted at dejection.

He had to relinquish the need to work for Wyatt just so he could see her once in a while. "I'll be busy. And so will you."

She stared off to the north. The forest fires that were still burning emanated an eerie glow, lighting up the pine trees and illuminating the outline of the peaks in the darkness. Without the strong winds, the smoke had lessened, leaving only a hint of it in the air.

He had to say something more, but as usual, he didn't know what. He could barely admit the truth about how he was feeling toward her, much less converse about it openly. Besides, what good would it do to talk about it? It would only dredge up more feelings that didn't need dredging.

On the other hand, not acknowledging anything between them would hurt her again. "I meant what I said before at the church, Ivy. None of this is your fault. It's mine for getting carried away."

"Carried away? Is that all this is to you?"

He didn't have to ask what she was referring to by *this*. He knew she was talking about everything that had happened earlier along with the attraction that was raging into an inferno between them more with every passing hour. "Yes, I'm sorry—"

"You ain't gonna give me an explanation?"

"I wish I could."

"But you're not, and you're aimin' to ride out of my life again, just like that?"

"You're better off without me."

"Fine." She sat up straighter in her saddle and gripped the reins tighter. "You're right. I am better off without you."

Protest stirred inside him, but he held it back.

Her mare shied, as though feeling the rising tension. "Go ahead. Leave. But this time I mean it. Don't come back."

"Hold on, Ivy. I don't want to part ways on bad terms."

She nudged her horse forward. "And I'm serious. I don't wanna see you again." With that, she dug in her heels and urged her mare into a trot that rapidly shifted into a gallop.

He wanted to yell after her to stop, to come back, to let him explain. But he stood mutely watching her ride away into the darkness, a sense of despair settling over him so thickly it was suffocating.

When he'd signed on with Pinkerton, he never expected to experience something like this—being torn in two by his desire to finish the job and a strange longing to walk away from it to be with a woman.

He lifted his hat off and palmed his forehead. Ivy was driving him to the brink of insanity.

With a growl, he slammed his hat down, spun, and stalked toward the hotel. He had to stick to his plan and couldn't let anything get in his way. Especially not his feelings for Ivy.

CHAPTER

16

Rock formations in the shape of a rattlesnake? Ivy knew of at least two areas that might fit the description.

The sky in the east was tinged with brilliant orange and red over the Kenosha and Tarryall Mountains, and the smoky haze from the forest fires to the north draped it all in a veil. Windy Peak stood at the forefront of the others, its bald head a shade of purple in the glow of the rising sun.

Bristlecones, ponderosa pine, and blue spruce covered the mountainside along with the enormous granite outcroppings that made the area a perfect place for hiding treasures.

She breathed in the cool air that would soon burn away in the heat of the July day. The earthiness of evergreens filled her nostrils along with the scent of smoke, which had grown more prominent the higher in elevation they'd climbed.

Behind her, Hance and Otis rode quietly, letting her lead the way up into the rocky areas she'd traversed plenty during the years she'd lived in South Park.

Ever since the Independence Day celebrations, she'd

known she had to strike out and search for hidden gold. Wyatt and Flynn had made it mighty clear they wouldn't tolerate her competing as Buster Bliss any longer in the cowhand contests. And without the prize earnings, she had no choice but to join the hunt for treasure or lose out on Steele's land.

She bit back a sigh. She'd probably lose the land anyway. Finding hidden treasure in the mountains was about as likely as locating a sober man in a saloon. But it didn't hurt to have a look. It was a heap better than sitting around waiting for gold to fall into her lap.

And it was a heap better than sitting around moping over Jericho.

At the thought of him, another piece of her heart crumbled away, just as it'd been doing ever since the other night. As she'd urged her horse across the barren prairie outside of Fairplay, she'd hoped and waited for the sound of him galloping after her, shouting her name, telling her he was being a pig for letting her go.

But only the lone howl of a coyote had resounded in the night above the pounding of her horse's hooves. By the time she'd ridden the five miles home, the truth had driven into her harder than a mule's back kick.

Jericho didn't want her.

Hadn't mattered that they'd shared a kiss. Hadn't mattered that he'd felt the same thing she had. Hadn't mattered that Wyatt and Flynn wanted him to marry her. Hadn't mattered that she'd asked him for an explanation.

Her throat tightened around a lump that wouldn't go away. This time she intended to put him from her mind and to stay as far from him as she could. She'd decided to skip out on the church service today to avoid him. She didn't know how she'd be able to sit in that small chapel with him nearby and not think on their kiss.

How was it he could kiss her like that one moment and then push her out of his life the next?

She shook her head, her long braid swishing sharply across her back.

"What is it?" Hance asked from behind her. "Do you see something?"

"Nope. We still got a ways before we're there." Half a day's journey at least, since the rocky terrain near the summit would slow them down.

The two men were like kids at Christmas in their zeal for finding treasure. They'd been consulting their map and checking off the locations they'd already searched. From what she'd been able to tell from the drawings of the Kenosha Range, they hadn't yet visited the sprawling rock formations that surrounded Windy Peak and several other peaks nearby.

Hance had pulled out a separate map, one drawn by someone else that had more precise markings on it. When he'd caught her staring at it, he'd stuffed it back into his coat pocket. Although he'd been as polite as always, irritation marked his expression.

It had given her a moment's pause and made her second-guess her decision to tell Wyatt he didn't have anything to worry about in letting her tag along with Hance and Otis. Maybe she should have taken him up on his suggestion to have Judd or Astrid keep her company.

Ivy hadn't even wanted to consider inviting Astrid, not after she'd blabbered the identity of Buster Bliss to the rest of the family.

Ivy had confronted Astrid about it that night after riding home from the dance. Of course, Astrid claimed she'd shared Ivy's secret to prevent any mishaps. But Ivy guessed the real reason was because Astrid was jealous of her getting all the attention from Jericho.

Whatever the case, Ivy reckoned she'd have to patch things up sooner or later. She couldn't stay mad at Astrid forever. Someone else would've figured out her duplicity eventually anyway. Ivy'd just hoped to hide her competing until after she'd saved up enough to beat Jericho in the bid for Steele's land.

She settled her attention on the granite formations ahead, the light of day bringing them to life. Maybe she needed to pray for a miracle. But she hadn't been in the business of praying in recent years. If she was honest with herself, she figured praying wouldn't do much good.

Father Zieber talked about God loving them no matter what they did or where they wandered, like a patient father always loving his children. But the closest thing she'd ever had to a father was Flynn, and she was always disappointing him. She didn't doubt she'd disappointed God too. He was probably sighing and throwing His arms up at her antics, especially lately.

She had to do better. And she would, once she had a place she could finally call home.

❧

Jericho's gut tightened as he stood outside the church after the service and searched up and down the street for Ivy, the wind slapping him hard. Through the swirling dust and the tumbling weeds, he didn't see her anywhere. He hadn't asked her family where she was for fear of seeming too interested. But it wasn't like her to miss the Sunday meeting.

The midmorning sun beat down on his black hat and soaked into his church clothes—black trousers, along with a matching suit coat and vest over a white shirt and tie. He'd taken extra time with his grooming, telling himself he wasn't doing it to impress Ivy. But a part of him couldn't deny that he had, and he was ashamed of it.

Though he hadn't wanted to, he'd arrived at the church early and watched for her, his chest thudding with anticipation. Even when she'd been absent, he'd kept on looking and waiting.

Now he was left with the unsettling conclusion that she'd accepted the offer to go treasure hunting with Hance Payne.

She had every right to gallivant around with Hance or any other man. Jericho had no claim to her, not after making the break with her on Independence Day. She'd given him a chance to explain things, but he let her ride out of his life. Because of that, he needed to honor her request not to see her again, needed to walk away and stop thinking of her.

Except, she was out there with Hance. And he didn't like it. Not one bit.

Was it because he was jealous? Or was it something more than that? Something Hance had said? Something someone else had said about Hance?

Jericho narrowed his gaze upon the barbershop and dentist office. Gordo had claimed Hance appeared familiar, like someone he'd known in Texas. Maybe Hance was lying about having lived in California. Had he sought refuge in Texas after the war before coming up to Colorado? Perhaps with one of the gangs of outlaws Gordo had mingled with?

And why was Hance so determined to hunt for hidden treasure? From what Jericho had gleaned, Otis and Hance searched every weekend and sometimes even closed up shop early during the week to go out. Clearly they took their hobby more seriously than most men. It was almost as if they were certain a treasure existed.

Not only that, but Hance seemed privy to details no one else knew, especially about the Spanish treasure. Most treasure hunters believed the fabled Spanish gold was located by the Purgatoire River east of Las Animas. No one had ever mentioned the Utes finding and moving the treasure. And Jericho had never heard anything about rocks in the figure of a rattlesnake.

The question was, how had Hance gleaned his information and where?

Jericho was half-tempted to break into Hance's shop and poke around to see what he could find. But the urgency inside prodded him toward the livery and his horse. He didn't like the idea of Ivy being alone with any men at this point, not until he whittled down his Rodney James suspect list.

Yet, he couldn't just ride out and drag Ivy home. She'd put up a big fight and refuse to come with him. And he couldn't offer to tag along with her, not after the way things had ended between them. It wouldn't be fair to keep pushing himself into her life and giving her hope when there wasn't any.

His sights shifted to the haze that had settled over the Kenosha Range. Billows of smoke rose into the air. Reports from those coming over Kenosha Pass all said the same thing, that the forest fires were burning in the Mount Evans area, that the flames hadn't made their way down into the Kenosha

Range. Ivy wasn't in any danger. But the smoke seemed to be drifting farther south.

Maybe he could ride out with the excuse that he was checking on the direction of the fire to bring a report back for any stagecoaches and teamsters considering traveling up the Kenosha Pass. Hopefully Ivy wouldn't see through his excuse and realize he'd followed her. Even if she did, he couldn't restrain himself any longer. His muscles were tightening with each passing moment with the need to go after her.

Within the half hour, he was on his way northeast up into the Kenosha Range, his weapons loaded and canteen full. He'd been there often over the years and was familiar enough with the rock formations to guess approximately where Ivy was taking the men. It was a long trip, and he wasn't taking any chances.

Still attired in his Sunday-meeting clothes, he rode at a punishing pace, sifting through the details he'd gathered about Hance and Otis. From all appearances and everything they'd said, they were just ordinary fellows trying to build successful businesses in the Fairplay community that Mayor Steele had worked hard to develop.

However, Jericho would use the opportunity today to spend time with them and hopefully discover more about their backgrounds and the treasure they were searching for—Spanish or otherwise.

By midday, as he traveled into the area known for its unique rock patterns, he found evidence of fresh tracks and horse droppings and guessed Ivy was headed to Windy Peak. He veered his mount in that direction, even though everything within him resisted the prospect of going to the area where his brother had died. He'd never been back, had promised himself he wouldn't return.

But today the urgency to protect Ivy drove him. He had to make sure she was alright.

The farther he traveled, the more the wind picked up and the smoke thickened, like fog settling over the evergreens. As he reached a high point with boulders towering from the earth, he reined in, took out his spyglass, and studied the land surrounding Windy Peak for any motion or color that would indicate Ivy's presence. From a distance, one of the rock formations wound upward from the bottom of a ravine, curving back and forth. Jericho guessed it could suffice for a snake.

Was that the spot Hance was seeking? Maybe they'd already discovered it. At the very least, Jericho needed to ride closer and scour the area.

Something in his peripheral vision caught his attention. He shifted his spyglass, and his stomach bottomed out. In the middle of thick clouds just to the north, red billowed above the treetops.

Fire. A swath of flames raged through the forest, the high winds fanning and causing them to jump from one tree to the next faster than he'd ever seen fire move. He didn't know if these flames were a part of the larger area that had been burning over the past couple of weeks or if this was a new fire altogether. But what he did know was that it was moving rapidly toward Windy Peak. If Ivy was anywhere nearby, she would soon be in grave danger.

Desperation clogged his airways. He had to find her. And fast.

CHAPTER

17

Smoke stung Ivy's eyes. But she blinked and attempted to focus. "We should be close now." Her voice came out scratchy after breathing in the smoke-laden air for the past hour of searching.

The high walls of the red-brown granite shielded them from the intensity of the wind but couldn't protect them from the smoke. Both Hance and Otis coughed into the neckerchiefs they'd raised over their mouths and noses.

"Maybe we should head back," Otis called from a dozen paces down the rocky mountainside. Laboring to breathe, the stout man had stopped and was studying the sky, now obscured by gray mounds of smoke that contained an edge of dark fury, like thunderheads before a storm.

Upon reaching the rocky slopes, they'd left their horses behind since the route was too treacherous, and they'd continued by foot, the sparse, dry brush providing holds that allowed them to make the climb.

Ivy peered up the steep incline through the haze. The

summit was within sight. "We've come this far—we can't quit now."

Lines of perspiration made trails through the grit on Hance's forehead, and his spectacles slid down his nose. "The smoke seems to be getting worse."

"Hopefully we'll move out of it once we get a little higher." She stepped up again, her nimbleness and her sturdy boots helping with the climb. She was having an easier time with the hike than Hance and Otis. Both were as clumsy as newborn calves, and Otis had been hacking and coughing for the past hour.

She hiked several more feet before glancing back. The two stood in the same positions as before. Their faces—at least what she could see of them—were red from the exertion as well as the heat of the summer afternoon.

Hance was staring up at the ever-darkening skies too. "You don't think we're in danger of fire?"

"Nope. I reckon the wind is causing a ruckus and blowing the smoke is all." She'd checked with teamsters yesterday and learned that the fiery area was still quite a way to the northwest. Even this morning during the ascent, the blackest smoke remained well out of this part of the range.

At the silence behind her, she halted again. The men were leaning against the rock.

"C'mon. Let's go."

"You're adventurous and brave," came Hance's muffled reply from behind his bandana. "More than we are."

With the way the wind was picking up, it wouldn't hurt to have a place to tuck into if the fire happened to head their direction. "If we run into trouble, we can always head back to that cave we explored just down around the bend. It ain't big, but it'll do if we need a quick place to wait things out."

Thankfully, their horses were tied loosely enough that they'd be able to get free and outrun the fire if it got close to them.

"That's a fine idea." Hance took off his hat and wiped his brow, clearly exhausted.

Otis nodded, but his chest heaved in and out as he labored for another breath.

"I tell you what. While you rest a spell, I'll head on up the last of the climb, take a look around, and call down to you if I see the rattlesnake rock formation."

Both men nodded eagerly.

Without another moment of hesitation, she continued upward, blinking against the hot, dry air and smoke that continued to swirl around her. As she came out from the crevice of boulders and into the open, she paused. She expected to see the forested valleys of the Kenosha Range, but the gray air hovered around.

She hopped from rock to rock as she crossed the summit, aiming for the even larger boulders that formed another craggy peak. The sides were sharply etched as if a giant had chopped away at them with an ax, scattering rocks over the hillside like wood chips.

Pausing, she peered through watering eyes, trying to spot anything that resembled boulders that twisted and turned like a snake. Too bad Dylan wasn't with her. He'd noticed a strange configuration of rocks the first time they'd been out in the area exploring and hiking and had commented on it. He'd likely be able to remember exactly where it was and take Hance and Otis right to it.

Dylan had pointed out a cave near the formation. But with so many caves and rocks all seeming so similar, identifying the spot was turning out to be trickier than she'd realized. And stumbling upon a lost treasure would be even trickier. Regardless, she thrived on a challenge and reckoned she'd get a day of harmless exploring out of her time, if nothing else.

She stepped over the craggy outcroppings and climbed around the center peak. At the sight that met her, she froze. The sky seemed to be on fire with flames shooting into the air and smoke bulging up in mushroom-like towers. Only it wasn't the sky on fire. It was the forest.

Strong winds were acting like bellows in a forge, pumping the flames hard and causing them to rage higher and hotter. Even from a distance, she could feel the heat. It blew against her face, drying her lips and mouth.

In seconds, the fire jumped from one tree to the next and was heading straight toward the summit of Windy Peak.

Her heartbeat stuttered with sudden urgency. She took a step backward but stumbled over the terrain. She had to get to Hance and Otis and tell them to hightail it down to that cave.

She started to backtrack over the rocks, but a glance over her shoulder showed the flames leaping as fast as a wild mustang racing across a mountain prairie. She wasn't gonna make it to Hance and Otis before the fire caught up to her.

She had to take shelter. Now. She scrambled down toward what appeared to be a grouping of large boulders.

"Ivy!" A call came from farther down the summit on the side opposite from where she'd left Hance and Otis.

She squinted, and through the smoke she caught sight of Jericho. What in the name of Saint Peter was he doing out in the Kenosha Range today?

He climbed up the incline toward her, his features taut with worry. "Come on! Hurry!"

With the heat pressing in behind her, she slipped and staggered until, at last, she met him and nearly collapsed into his arms with relief. But he didn't stop. The moment he had her, he raced toward another tall, jagged line of granite. "I saw a cave," he said without letting go of her.

The crackle of burning brush and the snapping of falling branches was much too close. Sparks popped into the air, and several landed on her arm. She swatted them and then brushed one off Jericho's shoulder.

How had the fire moved so swiftly without warning?

When they reached a narrow opening between two large rocks, he squeezed through and drew her along with him. She expected the space to be nothing more than a cleft where they might be able to huddle and hope the flames would pass over them. But Jericho tugged her in deeper.

She had to duck to keep her head from hitting the granite, but the interior was wide enough that they could stand side by side. Outside the glow of flames engulfed the rocks. And as the smoke seeped inside the cave, she cupped a hand over her mouth and nose to keep from inhaling it.

"Looks like we can crawl back farther." He lowered himself to his hands and knees and poked his head into what appeared to be a tunnel. Without a lantern or torch, they couldn't see where they were going or what lurked in the depths of the cave. But she followed him anyway, never one to let a little danger stand in her way.

The ground was smooth rock, cold to the touch. And the tunnel was tight, her head brushing the top. It was only a dozen feet, and they soon found themselves in another cave, this one bigger than the first.

Coughing, she sat back on her heels and tried to catch her breath. The light from outside barely reached inside the cavern, but it was enough to see that the room was narrow, the walls jagged, and a passageway continued on the other side. How deep into the mountainside did the tunnel go?

"Are you alright?" Jericho's shoulder brushed hers.

"Yep. Just inhaled a mite too much smoke."

"Hopefully it won't reach us here." His breathing was ragged too.

She wished for more light so she could examine him. "Did you get burned?"

"I'm fine."

"You sure?"

"Now that I've found you, I'm more than fine."

Had he ridden out all this way because he'd been worried about her?

She couldn't read into his words more than he meant. But something in his tone sent her pulse skittering, like the first rocks trickling down before a landslide.

He was sitting on his heels and took off his hat and wiped his brow. Only then did she notice he was still attired in his Sunday-meeting getup and looking real fine, in spite of being disheveled and dusty and sporting the bruise around his eye that Flynn had given him on Independence Day.

She shoved aside the attraction that rose against her will. She had to remember how they'd parted, that he hadn't made an effort to keep her, even though she'd given him every opportunity. She needed to stay mad. "What in the blazes are you doing out here, Jericho?"

"Do you want my excuse or the truth?"

"Do you want me to shoot you or punch you?"

He released a soft laugh. "The truth is that when you didn't show up for church, I got worried about you being alone with Hance."

His statement careened through her, leaving her off-balance. She was gonna have to be careful. Hadn't she just spent the majority of the ride out into the wilderness telling herself not to hope in Jericho again? After all the times she'd rebuked herself to let him go, she really had to do it this time.

"You didn't have to worry." She tried to infuse her voice with firmness even though her heart was on unsteady ground.

"You don't know enough about him."

"And I reckon you do?"

"More than you."

"He's harmless as a kitten."

"Maybe. Maybe not."

"I can handle Hance just fine."

Jericho harrumphed.

She elbowed him. "You know it."

He didn't respond, and she sensed an edge to him that hadn't been there before. Even though she could only see his outline, his jaw was rigid and his muscles taut.

Her nose tickled as tendrils of smoke wafted into their cavern. The growing red glow meant the flames were directly outside the cave opening.

In spite of being able to take care of herself, she could admit she was glad she wasn't alone in such dangerous circumstances and was with Jericho.

Another gust of smoke blew in, this one stronger than the last. She coughed and then pressed the crook of her arm over her mouth and nose.

In the next instant, Jericho wrapped his arm around her and drew her face against his chest. She found herself sitting on the floor, curled into him, his body shielding her from both the smoke and the heat.

She really oughta back away. But with his strong arms surrounding her and the solidness of his chest supporting her, she had no willpower to do anything but rest within the safety of his embrace.

As the smoke drifted around them, he coughed and bent his head so it rested against hers, his shallow breathing near her ear.

"Should we try crawling back even farther?" Her question was muffled against his shirt.

"We might have to. I just hate to go too far without light . . . just in case."

She didn't have to ask him about the possibility of drop-offs, cave-ins, or even wild animals. They could very well face danger inside as much as out. But at the moment, they had no choice but to push forward into the unknown depths of the mountain.

"Come on." Obviously drawing the same conclusion, he led the way toward the other side of the cavern and the next dark tunnel.

She crawled after him. This time the passageway slanted down. It was steep enough that they had to slide slowly and almost step their way down. At the bottom of the incline, the tunnel seemed to open up into a level room, but the blackness was too encompassing to see anything but the faintest of outlines.

The strike of a match was followed by a yellow glow. Jericho held up the match from the stash he carried for his pipe, giving them a better view of where they were. The room had definitely been inhabited at one time. The charred circle of a firepit sat at the center. A line of stones was pushed up against one wall and the dry, empty carcass of a deer against another.

Jericho crossed to the pit and retrieved a half-burned stick. He touched the end to the match, igniting a dangling piece of the bark. As the stick began to burn, he shoved together the remnants of the old fire.

She knelt and helped him, finding another charred stick and lighting it on fire as well. Within minutes they had a small blaze going. By adding the dried bones in small increments, they could buy enough light for an hour or two. If they got lucky, they wouldn't need more time than that before the forest fire moved on and it was safe to leave the cave.

"Hope Hance and Otis are okay." She pressed a hand to her forehead to ward off the frustration with herself for putting their lives in jeopardy.

"Where did you leave them?" Jericho crouched low and blew on the flames.

"On the other side of the summit. They were too tired to hike to the top."

"Let's pray the wind didn't blow the flames that way."

At the very least she prayed they'd been able to take refuge in the cave they'd passed.

"Might as well sit a spell." She lowered herself to the ground—a mixture of granite and dirt. While the floor was mostly smooth, the walls were jagged, as if they'd been hacked at to make more room. The rocky remains of such hewing had long ago been removed, leaving no debris behind except the line of stones.

Jericho stood and paced around, studying the walls and crevices.

"See anything?" Her eyes followed his every move. He was much too dashing in his suit coat and trousers.

"It hasn't been occupied recently." He swiped at a spiderweb dangling across the ceiling. "But from the remains of the fire and bones, I'd say people have used the cave within the last five years at least."

"Maybe Irregulars during the war?"

"It's possible."

Since Colorado was still a territory of the United States and hadn't yet been given the status of statehood, it hadn't officially entered the war for either the Union or the Confederacy. Instead, both sides had leveraged the territory to their own advantage, primarily in using gold and silver mines to finance the war efforts. The governor had called for regiments of Union soldiers. But Confederates had formed militia groups as well. While no major battles had occurred between the two warring sides, the Confederates had engaged in irregular skirmishes, thus gaining the name Irregulars.

Jericho brushed a hand over the trail of stones, and as he did so, Ivy's racing thoughts came to an abrupt halt. She pushed up from the ground and joined him in front of the formation. The fire wasn't big and didn't provide much light, but it was enough to recognize the rocks had been placed in the pattern of a rattlesnake.

CHAPTER

18

"Are you seeing what I'm seeing?" Ivy radiated with excitement.

"Blazing smoke." It had taken him a minute, but he'd finally recognized the winding snakelike pattern. The front stone was shaped like a head, and each of the other rocks varied in size, none bigger than a bushel basket, easy enough for a man to carry.

"This has got to be what Hance is looking for." Ivy knelt and picked up the front rock. "Reckoned it'd be on the out-side of the mountain marking the spot, not tucked away deep in a cave."

"I think it's in both places." Jericho crouched beside her and ran his hand along the ground, feeling for any indenta-tion that would signify the granite had been cut. "Back a ways as I scanned Windy Peak with my spyglass, I noticed a line of rocks curving up from the bottom of the ravine." He'd aimed directly for it.

With the fire roaring toward the peak from the connecting mountain, he'd been frantic with the need to find Ivy and the men. He hadn't expected to see her scrambling around the summit and attempting to outrun the fire, but he'd been so relieved, he hadn't had time to revel in the fact that he'd found her.

"That means the treasure's in here somewhere." Ivy stood and began to search around the cave, prodding and poking at the walls.

"Don't get your hopes up too high." He continued to run his hand along the ground, moving the rocks and checking under each one.

"You know if I find the treasure, I'm gonna have to hog-tie you and leave you behind?" Her tone was turning light-hearted, and he loved this playful side of her, knew it was his fault that she wasn't like this more often around him.

"Hate to break it to you, but you'd never be able to hog-tie me." He bantered back, hoping to keep the mood light for as long as possible. Because sooner or later, all that had happened at the Independence Day celebrations would come calling. They couldn't hold the frustrations at arm's length forever.

"Oh, I'll hog-tie you." She was on her hands and knees feeling along the perimeter. "Leastways until I can take my part of the treasure on back to Mr. Steele and buy that piece of land."

Buying the land. That's why she'd agreed to the treasure hunt with Hance. Because she was seeking a new way to earn money now that she couldn't join in the cowhand competitions. He should have guessed as much. "You might think you're the best roper this side of the Rockies, but you haven't gone against me."

"Think you're good at it, do ya?"

"Don't think it. I know it."

She laughed lightly. "Reckon we oughta have a competition then. To prove who's the best."

"You're on."

A beat of silence passed. "I hope you know I'm serious about buying that land, and if I find the treasure, I'm aiming to use it for the purchase."

He let another quiet moment settle between them. Should he just tell her he wasn't interested in the land, that she could have it? His muteness on the matter was making things so much harder for her. And yet his reserve could mean the difference between her life and death when it came to Rodney James.

"If you find the treasure"—he tried to lighten his tone—"then you deserve the land, no question about it."

She paused, and he could feel her attention shift to him. "Then you don't think the treasure's here anymore and that we're on a wild-goose chase?"

He glanced around the cavern that was no bigger than the front parlor of the average farmhouse. "Should I tell you what you want to hear?"

"Are you some kind of mind reader now?"

"With you, yes."

"Just shoot straight with me."

"Fine."

"Fine." She had that feisty look in her eyes, a look that always made him slightly crazy for her.

"If this place had a Spanish treasure from the early nineteenth century, then it's been found." He hated to disappoint her, but the fact was, if the Utes had really brought the Spanish treasure to this particular cave long ago, then someone would have stumbled across it by now.

"Why would Hance be looking for a treasure that's been found? And how would Hance know about the rattlesnake formation?"

It was turning out that Hance was more knowledgeable about this spot than he'd let on, more so than anyone else. Ivy's question echoed all the questions Jericho had been asking himself. How had Hance gleaned the information? Had he heard about it from Confederate groups or outlaws who might have used the cave? Was it possible he'd moved to the area for the very purpose of finding such a treasure?

"If there's a treasure, maybe it ain't Spanish gold. Maybe a group of Irregulars hid some gold."

"Maybe. But even that's a long shot."

"You're such an optimist, Jericho. What would the world be like without your cheery outlook?"

He snorted but kept on searching. For her sake. She wouldn't be satisfied until they checked every inch of the place.

They scoured each rock and crevice but could find nothing that indicated a treasure had been hidden there—either by Utes, Confederates, or outlaws. Finally, Jericho sat down and leaned against one of the stones forming the body of the snake. The fire was only a tiny flicker of flames but gave off enough light that the discouragement etching Ivy's features was obvious.

"You should rest." He patted the spot on the ground beside him.

Expelling a sigh, she crossed and lowered herself beside him. "Maybe God's telling me I'm taking the easy way out by trying to make good on stolen gold instead of earning my land the honest way through hard work and sweat."

She reclined against the rock next to his, stretching out her long legs and fixing her split skirt so it covered her modestly. Just the motion reminded him of how womanly she was and set off a chain of explosions inside him.

They were together. Alone. Without anyone to interrupt them this time.

He swallowed hard, crossed his arms, and stared straight ahead.

She fidgeted with a loose thread on her skirt, folded her hands, and then plucked at the thread again. "After the other night, I'm surprised you noticed I was gone from church." Her statement was quiet—and surprisingly devoid of anger. "Didn't think you'd be paying me any attention and would be ridin' clear 'round me as far as you could go."

Yes, of course she was thinking about their last parting and wondering why he was following her when he'd told her she was better off without him.

How could he possibly explain things to her when he couldn't figure it out for himself?

"Just because I can't have you doesn't mean I'm able to stop looking at you." The second his words slipped out, he wanted to smack himself across the head. What was he doing? He couldn't lead Ivy on, not again. He didn't want to keep on hurting her.

She didn't move.

"I'm sorry. I shouldn't have said that."

"It's okay. I like knowing you can't stop looking at me."

He could feel her studying him. He needed to get up and walk to the other side of the cave. But he couldn't make himself do anything.

"What do you mean that you can't have me?" she asked.

Didn't she deserve some kind of explanation? Couldn't

he give her enough of an answer so that she'd understand she truly was better off without him?

"Does it mean you want me even after all you keep saying?" Her question was soft, beckoning.

Lord help him. He fisted his hands to keep himself from reaching for her. "You're a beautiful woman, Ivy."

She hesitated. "I always thought you didn't like me because I needed to grow up."

"Well, there's that. You were too young—"

"Not anymore."

"I know."

She sucked in a breath at his admission, as though she hadn't expected it.

While he was confessing, he might as well keep going. "Dylan made me promise to treat you like a sister and nothing more."

"What? Why?"

"Guess he thought he was protecting you. Can't say I blame him with how pretty you've always been."

"That scoundrel."

"I would have done the same thing if I'd had a sweet little sister tagging along. Would have told all my friends I'd break their hands if they touched you."

She laughed lightly.

He let himself relax against the stone.

"You didn't answer my question. Do you want me?"

He'd barely had time to lean back before he stiffened. Leave it to Ivy to persist so bluntly. Of course he wanted her, but he couldn't tell her that. Or could he? Maybe if he just admitted his feelings, he'd assure her that she was fine, and he was the one with the issues.

"Don't you go and tell me what you think I wanna hear. Tell me the truth." Her hands twisted in her skirt, her knuckles white.

"Yes." He let the word out, couldn't hold it back.

She held herself still. "Yes?"

"Blast it all, Ivy." He shifted, then met her gaze. "Yes. I want you."

Her eyes were as dark and vast as a starless night sky. Surrounded by long, thick lashes, they seemed to peer inside him down to his soul.

All he could think about was the seriousness of her expression and how it made her more mature and desirable. He wanted to frame her cheeks with his palms, run his fingers through her hair, and let his lips explore hers. But he couldn't.

She sat up, then pushed to her knees.

What was she doing? Had he offended her again?

As she turned to face him, a spark lit up her eyes. She scooted closer.

A clanging inside warned him to move. Right away. And put a safe distance between them.

But as he pressed against the cave floor in an effort to rise, she settled both her hands on his shoulders, pushing him back in place. When she lowered a hand and rested it on his chest over his heart, another warning passed through him. But as she bent in closer, he gave himself over to her. He didn't want to resist her and whatever she intended to do to him.

In fact, his blood pumped hard at the prospect of letting her have her way.

Her fingers dug into his shirt and formed a fist at the same time that she slipped a hand up and skimmed his neck.

The very touch sent fire through his veins.

She lifted his hat off and tossed it to the cave floor beside him, all the while keeping her gaze locked with his. Something in her eyes dared him to make her stop. But all he could do was silently dare her to keep going.

As her hand rose into his hair, the spark in her eyes burned brighter and her lips twitched with the beginning of a self-satisfied smile. So she thought she had power over him? Well, she was right. She did. He'd let her toy with him for a few more minutes and then show her the kind of power he wielded over her.

Her fingers delved into his hair, and at the touch he nearly groaned. She combed deeper, locked into his hair tightly, then tugged him forward, using her fist in his shirt to drag him along.

When his face was only an inch from hers, her breathing bathed his lips, and her eyes were heavy lidded. But she held him in place and didn't move the final distance to kiss him.

His chest rose and fell raggedly.

"Say it, Jericho."

"Say what?"

"You know." Her voice was sultry and was doing crazy things to his insides.

At this point, he'd say anything for her kiss. Even that he loved her, because it was the truth. He couldn't deny it any longer. But he had a feeling she wasn't asking for words of love. Not yet.

Her fist in his shirt tightened. "Tell me you want me to be yours."

"I want you to be mine, Ivy."

Her smile curled higher.

"I want you to be mine more than you know—"

Her kiss cut him off, capturing him body, soul, and spirit. He let her take the lead, kept his hands at his sides. Even with the power of the desire between them, her kiss was gentle and delicious.

It only made him hungry for more.

When she pulled back, she didn't meet his gaze. As her fingers loosened within his hair and shirt, she bit her bottom lip, her uncertainty calling to him. He could almost hear her asking if she'd been too forward, second-guessing herself for kissing him.

He wanted her to have no doubt just how much he desired her. And it was his turn to make sure she knew that no matter the power she might have over him, he could affect her too. He situated his hands on either side of her waist and lifted her so that she was sitting on his lap. In the same motion, he leaned in and took possession of her mouth.

He wasted no time deepening the kiss, claiming her in a connection so bottomless that he lost himself, forgot where they were and what was happening. All that mattered was being with her and loving her and having this passion, their mouths almost desperate, as though they were both starving for each other.

At her soft moan, he jerked himself back to reality, to the fact that he was nearly crushing her with his need, but that she was responding with equal fervor. Somehow, they'd started a forest fire between them, and if they weren't careful, it was going to burn them both up.

Even now, his hands itched to slip higher, to roam farther. And though he might indulge in this kiss with her here and now, that didn't change anything about his situation. Or about the danger his job could bring to her.

Danger.

He broke away, needing to put space between them. He set her aside and then scrambled to his feet. Shaking his head and inwardly cursing himself, he stalked to the opposite side of the cave. He stopped, faced the wall, and palmed the back of his neck.

Why had he given in to his affection for her again? It was all wrong and couldn't lead anywhere. Could it?

CHAPTER
19

Ivy's breathing was fast and hard, echoing in the cave as loudly as if she'd run a mile up and down a mountain trail.

What was she doing? She'd told herself she had to let Jericho go, stop allowing herself to hope there could be something between them.

She pressed a hand to her chest and tried to calm her erratically beating heart. Land sakes, that man could kiss. She'd thought she was proving something to him by initiating a kiss—proving how she was in control of herself and her feelings for him. But she'd been wrong. She'd only demonstrated just how much control he had over her. Her kiss had been timid compared to the consuming nature of his.

He stood a dozen feet away, his back rigid. He'd made it clear enough both with his words and his actions that he cared about her. So what was the matter?

She needed to reassure him whatever was wrong didn't have to come between them, that they could work through anything. Because that's what she wanted . . . to be with him. That's all she'd ever really wanted.

But how could she convince him?

He blew out a taut breath and kneaded his neck.

She pushed up, a quiet desperation slithering through her. If she didn't say or do something, he was gonna drive a wedge between them again. She could sense it, just like she could sense when the weather was about to change.

She crossed and stood behind him. For a second, she waited for him to acknowledge her. But he stared straight ahead at the roughly hewn wall.

Fine. She'd have to make him turn somehow. Taking matters into her own hands wasn't something she was afraid of doing. She'd done it aplenty in her life. But this time, the stakes were higher than ever. If she couldn't get through to him, she was gonna lose him. And in doing so, she might lose herself.

She laid a hand on his back.

He didn't move.

She wasn't sure if that was a good sign or bad. Whatever the case, she grazed her fingers up his spine. When he still didn't protest, she took more courage and slid her arms around his waist. She leaned into him, hugging him from behind and resting her cheek against his coat.

His body was hard, unyielding. Just like his spirit. Most of the time, she loved that he was so determined. But this was one occasion she wished he wasn't strong-willed.

She started to pull back, but in the next instant, he folded his hands across hers, then his arms, pinning her in place.

"I should say I'm sorry." His whisper was harsh.

"Don't."

"I won't."

"Good."

His fingers circled hers. "You're a beautiful woman." He hesitated half a heartbeat, enough to know he had a heap more to say.

"But . . ."

"But I'm no good for you."

She tightened her hold. "I reckon I can be the judge of that."

"If you knew the truth, you'd agree."

"Try me."

"I can't tell you. It's better for your safety that way."

"Why? Are you an undercover agent or somethin' like that?"

When he didn't answer, she stilled. She'd only been jesting, but apparently she'd hit close to the truth.

She pressed on, trying to piece together all the clues she'd gleaned about him since his return. "You're not a police officer like Dylan. But you're working for the law in a different capacity."

"I guess you could say that."

"Are you here in Colorado looking for a criminal?"

He shrugged. "Might be."

No doubt about it—she'd hit on the very thing he'd come back for.

"I can't say anything more about what I'm doing, Ivy. So please don't ask."

She nodded. "You're aimin' to leave once you get what you came for?"

"That's right."

"And what if I don't want you to leave?"

"I have to."

"Then you can come back when you're done."

"I'll never be done." His words carried the weight of the world, telling her exactly how seriously he took his work.

"Fine. I'll go with you."

"No. Never." His answer slammed into her harder than a gunshot.

She closed her eyes at the sudden sting of tears and started to slip away, but he spun and grabbed her upper arms.

"I'll never put a woman in danger the way my dad did to my mom." His handsome features were haunted.

Though Jericho had talked about his frustration with his past, he'd never shared exactly what had happened. All she knew was that his mom had died, his dad was a lousy drunk, and Nash had looked out for him. Jericho let them all believe he was from Missouri when he was really from Chicago. What other secrets was he harboring?

He stared at her intently, almost as if he wasn't there but was reliving the trauma from his childhood.

She lifted a hand to his cheek and tried to smooth away the shadows. "What happened to your mom?"

Her touch seemed to pacify him just a little, enough that he loosened his grip. He stared at the fire again, lost some-place in the past.

"Never mind. You don't have to tell me—"

"A crime boss my dad was hunting trailed after her one Sunday night when she was walking home from church. He kidnapped her. Told my dad he had her but wouldn't release her without a hefty ransom. When Dad couldn't come up with the money fast enough, the guy and his gang tortured and murdered her."

Ivy's insides curdled. She could only imagine what the experience must have been like for Jericho. He was sensitive and felt things deeply. He'd likely agonized every second his mom had been held by the crime boss. No one could go through something so traumatic and not have scars.

She grazed his hard jaw, wishing she could take his tension upon herself. "That's an awful thing. Worse than awful. I'm sure the memories have lived right alongside you all this time."

He nodded. "Told myself I never wanted to become like my dad. But here I am."

"You're not like him."

"When I returned to Chicago, I realized I wanted to hunt criminals. I *needed* to hunt them. For my mom's sake and all the innocents out there like her."

"That doesn't mean you're like your dad—"

"It means I'm living a dangerous life. And I refuse to drag anyone else into it. Especially a woman I love."

Her heart fluttered. A woman he loved?

As if hearing her unspoken question, he dropped his attention to her face. His eyes radiated with an agony that left her lungs stinging. "I can't do it, Ivy."

She understood what he was saying but didn't like it. She could never think of asking him to stop doing the work he was passionate about. But at the same time, she couldn't fathom losing him forever. "You know I'm a strong woman, and I won't let nobody hurt me."

It was his turn to cup her cheek, and he did so gently. "You're a very strong woman, one of the strongest I've ever met."

"I can handle anything that comes my way."

219

He pressed his lips together, clearly fighting back words. He wouldn't give up this beautiful thing happening between them, would he? He'd walked away from her after the confrontation with Wyatt and Flynn at the church. He'd let her ride off after the dance. And from the sounds of things, he was intending to push her aside again today.

"Don't leave me again," she whispered.

The firelight was dying, and it was time to add more fuel. But the dim light couldn't hide the tempest raging in his blue eyes. "I knew it was a bad idea to come back to Colorado. I should have given the assignment to someone else."

Irritation speared her. "Maybe you should've."

His jaw flexed.

"Maybe you oughta just tuck tail and run. Since that's what you're good at."

"Are you calling me a coward?"

"I ain't saying it. But from where I stand, sure looks like you're trying to cut me loose as fast as you can."

"That's because being with me will only put you in danger."

The thread of desperation in his voice snuffed out her ire. After all he'd revealed about his mom, Ivy couldn't blame him for being afraid. But somehow, someway, she needed to show him she was different, that he didn't have to worry about her.

She had to win him over. Maybe if she could make him care about her enough, he'd put aside thoughts of having their separate lives. Maybe he'd work harder to find a way for them to stay together.

The only means she had to convince him was a kiss. Without giving him a chance to set her aside or stalk away again, she stood on her toes, wound her arms around his neck, and dragged him down, chasing and catching his mouth with hers. She moved with the same force and precision she used when roping cattle, knowing she couldn't waste a single second with indecisiveness, or she'd lose her chance.

For a moment, he held himself back, as if he had every intention of resisting, perhaps even of bolting. But she deepened the kiss, delving in passionately. In the next instant, he released a murmur and slipped his arms around her, drawing her close, almost fiercely so. He returned the kiss with an intensity that stirred her emotions into a whirlwind.

His powerful wanting seeped through her. She sensed that she could keep going, that he wouldn't stop her. In doing so, she'd capture him, and he'd be hers.

But as quickly as the thought came, she slowed the kiss. She didn't want to win him through manipulation. She didn't want him to be with her because she'd trapped him into doing so. If he stayed, she wanted him to choose to do so.

She pulled back and broke the kiss. His hands on her back tightened, and he followed her lips, clearly not sated. She wanted to meet him kiss for kiss and didn't want to sever their bond, not after wishing for it so long and finally getting it. But she turned her head, caring for him too much to win him this way.

His lips landed on her jawline and made a trail to her neck. His breath was hot and his kisses hungry, almost as if he needed her more than he'd recognized. What if he loved her? He hadn't come right out and said it, but how else should she take what he'd alluded to moments ago?

She'd always loved him. She could admit it. Even though she tried to stop herself from caring, deep inside her feelings for him ran strong and steady and unshakeable. But she couldn't say so, not now.

Instead, she said the next best thing. "I'm willing to face danger to be with you, Jericho."

His trail of kisses came to a halt. "No." His answer was hoarse, as though he was battling himself to say it.

"Don't say no yet. Think about it first."

He shook his head and started to speak, but she touched her finger to his lips, cutting him off. "Please?"

His brow furrowed.

She peered up at him, loving every nuance of his chiseled features, the strength of his mouth, the hard lines of his jaw, the purpose in his eyes. He studied her face too, and in that moment she felt as though her heart was inextricably linked to his. The thought of him walking away and out of her life again was too difficult to contemplate.

He retreated a step, putting some distance between them, almost as if he needed it to bring his thoughts into coherence. "If I say I'll think about it, in the end will you accept my final decision?"

Could she? What if he said no to being together?

"It's not you, Ivy. Remember that."

She buried the rising need to cling to him no matter what. "Fine. If you decide to move on, I won't pester you."

He watched her as though testing the sincerity of her words. "And I promise not to hang on to you."

Even though she wanted to give him permission to hang on to her all he wanted, she couldn't make herself say the words. She already sounded too desperate and needy.

The flames from the small fire flickered even lower, settling the darkness about them. The cave opening was still shrouded in smoke, which had sifted inside their cavern but thankfully hadn't permeated enough that they couldn't breathe.

The lack of light only made her want to curl up against him, just be with him, and make the most of the time they had together before it came to an end.

As if sensing the direction of her thoughts, he took another step away. "We can't kiss again." His attention dropped to her lips, and the heat that sparked in his eyes only ignited something inside her.

"Why not?"

"Because I can't think straight when I'm kissing you."

"What if I don't want you thinking straight?"

He closed his eyes for a second. And when he opened them, he stared past her at the fire.

She was half tempted to brush against him, run her hands up his chest, and tease him until he couldn't resist any longer and bent down to kiss her. But she held herself back. She had to wait for him to give himself—and kisses—of his own accord, not because she coerced him into it.

"Alright." She released a sigh.

"What?"

"I won't kiss you until you ask me to."

He opened his mouth to respond, then stopped abruptly, narrowing his gaze, which was still trained upon the firepit.

He started toward the remains of their fire, and when he reached it, he crouched and used a bone to brush back the embers. Then he smoothed his fingers over the now-empty spot, revealing a groove in the granite.

Was it a crack in the rocks? What did that mean?

She knelt beside him and swept away more of the ashes,

uncovering a deep line that ran underneath the center of the firepit.

It wasn't long—only about a foot—and might not be anything at all. But it was a heap more than they'd discovered yet.

She dug harder, and the rock shifted. She didn't want to get her hopes up, but was it possible they'd discovered the spot where the gold had been buried?

CHAPTER
20

The cut in the cave floor was too perfectly rectangular to be anything but manmade. And the position was too calculated to be anything other than a hiding place beneath the firepit. Not many who took refuge in the cave would clear the ashes.

Jericho wouldn't have noticed it if not for the last glow of the firelight falling on the crack in just the right way.

At first, he'd thought he was seeing a small snake driven into the cave by the forest fire outside. In fact, he was surprised wild creatures hadn't yet joined them to escape the heat and the flames. But when he'd taken a second look, he'd realized the dark line was too motionless to be an animal.

"It's gotta be where they hid the treasure." Ivy dug alongside him eagerly.

"Seems like it."

Someone had hidden treasure there, no doubt about it. But who? Why? And more importantly, how did Hance know about it? The questions nagged him as they had ever since he'd left town. But now the need for answers grew more demanding.

The stone head of the snake pointed toward the center of the cave, right where they were digging. How had he overlooked the clue?

He knew exactly how. Because he'd been too enamored with Ivy, too caught up in admiring her, too occupied with battling his attraction to her. She was a huge distraction. And if he wasn't more careful, he'd miss something bigger the next time and possibly put her in terrible danger.

He unsheathed his knife from inside his boot and wedged it down into the crack. Using the hard steel blade, he leveraged the stone upward. It didn't move far, but it was enough that they could get their hands underneath and lift.

As they hauled at it, he wanted to warn Ivy not to get her hopes up. Whoever had buried a treasure here had more than likely come back for it. But seeing the brightness of her eyes and the anticipation on her face, he couldn't make himself speak words of caution. She'd find out and be disappointed soon enough.

Besides, now that she'd figured out the nature of his work in South Park, he could tell her the truth about Steele's land. He'd have to keep up his public pretense of wanting to buy it, but at least she would know she didn't have anything to worry about.

"I can't believe this." She dragged on her end of the stone, inching it upward.

The opening widened until they could see a dark pit underneath like a yawning mouth. As they set the slab aside, he leaned forward at the same time she did in order to peer into the hole. Their faces were close enough that he could feel her breath against his cheek.

He went to the brink of heaven and back every time he kissed her. Even now, he wasn't sure how he'd been able to stop, why he wasn't still kissing her. Because that's all he wanted to do.

He forced himself to focus on the pit. He'd told her they couldn't kiss again. She'd promised she wouldn't kiss him until he asked her to. Which he wasn't planning to do. He couldn't. He wouldn't. Even though he'd told her he'd think about their relationship and a future together, he had no intention of dragging her into his world—a world filled with brutality, lawlessness, and death.

Into his mind flashed the image of his mom's dead body. As the coroner pulled down the sheet covering her, his stomach had roiled at the sight of the bruises marring her pretty face and the realization of the pain she had suffered, how scared she must have been, how she'd probably begged her captors for mercy, only to have them hurt her even more.

He'd learned that day exactly how cruel and soulless some criminals were. All because they believed they were above the law and could live the way they wanted, destroying people— entire families—for their own personal gain and pleasure. Those men needed a reckoning. And he planned to make sure they got it. He might not be able to bring back his mom, but he could make the world a safer place for others. It was what God had called him to do, and he couldn't toss that aside, not for anyone. Not even for Ivy.

Rodney James was one of those cruel and soulless men. He'd been caught near the end of the war and charged with murder, but he'd escaped from jail and disappeared. Until last year, when the Department of Justice had relayed to Pinkerton that the war criminal was living in South Park. Apparently, he'd bragged to a Denver prostitute about his crimes as well as his plans to settle in South Park, most likely in Fairplay. She'd told a fellow prostitute about the strange man. Clearly she hadn't anticipated that he'd murder her before he left town. But he did, and he cut out her tongue.

Unfortunately, Denver investigators hadn't been able to get a detailed description of Rodney to help update his profile. So they were still working with one of the pictures taken during the war.

The fact was, even though Jericho was narrowing down his list of suspects, he still needed more time. Which meant he had to warn Ivy not to speak a word about his mission to anyone—for his sake and hers.

She was already reaching her hand down into the hole.

"Hold on. What if there's a nest of rattlers at the bottom?" It was unlikely, but she was too impulsive at times.

She paused, grabbed the end of a flaming bone from the fire, and held it over the opening. The light illuminated the hiding spot. Approximately two feet deep, it was shadowed with dust and debris. But at the bottom sat two satchels.

Before he could stop her, she grabbed one and hefted it up. The leather was crinkled and worn, a knotted drawstring at the top. "It's heavy." She plopped it onto the cave floor, and something inside clanked.

"This has gotta be the treasure." She fumbled at the drawstring. "What else could it be?"

He sat back on his heels and waited. The leather knot wouldn't budge, and Ivy grew flustered the more she worked at it. Finally, he reached over and sliced the strip with his knife. The binding fell away, and the bag opened.

She grinned. "What would I do without you, Jericho Bliss?"

"Land yourself in trouble up to your neck."

"I can manage just fine, and you know it."

She was capable, but he couldn't pass up the opportunity to tease her. "Then why are we trapped in a cave in the middle of a forest fire?"

"Because I need this." She patted the bulging bag.

"Treasure or not, you can have Steele's land."

She paused in peeling back the satchel. Her brows rose above her expressive eyes.

"I don't need the land, was only buying it to keep up appearances so no one would grow suspicious of why I came back to South Park."

"You put me through all that worrying for nothin'?"

"Figured a little hard work and sweat wouldn't do you any harm."

She shoved his arm.

He toppled back in an exaggerated fashion, pretending her playful push had more power than it did.

Her expression was somber, anything but playful. "I was real worried."

"I know and I'm sorry." He sat up. "You don't know how bad I wanted to tell you that day after meeting at Steele's office. But I knew then I'd have to explain the nature of my work."

"I wish you would've."

"I can't chance anyone knowing what I'm doing here. It could ruin everything. And, worse, it could put you in danger."

She watched him, questions flickering in her eyes. She likely had a thousand of them as usual.

"Don't ask." He'd already said too much and wouldn't say anything more.

"You know you can trust me."

"The less you know, the better."

She pursed her lips, then began to tip the bag. Small pebbles slid out first, then larger uneven stones followed by a big piece. In the shadows of the cavern, the rocks didn't appear to be extraordinary at first glance. But as Ivy lifted a flame above the heap, the specks in them glittered.

"Is it gold, Jericho?"

"Looks like it." He picked up the largest of the chunks and held it up to the firelight. From all appearances, the odd-shaped stone was solid gold. Although he'd seen gold, especially during his year or so of mining with Nash, he'd never touched any. If he had to take a guess, he'd say the nugget was ten ounces, maybe more. The others were smaller but contained a mixture of granite and gold.

Ivy examined one of the medium pieces. "How much is all this worth?"

"Likely thousands of dollars."

She released a low whistle, then she reached inside the hole and withdrew the second satchel. He helped her cut the drawstring again and dump the contents onto the floor next to the first bag, revealing more of the same gold-tinged rocks.

They studied the pieces for a short while, and Ivy remarked excitedly about them.

"We should put them back," he finally suggested.

"Let's take some with us." Her hand hovered above a larger stone. "We deserve a share since we found it."

He started depositing the nuggets back into one of the

satchels. "If the gold was stolen, then we can't take any. We'd be just as guilty of stealing as the original culprits."

"But if it was taken from the Spanish a long time ago, then it doesn't belong to anyone now, does it?"

He scooped up more of the rocks. "I thought we already concluded that kind of treasure wouldn't have lasted."

"Even if it's stolen, how would we trace who took it and where it came from?"

"We might not be able to, but we should at least try." He buried the gold out of sight in the bags, where it wouldn't tempt either of them to do wrong.

She snatched a medium-sized nugget before he could stow it away. "Are you sure I can't have one piece? Just to prove to myself that I found it . . . and maybe to use on buying Steele's land?"

He hesitated in giving her permission. If anyone learned they'd discovered a treasure, they'd draw all kinds of attention— something he didn't need. And he wanted the chance to find out more about any stolen gold in the area over recent years before they hauled the treasure away.

She turned the nugget over in her hand. "If we find the owner of this stash, I'll do the right thing and give the gold on back. But you know as well as I do that's gonna be real hard."

The territory had always been rife with thieves and out-laws stealing silver and gold from stagecoaches and wagon trains. Even if he tracked down all the miners in the area who had lost gold at one point, how would he be able to narrow down which one of them the gold belonged to?

"Alright." He finished stashing the last handful into the pouch. "But keep the nugget well hidden, and don't tell a single person you have it. We don't want anyone getting wind of our find, not until I have the chance to come back for it and haul it down to Denver."

"We're not taking it with us today?"

"It's safest here for now. As long as we don't say anything, no one will find out about it."

"What about Hance and Otis? Don't you think they deserve to know and have part of it? After all, we wouldn't have discovered it if not for them."

"Let's hold off." Jericho lowered one of the satchels into the hole. "Something about them doesn't sit well with me."

She gave a soft laugh. "Reckon that something is called jealousy."

"I admit I get worked up seeing you with other men." That was an understatement. He turned into an enraged grizzly about to charge when she was with anyone else. "But that's not what's bothering me with Hance."

"Hance is a really nice fella and decently handsome." Her words contained a note of teasing.

"He's not as nice or as handsome as me."

"Maybe just a little."

He glared at her, and she smiled innocently. He wanted to lean over and steal a kiss from her and show her that no other man could compare to him, but he shook his head, trying to shake off the desire.

He slid the stone lid back into place, and she joined his efforts. Then they spread out the ashes and embers, filling in and packing the crevices of the secret hole, disguising it as best they could.

When they finished, he crawled up through the series of caverns. He wanted Ivy to wait in the cave until he had a chance to make sure things were safe, but of course, she wasn't content to stay behind. As he cautiously peered out of the narrow opening, he could see that the smoke was still heavy in the air, but the flames had moved on, leaving a charred landscape in their wake—blackened rocks, skeletal trees, and every spot of green turned to ash.

"Is it okay to leave?" she asked from behind him.

"I think so."

He didn't count on their horses being in the area. They'd likely galloped away in a frenzy at the first sight of the flames. Without their mounts, they had a long hike ahead. And before they could start back, they had to seek out Hance and Otis. It was possible the two had already headed down. But the decent thing to do was make sure they'd survived.

He doubted any of them would make it to South Park before nightfall. But it wouldn't hurt to try, since once they reached a main wagon path, they might be able to find a ride the rest of the way to Fairplay.

As long as the fire didn't change directions, they'd be fine. The least that could happen was having to camp for the night at a lower elevation. He didn't want to end up spending the night alone with Ivy. He'd only be asking for trouble if he did so. But he prided himself on being a strong man. And this time, he needed to be extra strong so he could protect the woman he loved from himself.

CHAPTER

21

"Over here!" Ivy halted and waited for Jericho to catch up. Blackened rocks and embers crunched beneath his boots as he climbed over the rough boulders that made the mountaintop a challenging place to cross. But, of course, Jericho made it seem effortless.

For a second, she let her eyes feast upon him, the surety with each step he took, the proud bearing in his shoulders, and the rounded muscles in his chest and arms that made his suit coat stretch tight. Even coated in dust of ashes and smoke, his handsomeness made her heart patter faster.

Jericho paused on top of a large boulder, his feet spread. He glanced around as though trying to find the object of her fascination. "What's wrong?"

"Nothin'." She trailed her gaze over him again. "Just admiring the view. Ain't I allowed to do that once in a while?"

At the sight of her so blatantly staring, he ducked his head, but not before she caught sight of his crooked grin. "No, Ivy. Admiring the view wasn't part of the bargain."

Her chest bubbled up with pleasure. "The only promise I made was that I wouldn't kiss you. Everything else is fair game."

"So you intend to make it impossible for me to resist you?"

"Sounds like a real fine idea to me."

He shook his head, still grinning, and resumed his hiking.

She turned and started forward. She loved being up here with him, hadn't wanted to leave the cave, would have lingered longer if he hadn't been pushing to start out. The only thing that had needled her to go was the possibility Hance and Otis had been hurt during the fire, that even now they might be lying unconscious somewhere from the smoke. Or, worse yet, burned.

She blamed herself for bringing them up so high with the danger nearby. Even if she hadn't known the fire was close and moving so fast, she still should've used more caution. Hopefully the fire hadn't reached them. But if it had, the ravine where she'd left them had been fairly safe, especially with the cave nearby.

The problem was, the mountaintop looked the same from every direction, and she was starting to wonder if she was going in circles.

"This is the second time we've passed this location," Jericho said.

"I left them here somewhere."

"I'm sure they made it down."

She fisted her hands onto her hips and tried to see through the heavy smoke to the mountainside below. But as far as she could make out, the area was deserted.

Jericho climbed down behind her. When he hopped onto the rock beside her, she could feel the power of his presence and wanted to sink against him and into his arms. As much as she longed to revel in his nearness, she clasped her hands together to keep from reaching for him. She'd already made up her mind that if he wanted to have a relationship with her, he'd do it of his own free will or not at all. That was her resolve, and she had to stick to it.

"Once we find them, I'm gonna feel bad not telling them about the treasure." She pulled the gold from her pocket and admired it again. Even with the haze obscuring the sky, the rock sparkled in the daylight. It was stunning, and she couldn't keep it in her pocket despite Jericho's warning that he'd take it from her if she didn't leave it tucked out of sight.

"Put it away."

"Make me."

He reached for it with a growl, but she leapt to the boulder beneath them and smirked over her shoulder, hoping he'd read her challenge to come and get her . . . if he could.

His eyes took on a glint, one that made her blood race with delight, anticipation, and desire all mingled together. When he began to chase her, she was half tempted to cheat and go slow, just so he could catch her. But she was too competitive to allow him to win that easily. If he wanted her, he was gonna have to capture her fair and square.

She descended several more paces before glancing at him over her shoulder. He was still in pursuit. She released a breathless laugh and started forward only to smack into someone. The hard jolt threw her off-balance.

Fingers bit through her sleeve, pinching her arm hard, but the grip steadied her and kept her from toppling.

As she tilted up her hat, she took in Hance's long, lean form. Relief washed through her like a flooded creek in a narrow gully. "Oh, Hance. Thank the Lord Almighty you're alright. We've been searching for you. Where's Otis?"

She glanced beyond him to find Otis standing with two other fellas a dozen paces away. In their stained trousers and scraggly shirts, the newcomers looked familiar. Had she competed against them in a cowhand contest? Or were they miners who'd come to town from time to time?

"See we've got some company." She attempted to twist away from Hance, but in the next instant a cold, hard barrel pressed against her temple.

"Stop where you're at, Bliss, or I'll shoot her." Although Hance was as even and calm as always, his demeanor contained a deadliness that sent a shiver up her spine.

Before she knew what was happening, he maneuvered her in front of his body so that she was acting like a shield. He dragged her backward toward Otis and the two other men. The revolver barrel against her temple didn't budge.

She was facing Jericho now, and he had a gun in each hand, both aimed at Hance. Jericho had always carried one in a holster at his hip. Where had the other come from?

"Let her go." Jericho's voice was harsh and demanding.

"What's going on, Hance?" she asked, more confused than a tenderfoot on his first day on the range.

"You've got my gold." His response was low, almost pleasant, but as he spoke the last word, he jabbed the barrel harder, this time against her neck.

She couldn't keep from crying out at the bruising pain, losing her grasp on the piece of gold as Hance wrenched it from her.

Jericho took a step down, but a bullet pinged the rock in front of him. One of the other fellas was shooting, but

Jericho didn't take his aim off Hance and advanced another step. "If you release her, I'll take you to the gold."

Hance tugged her harder against him. "She's staying with me. And if you don't want me to hurt her, then you'll do whatever I tell you to."

"C'mon, Hance." She wiggled to free herself. "You don't need to be so angry about things. We'll show you where the gold is without any threats. Alright?"

A sting against her neck stilled her. It was followed by the warm trickle of blood down her neck. Did Hance have a knife pressed against her?

"Put down your guns, Bliss," Hance's command rang out. "Or I'll start carving her up."

Start carving her up? Who was this madman? He sure as the sun rises wasn't the doting suitor who'd danced with her only days ago.

Jericho set one gun down on the rock in front of him and then placed the other next to it. "There. Now take me instead of her."

Hance gave a curt nod at the other fellas. They skirted close to Jericho, picked up his revolvers, and then circled him warily, their guns trained on him.

Jericho didn't move. "Let Ivy go."

Hance still didn't remove the blade from where it scraped against her neck. "I'm not a fool. I know exactly how much you care about Miss McQuaid. You made that quite clear since your return. And I know you'll do anything to keep her safe."

⁂

Jericho's fingers itched to snatch up his guns and put bullets into the heads of both men drawing near. But with

Hance's knife already cutting into Ivy's flesh, he couldn't risk it. He'd have to go along with the fellow for the time being until he could find a way to free Ivy.

As one of the men grabbed his arm, Jericho tensed but forced himself not to strike. The second one latched on to Jericho's other arm, and within an instant, the two had his wrists tied together in front of him.

Even then, Hance kept the blade against Ivy's throat. Thankfully, she'd stopped resisting, clearly sensing her life was at stake.

As the two men led him down toward Hance, Jericho's mind whirled in a hundred directions. Hance was definitely not who he claimed to be, not if he had a team of men working with him. And not if he could so easily hurt Ivy.

In fact, his calculated brutality hinted at the emotional profile of someone like Rodney James, who had no value for life, who used people for his own gain, and who slayed the innocent in the blink of an eye.

And, of course, Hance fit the physical profile in nearly every way too.

If Hance was Rodney James, then Ivy was in real danger of losing her life. And Jericho couldn't take any chances in angering the man. He just prayed Hance hadn't figured out his true motive for being in South Park.

"Tie him up tighter." Hance's gaze connected with Jericho's, and the coldness behind the spectacles told Jericho more than any words. Hance had been playing a part these past weeks, pretending to be a normal man with a normal past. But now on the mountaintop, where no one else was around, he'd stopped acting and was revealing his true nature.

No doubt about it. The man was Rodney James.

Jericho kept his own eyes and face from revealing anything except the emotions expected of a man in his situation—bravado and fear. The fear wasn't all that hard to conjure, since he was terrified for Ivy.

Hance's lips curved into a semblance of a smile, as though satisfied with seeing the distress. Most of the worst criminals seemed to thrive on fear, almost as if it sated their appetite. The more Jericho could feed the man's lust for fear, perhaps the more he could throw him off guard.

"You can do anything to me, but please leave Ivy out of this." Jericho's words came out desperate without his having to try too hard.

Ivy's eyes had widened, and her face was growing pale. He guessed his show of panic was only frightening her more. But if he could somehow get her away from Hance and the knife blade, he could work at freeing her.

"Tie her up," Hance ordered the men.

As they moved to obey, Jericho guessed the two as well as Otis were a part of Rodney's regiment during the war. No doubt they'd escaped to Texas, mustered there in one of the outlaw camps, and then come up to South Park together. Not to hide out and live here. But to search for this specific treasure, a treasure they obviously knew a great deal about.

Who had given them the information? Another band of outlaws? Perhaps even someone who'd been in the original group that had hidden the treasure in the first place? It was entirely plausible that Hance—Rodney—had gained knowledge about the treasure by killing and stealing for it.

Records indicated Rodney had been a brick mason before the war. When coming to Colorado, he'd probably settled on being a barber because the trade wasn't all that hard to learn, especially if he'd given haircuts to other soldiers during the war.

Of course, it stood to reason that Hance had needed to stop in Denver to purchase supplies for his barbershop business. Somehow he'd gained the money he needed for equipment and transportation to South Park—likely through gambling or thieving.

Whatever the case, Hance wanted the gold, had been seeking it for months. And now that it was within his grasp, he'd do anything to get it.

As soon as Ivy's hands were tied together, Hance pulled his knife away from her throat. But he kept her firmly within his grasp, the knife close enough that he could hurt her if Jericho made the smallest move to try to escape or defy him.

Hance still held Ivy's gold nugget in his free hand. He examined it again, unable to hide his excitement. "Let's go." He prodded Ivy so hard that she nearly tripped.

Fury burned a trail through Jericho. He wanted to rip the fellow apart with his bare hands for hurting her and treating her with such disrespect. As ungodly as his attitude was, the anger festered inside him so that he was afraid of what he was capable of doing once he freed himself . . . because he would free himself. He had no choice if he wanted to save Ivy.

The two men led him forward between them, while Hance followed behind with Ivy. Otis, as quiet as always—except for his coughing—took up the rear, his gun out and trained on Jericho.

"Take us directly there, Bliss," Hance called out before erupting into a fit of coughing too. The smoke wasn't nearly as thick as it had been when they'd left the cave, but it was still irritating.

Jericho traversed the mountain back the way he and Ivy had come. As he headed toward the cave opening, he considered the possibility of leading them astray for a while longer and pretending he couldn't find the gold. He'd buy himself more time, as well as tire and weaken them.

However, when they finally reached the cavern, he stopped. Dragging out the search was too risky. He couldn't chance angering Hance and having him harm Ivy. "It's in there." He nodded toward the line of boulders that swiveled back and forth, forming the body of a snake.

Hance paused, his hold on Ivy's arm unwavering.

Jericho glanced at her, hoping she would behave for as long as possible. He'd learned years ago that she was unpredictable—he never knew what to expect from her. And in this case, he needed her to cooperate.

She met his gaze and gave him an imperceptible nod, as if she was attempting to signal him.

He shook his head, warning her not to try anything. As the men shoved him forward, he had the terrible premonition that Ivy had a plan—a plan he wouldn't approve of. He wanted to turn around and shout at her to let him take care of things in his way and his timing.

But all he could do was duck into the dark cave and pray he'd get them out of this trouble before she made things worse.

CHAPTER
22

Ivy stumbled ahead of Hance, nearly bumping her head against the ceiling of the passageway.

How had she been so wrong about him and missed the signs that he was such a brute? This was all her fault. If only she hadn't run off to go treasure hunting, especially with a man she barely knew. In fact, she'd been downright immature about stringing Hance along to make Jericho jealous, that's what. And it was past time she grew up and started acting like an adult.

Behind them, Otis held a lantern he'd retrieved from the supplies the other men had brought along. The light guided them through the hazy tunnel. With her hands tied together in front of her, she had a difficult time crawling but forced herself to keep going, especially with Hance using the tip of his knife to urge her along.

When they finally made it to the back cave and were standing, Hance once again pressed the knife to her neck. The skin there stung and was sticky with blood already. As the blade bit into her flesh, she pinched her eyes closed and prayed.

If ever in her life she'd needed divine help, now was the time, now as she worked to free them from the mess she'd gotten them into.

"Hurry up and show us where it's buried, Bliss." Hance motioned impatiently.

Jericho dropped to his knees in front of the embers of their fire. He swept the ashes aside and ran his fingers along a groove, his hands still bound and making the effort more difficult.

As soon as he opened the hiding place and these men got their hands on the treasure, they'd have no need for Jericho and her. Hance wouldn't think twice about murdering them, throwing their bodies into the charred woods, and then setting them on fire to make it seem like they'd gotten trapped and burned to death.

That was why she had to act now. "Jericho Bliss, you've got about as much spine as a snail."

He paused and shot her a dark look.

"That's right, figured you'd try to stand up for us, for me. But you're just too weak, ain't you?" She worked her expression into one of disgust. She didn't mean a word of what she was saying, but if she could cause a commotion, then she might be able to distract the men enough that she could break loose. And once she was well away from any threat, then Jericho could fight, even if only with the knife in his boot that they hadn't confiscated yet.

Jericho kept digging, not taking the bait. "It would be easier to lift the stone with a knife."

The knife against her neck wavered, then Hance shoved

her toward Otis. "Hold on to her and don't let her go for anything."

Otis fumbled but clamped his fingers around her arm, then pressed his gun into her side. From what she could tell, all four of their captors were armed. But Otis wasn't as strong as Hance. Could she wrestle the gun from him and shoot Hance while he was busy with the gold?

She had to continue making everyone think she was mad at Jericho and cause an upheaval. "You were aimin' to get the gold and hightail it away from me as fast as you could go."

"Stop talking, Ivy." Jericho ground the words out.

"Oh, so now you're back to acting like my brother?"

He focused on digging his fingers into the crevice while Hance slid his knife down inside and began to try to heft the stone upward.

"I thought we'd moved past that." She lobbed the accusation with as much derision as she could muster.

"We have."

Hance released a choice cuss word. "You know what I did to my wife when she sassed off to me? I made sure she knew I was in charge."

"I ain't sassing."

Jericho slanted her a dark glare. "This isn't the time or place to discuss this."

She was making Jericho madder than a cornered skunk, but if she could save their lives, it didn't matter. "After all the kissing, I reckoned you were done bossing me around like I'm nothin' more than a child. But I guess I was wrong." She'd raised her voice with each word until she was practically shouting.

At the mention of kissing, she could feel Otis's grip

slacken. The other two men shifted to look at her, something changing in their eyes, something hungry and dangerous.

Maybe she shouldn't have spoken so freely about the kissing, but it was too late now. She was causing a ruckus and had to keep going. Even Hance was getting distracted by the arguing. "All along you were just hankerin' to get me in your bed before riding away, weren't you?"

"Blast it all, Ivy!" Jericho sat back on his heels, scowling.

It was the perfect moment to strike. With Hance's knife wedged in the stone, Jericho had a fighting chance. She just had to get Otis's gun first. With a firm nod at Jericho, she squared her shoulders.

"No!" he shouted.

But it was too late—she slammed Otis backward and in the same moment wrestled for his revolver. His grip was loose, and though he fumbled to keep hold of it, she had it out and in her grasp an instant later.

With the rope constricting her hands, she fought to find the trigger. Otis lunged at her, but she dove out of his way.

The crack of a gunshot came from somewhere near Jericho. She glanced his direction to find him on his feet with a gun in his bound hands. Where had he gotten the weapon?

With the knife still wedged in the stone, Hance cursed and reached for his holster. He cursed again as his hand came up empty. Jericho had Hance's gun and was taking aim at one of the other men.

Only then did she notice the man was pointing his revolver at her.

"Shoot her now," Hance called irritably.

But the man was too late. Jericho had already pulled the trigger and the bullet hit the fella, knocking him backward.

Otis caught his balance and came after her again, his face red and perspiring.

She easily sidestepped him. Then without a moment's hesitation, she aimed the revolver. She wasn't a sharpshooter like Dylan, but she knew enough about guns to hold her own. She had no intention of killing, only causing him enough pain that he'd be disabled from the fight.

She squeezed, and the gun blasted. As the bullet tore into him, he shouted and fell back, grasping the arm she'd shot.

Without waiting to see what Otis did next, she spun and pointed her weapon at Hance only to find that he'd freed his knife and was coming after her. She squeezed the trigger, but the bullet missed and pinged against the opposite wall, coming too close to Jericho, who was still exchanging shots with the other man.

She wanted to shoot at Hance again, but what if the next time the bullet found Jericho?

As if sensing her hesitancy, Hance advanced more quickly.

She bolted up the incline. She couldn't let him get a hold of her again. If he did, he'd use her to control Jericho like he had before. She needed to get away, and fast, but she couldn't use her hands to help in her escape, not with them tied in front of her.

As she scrambled toward the passageway, Hance grabbed her foot. She kicked him hard, nearly hitting him in the face, but in the next instant, he dragged her down as if she weighed nothing more than a gunnysack full of goose feathers.

He slammed an elbow against her hands, and the revolver flew from her grip. Before she could get her bearings, he held the knife up to her chest. With a triumphant gleam, he spun toward Jericho. "Put the gun down, or I start carving."

Jericho was in the process of shooting, and this time the bullet hit its mark and his opponent collapsed.

"I said put it down, Bliss!" Hance pressed the blade into her chest by her upper arm, piercing through her garments and into her flesh. It sliced deep, and she cried out at the burning agony. "Next cut will be on her face!"

Jericho spun, took aim at Hance, and this time, he didn't wait. He squeezed the trigger.

Hance's eyes widened in a brief moment of surprise. As the bullet blasted into his chest, he rammed the knife into her. She screamed, the pain unlike anything she'd ever experienced before. Black dots flashed in front of her eyes. Bile rose swiftly. And in the next instant, the world went dark.

CHAPTER

23

"Ivy!" Jericho bolted across the cave toward her. His heart thudded worse than a whole herd of buffalos stampeding. She'd collapsed onto the floor, and Hance's knife was wedged deep in her upper arm beneath her shoulder.

Before he could reach her, Otis grabbed the gun beside him, the one Ivy had dropped, and he pointed it straight at Jericho. "Stop right there." The stout man's face was creased with pain, and he was wheezing hard. Blood seeped into his shirtsleeve, staining it crimson.

Jericho slowed his steps and pointed the revolver at Otis. He'd used the last bullet of the six-shooter on Hance, but hopefully Otis wouldn't realize it.

"I mean it. Stop. Or I'll finish her off." Otis swung the gun toward Ivy, aiming the barrel at her head. His hand shook with the effort, but his finger closed about the trigger and started to squeeze.

Jericho halted. "Don't do it."

"Give me one reason why I shouldn't."

"Because I'm the one who knows who you really are. Not her."

"And who do you think I am?"

"You're Rodney James."

Otis shifted the gun back onto Jericho just as he'd hoped, confirming his suspicion.

At first Jericho had assumed Hance was the notorious outlaw, but the truth had fallen into place once they'd reached the cave.

Hance's comment about having a wife had been a major clue, coupled with the realization that Hance had some skill in interacting with women—albeit mediocre skills. Otis, on the other hand, bumbled around anyone wearing a skirt. He was the type who would have remained a bachelor living with his grandmother well into old age.

Although the person in the photograph from the war hadn't been hefty, it was possible Otis used the weight gain as part of his disguise. It had certainly rounded out his facial features and made him less recognizable.

And then, of course, there was the asthma. Otis had it in full force and was still wheezing even now. The fellow had learned how to survive over the past years by hiding in the shadows of other people. Namely Hance.

"Let me guess." Otis studied Jericho's face. "You're a bounty hunter intent upon bringing me in for justice."

Jericho had to put an end to his conversation with Otis and tend to Ivy. From what he could see of the knife wound, he had to get her back to Fairplay as soon as possible. She wasn't bleeding profusely—which meant the knife hadn't hit a major artery. Even so, she needed the care of a physician, and the trek down the mountain would be long and hard.

The trouble was, Otis had a loaded gun along with every reason to put a bullet in his head.

"The question I have"—Jericho had to distract the fellow—"is where you got the information that the treasure was here."

The gun in Otis's hand shook. The man was weak and short of breath. Jericho could take him down in an instant if he didn't have to worry about Otis shooting Ivy. He still had his knife, but with his hands bound together, he might not be able to unsheathe it fast enough to stop Otis from doing damage.

Otis glanced at Hance's prostrate form near Ivy. Jericho hadn't wanted to kill any of the men, only wound them enough to disable them. He'd succeeded with the other two in knocking them out. But with Hance threatening Ivy's life, he'd done what he needed to in order to protect her.

"Hance's brother was the head of the Kingston Gang."

Kingston Gang? Jericho's pulse took a dive. That was the same gang whose treasure he'd been seeking the day Nash had fallen to his death.

"Hance found the map among his brother's belongings," Otis continued, "after his brother was hung for crimes. The trouble with the map was that it didn't specify the mountain."

With each word, Jericho's muscles tensed even more. If only the Kingston Gang had never been in the area. If only they'd never buried any treasure. And if only no one had known about it, including him.

Loathing pushed up into Jericho's chest—loathing for all the criminals who'd brought so much pain to his life. Not only had they taken his mom, but indirectly they'd taken his brother. And now they threatened to take the woman he loved.

As Otis peered again at Hance, Jericho acted on impulse. He darted forward.

Shifting his attention back to Jericho, Otis squeezed the trigger.

Jericho dove to the ground, the bullet nearly missing his head. He hit the cave floor hard, knocking the breath from his lungs, but he rolled forward and barreled into Otis. Before the outlaw could shoot again, Jericho slammed his arm and dislodged the gun, causing it to fall to the cave floor and skitter out of reach.

In the same motion, Jericho slipped his knife from his boot and pointed it at Otis. "Time for your reckoning, you piece of scum."

Otis breathed in and out with a quick, shallow burst, then nodded. "Do it. Kill me."

Jericho's gut churned with the need to plunge the knife into Otis and twist it, making him pay for Nash, his mom, and every other innocent victim who'd suffered at the hands of criminals like him.

Otis shifted his fingers against his bloody arm wound and then winced before closing his eyes. "You're not planning to turn into a coward now, are you?"

At the dare, the churning pushed into Jericho's lungs, fanning the air there hot with hatred. He slipped the blade up and sawed at his bindings. The moment his hands were free, he slipped his fingers around Otis's neck and squeezed hard.

Jericho jabbed the blade into Otis's chest and drew blood. At the same time, he put pressure on Otis's windpipe and cut off the man's air supply. Already lacking oxygen, it wouldn't take long to strangle him.

"That's right," Otis rasped out the words. "Punish me."

Punish him? Jericho blinked. Was he wanting to yell, hit, and kick so that he could punish someone else for everything bad that had happened to him?

Was that why Otis had hurt others?

Jericho dropped his hand away from Otis's throat and lessened the force of the knife blade. "That's why you hurt so many people. You couldn't punish the one person who'd inflicted so much pain on you. Your dad. So you had to punish others."

Otis's eyes flew open, and the agony there testified to the truth of what Jericho had spoken.

Before Jericho could react, Otis lunged forward, wrapped both hands around Jericho's neck, and squeezed. His grip was like an iron manacle, unyielding and unmoving.

Jericho tugged at Otis's fingers in a desperate attempt to loosen them. But the veins in Otis's forehead bulged, and his cheeks reddened, his fury giving him a burst of strength that defied human capabilities.

Strangely, Otis's eyes were dull, almost as if he wasn't present any longer. Maybe he was indeed somewhere in the past, picturing his dad's face in place of Jericho's—the dad who had not only failed to love him but, if the reports in the files were true, had treated him worse than a mangy mutt, kicking, beating, and starving him.

No doubt Otis's hatred and bitterness had fueled his brutal murders of so many others. And if Jericho let his own hatred and bitterness fuel the murder of this man, where would his depravity stop? What kind of man would he become? Certainly not much better than Otis.

Jericho slipped his knife up and cut Otis's hand, forcing him to release his hold. As the outlaw screamed and dropped his hand, Jericho tore off a strip of his shirt and quickly wrapped it around Otis's new cut to staunch the bleeding.

As much as Jericho wanted to make the man suffer for all he'd done, he couldn't let revenge have a greater need inside him than justice. After all, revenge had to do with payback for selfish satisfaction. But justice was about righting wrongs for the good of everyone.

"I'm making a litter for Ivy, and you're helping me carry her down the mountain." He fastened a cord around Otis's hands, binding them together. The man would be weak from his wounds and asthma, but he could brace the poles on his shoulders, at least until Jericho found a horse or a passerby who could assist him.

Otis leaned back against the wall, his eyes closed. "Told you to kill me."

"I'll be taking you into Denver and to jail so you can stand trial for all you did." Jericho secured Otis tightly, making sure he wouldn't be able to get loose. Then he checked him for any hidden weapons.

"They'll end up hanging me, so might as well get on with it."

Jericho unsheathed a knife tucked away under Otis's shirt. "I'm not the judge. I'm just the bounty hunter." He found another knife in Otis's boot.

"Why not save everyone the time and effort and tell them you were defending yourself and Miss McQuaid?"

Jericho had considered the possibility. But as he swallowed more of his rage, his head began to clear, and he knew he had to do some work on his own heart once he had Otis locked away.

"I need your help in carrying Ivy down the mountain."

"And what if I don't help you?"

"You will. Ivy's a good woman, and you know she doesn't deserve to die out here."

"She shot me."

"Because you would have shot her first."

Otis dragged in a shuddering breath, as if gathering the strength to resist.

"Then do it because you know this will be your last chance to make up for your wrongs."

Otis was silent for several heartbeats. Jericho would carry Ivy out on his own if he had to, but she'd suffer less if they worked together to transport her. Finally Otis nodded. "Alright."

Jericho nodded his thanks in return.

As he crawled toward Ivy, his gut cinched again at the sight of the knife handle and the blood covering her bodice. He examined the entry point and the wound. Although he wanted to pull out the knife, he knew he needed to wait and let a doctor take care of it, especially since the knife appeared to be plugging the wound and preventing too much blood loss. Instead, he did his best to form a makeshift sling to keep her arm immobile during the long trek.

Next he tied together the coats and shirts he divested from the others, and he created a litter. Then using two long charred but sturdy branches, he knotted the litter to the poles.

After securing the remaining prisoners, he carried Ivy out of the caves as carefully as he could. As he placed her gently on the makeshift litter, she moaned but didn't awaken. Finally he prodded Otis out of the caverns into the smoke-laden air. With watering eyes and a hacking cough,

Otis cooperated with bracing one end of the litter on his shoulders, even though he grunted from the pain of his arm wound.

The climb down through the scorched forest was steep and difficult. But without the tangle of brush to slow them, the hike went faster than Jericho expected. Thankfully, Ivy mostly remained unconscious, awakening only on and off.

When they entered a swath of forest that hadn't yet been burned to the ground, he prayed he'd soon locate their mounts. But as the shadows of evening stretched longer and darkness crept in around them, he began to despair that he'd find a faster way to transport Ivy so she could get the doctoring she needed.

Eventually they reached the wagon road that led into Fairplay. It was smoother and wider and less jarring for Ivy on the litter. Even there, Otis's steps dragged more, until he fell to his knees. "I can't go on."

Overhead through the canopy of spruce, Jericho glimpsed a hawk circling in the sky, its long wings spread, revealing the streaked pattern of either a Cooper's or sharp-shinned hawk. The smoke had thinned, showing the pale blue of the evening sky. Though the scent of burning forest lingered in the air, Jericho had taken them far from the flames that still glowed an orange red over long portions of the range.

He lifted the poles off Otis's shoulders to give him a rest. The outlaw leaned back against a lodgepole pine. The bandage around his gunshot was saturated with blood. And he closed his eyes, weak from blood loss as well as from the continued battle with his asthma.

Jericho knelt beside Ivy. Smudged with soot, her face was still so beautiful. His chest ached with the need to take her pain upon himself. He sighed as he had a hundred times since leaving the cave. He should have done a better job protecting her, should have warned her not to try anything and to let him make the first move.

Pressing the canteen to her lips, Jericho dribbled in as much water as he could get her to take. Then he handed the leather container to Otis.

The man shook his head. "Let me die, Bliss. It's what I deserve, and you know it better than anyone."

Jericho couldn't argue with Otis. But after how close he'd come to choking the man, he reckoned he had his own struggles that could have taken him down the wrong path too—if not for the grace of God. "From what I learned in the Good Book, we all have sinned and deserve to die."

"Some sinners—like me—deserve to die more than others."

"Maybe. Or maybe God's giving you an extra chance to make your peace with Him before you pass out of this life."

Otis scoffed. "He won't want to hear from someone like me."

Jericho shrugged. "I'm no preacher, but Christ, in the middle of suffering the worst kind of torture while being nailed to a cross, made time to listen to the thief crucified next to Him. If He could forgive that man, He can forgive anyone."

Otis opened his eyes and stared through the pine branches at the clear sky. "Doesn't make sense."

"Reckon forgiveness doesn't make sense to most people." It didn't make sense to Jericho either. It was a whole lot easier to harbor anger. Yet, if God could forgive the worst of them with so much generosity, then maybe Jericho needed to start doing some forgiving of his own, starting with himself.

As much as he still wanted to take the blame for Nash's

death, he had to forgive himself and move on. It was what Nash would have wanted. His brother had only ever sought the best for him and wouldn't want him to live under the weight of the accident. Because that's what it had been. An accident. Jericho just needed to accept it.

At a groan from Ivy, Jericho brushed back the strands of hair from her face. Her lashes fluttered and her eyes opened. As she focused on his face above hers, confusion pooled in the dark brown. "Jericho?"

"I'm here." He rested his hand against her cheek and stopped himself from bending down and pressing his lips to hers.

"Where are we?"

"On our way home." If only they were a little farther.

She reached up as if to touch her wound, but at the movement she cried out. In the next instant, she leaned her head to the side and vomited. She had nothing in her stomach to empty except the water he'd been giving her.

When she finished, her lashes fluttered back down. And she was so still, he guessed she'd passed out again from the pain. Even though she was a strong woman, her body could only handle so much.

"We need to keep moving." He stood, the desperation prodding him as it had since they'd left the cave.

Otis tried to push to his feet but couldn't make it more than halfway up before collapsing. "After your efforts to turn me into a saint, I'd like to prove I'm good for something and help carry her the rest of the way to Fairplay. But I don't think I'll make it."

The long summer day was working in their favor, but Jericho guessed they had another hour of daylight at most.

Would he have to leave Otis behind and finish carrying Ivy to town on his own? If so, he'd have to bind the man to a tree to ensure he didn't run away. But such a defenseless position could put him in danger if any wild animals came upon him before Jericho had the chance to return.

It was also possible the conniving outlaw was acting weak in order to get Jericho to go on without him.

"Stop wasting time and tie me up." Otis spoke matter-of-factly. "If you hurry, you'll make it to town with her before daybreak."

The dusty wagon path ahead was cluttered with dandelions amidst patches of sparse dry grass. From here on out, it was worn enough that he could pull the litter. It would be bumpier for Ivy, but it would allow him to move more quickly than if he carried her.

But he also had the feeling if he left Otis, somehow the man would figure out a way to go back for the gold and disappear forever. Then all the efforts Jericho had made over the past weeks would be for nothing. He'd lose Otis and lose the Department of Justice contract for Pinkerton.

"I'll carry Ivy," he said. "But you have to stay with me. I can't leave you here by yourself."

"If you tie me up, I won't be able to get away."

"Come on. Let's go." Jericho reached out and hefted Otis back to his feet. The man swayed and braced himself against the tree. Otis appeared genuinely sick and tired and weak. But that's what a good con man could do. Fool everyone around him into pitying him.

At a shout from down the wagon path, Jericho's pulse skipped. Someone was near, hopefully someone who could assist him.

"We need help!" Jericho called and waved his hands in the direction of the lower elevation.

Another shout came in reply. But Jericho couldn't distinguish the words, and with the aspen and pine blocking his view, he wasn't able to get a view of the newcomer. He hoped help was coming, but he took out his gun and readied it, just in case.

Seconds later, several riders came into view on the path below, and they were galloping hard and kicking up dust. Three muscular men who held themselves with confidence and determination.

Jericho would have recognized them anywhere. The McQuaid brothers: Wyatt, Flynn, and Brody.

"Hey!" Jericho called out, fighting back the strange need to weep with relief.

Brody was at the forefront and urged his mount faster over the gravelly rocks. Slightly bulkier than his brothers, Brody had the same dark hair and eyes as Wyatt and Ivy. Even if he resembled them in appearance, he was much quieter, almost brooding.

Brody must have returned from the Front Range over the past couple of days after Jericho started staying in town. As the burly man climbed the last bend of the road, his dark gaze swept over Ivy and halted on the knife in her chest. He charged the last of the distance and hardly gave his horse the chance to stop before he was sliding off and kneeling at Ivy's side, his fingers on the pulse in her neck. "What happened?"

Jericho hesitated. How much should he reveal? "She got in the middle of my fight with a band of outlaws."

Brody's gaze flicked to Otis standing in the shadows of the darkening forest before returning to the wound. He carefully peeled back the section of her bodice so he could get a better view of the puncture. At the sight of the flaming skin and blood, his brows furrowed into a scowl—the typical anger Brody had always worn.

Wyatt and Flynn reined in beside them, their horses snorting after so strenuous a ride. They'd clearly pushed hard. "Ivy's horse came back to the ranch without her," Wyatt said, his face etched with worry. "She told me she was going treasure hunting, and I reckoned she must've gotten into some kind of trouble."

"Did you get caught in the fire?" Flynn directed his question to Jericho as he dismounted.

"Yes, the fire trapped us for a bit. But that's not the problem now."

"Then what is?" Flynn scanned Ivy and then blanched. "Thunderation, Jericho! How'd she get stabbed?"

Brody tipped up the brim of his hat and peered at Jericho as if he'd turned into the devil himself. "He claims she got in the middle of a fight with outlaws."

Now that he'd captured Otis—Rodney James—what was the point in hiding the nature of his bounty hunting work from them any longer? He might as well confess the truth. "I'm an agent working for Pinkerton in Chicago with my dad. I came here to hunt down Rodney James, wanted for war crimes." He cocked his head at Otis.

Wyatt glanced at the outlaw, who'd slouched down against the tree again. Otis hardly had the menace of a crook, especially now with his pained expression and labored breathing.

"There were four of them." Jericho felt as though he had to offer the additional explanation. "The other three are tied up in a cave."

"You mean to tell me you've been here all this while tracking down outlaws and putting Ivy in a heap of danger?" Flynn took a menacing step toward him, his fists taut as if he wanted to slam them into Jericho.

Jericho stiffened, his face still smarting from his last altercation with Flynn. "That's why I was trying to keep my distance from her."

"From everything I've seen, you ain't been keeping your distance." Flynn was practically shouting. "And being out with her again today ain't either."

"I followed her because I was worried about her being alone with Hance and Otis." Jericho couldn't keep his tone from rising too.

Flynn shook his head, his eyes flashing. "If you were so blamed worried, you should have steered a mile clear of her."

He'd tried. But he wasn't about to give Flynn any excuses because he could have tried harder, even if it'd killed him to do so.

Brody began to lift Ivy into his arms. Jericho reached to help him. Before he could touch Ivy, Flynn shoved him away with a force that made him stumble backward and almost topple to his rear end. "Don't you dare get anywhere near her again."

Jericho righted himself and reined in his frustration.

"Take it easy now, Flynn," Wyatt said. "Fighting each other ain't gonna do us a lick of good."

"Agreed." Brody started back to his horse. "Let's stop wasting time and get her to the doc."

Jericho wanted to be the one carrying Ivy and taking her for help. But if anyone could do it safely, Brody was the man. He had a gentle way about him that worked wonders with horses and all creatures.

Brody shifted Ivy gingerly, but even then she moaned. "Once I'm in the saddle, I need someone to hand her up to me."

Wyatt jogged toward Brody. Jericho started to follow, only to have Flynn shove a palm into his chest and stop him. "I said stay away from her. Do y'hear me?"

Jericho balled his fists at his sides to keep from brushing past Flynn and going with Ivy.

"You could have gotten her killed." Flynn punched a finger against Jericho's sternum.

Killed. The word hit Jericho with the power of a gunshot. Flynn was right. He'd almost gotten Ivy killed.

Jericho retreated a step, his body suddenly weak, his blood cold.

If she died, it would be because of him and his not staying far enough away from her. If he hadn't come back into her life and threatened her plans to buy Steele's land, she wouldn't have felt the need to hunt for treasure, likely wouldn't have gone out with Hance and Otis, and wouldn't have been involved in the gun battle.

Everything that had happened to her was his fault.

With a final warning glare, Flynn spun and stalked away. As he reached his horse, he paused. "If you love her the way it seems you do, then go back to Chicago and leave her be."

"That's what I was aiming to do all along."

"Then stick to it." Flynn shoved his boot into his stirrup and climbed onto his horse. Already Brody had Ivy situated in front of him in the saddle and was heading out. Even as carefully as Brody was holding her, the jarring would hurt her. Jericho just prayed she'd stay unconscious for the rest of the ride back to Fairplay.

Wyatt had mounted and was waiting for Flynn. From the dark expressions of both men, Jericho guessed they'd be happy if they never had to see him again.

As they urged their horses into a gallop, Jericho watched them until they moved down the mountain out of sight. Even then, he stared at the ruts in the wagon path, a new sense of despair settling over him.

Somehow he'd let his infatuation with Ivy blind him. And earlier today, during their kissing in the cave, he'd almost convinced himself he could find a way to be with her, that he could make things work.

But all along he'd been a fool to get involved with her in any form. Everything that had occurred today was the perfect example of what could go wrong because of her association with him. This time she might survive. But what would happen next time? Because with his work, there would always be a next time.

From the corner of his eye, he could see Otis attempting to wiggle out of his binding. No doubt about it, the man was sly and would come up with any angle he could find to free himself. It was for the best Ivy was gone, away from Otis and any further danger.

Besides, without Ivy around distracting and worrying him, maybe now he could finish the job he'd come to South Park to do.

He swiped up a log and made his way to Otis. Without saying a word, he knocked the fellow unconscious. Then Jericho dragged him to the litter, tied him in place, and started on the way to town.

CHAPTER
24

Burning heat prodded Ivy awake. Her stab wound throbbed, starting at her shoulder and pulsing down her arm. But it wasn't as awful as it had been at first.

She pried her eyes open only to feel the room spinning around her.

"How you doing?" Tender fingers combed back her hair.

A glassy haze made her vision fog up, but she tried to focus on the face hovering near hers. "Jericho?"

"Nope. It's me. Brody." His hand was cool against her hot face.

She didn't want to be disappointed, she adored Brody, but the letdown came anyway. She hadn't wanted her time with Jericho to end. She'd wished to go on being with him forever in a world where just the two of them existed. It was irrational, she knew. But she'd loved every second together in the cave.

He'd all but come out and admitted he loved her.

Brody's hand slipped behind her head to lift her up. "You gotta drink something."

Her throat was dry and her lips cracked. And she was hot. All over. As Brody pressed the brim of the cup against her lips, she drank greedily. When she finished, he situated her again, and this time she could see that she was lying in the big bedroom on the main floor of his house, a bright, airy room he and Savannah shared.

"How'd I get here?" Her voice cracked.

"We found Jericho dragging you down Kenosha Pass. Flynn and me brought you here, while Wyatt went on and fetched the doc."

She tried to recall the faintest smidgen of the trip, but her mind was shooting with an empty chamber. The last thing she remembered was her attempt to escape from Hance. "How long have I been out?"

"Since we got here late last night."

From the way the long rays of sunlight slanted past the lacy curtains in the open window, she guessed it was going on evening. She shifted her shoulder and winced at the twinge of pain, which was nothin' compared to the gut-emptying agony from before.

"Doc sewed you up and gave you morphine." Brody dipped a rag in a basin on the bedside table, wrung it out, and then laid it across her forehead.

The coolness soothed her skin, and she closed her eyes, suddenly too weak to do anything other than rest. The morphine was easing her pain, but it was also making her tired and dizzy.

"Is Jericho alright?" She could only imagine how difficult his journey off the mountain had been.

Brody hesitated.

Her heart sped. "Where is he? He ain't hurt too, is he?"

"Naw, he's fine." Brody's tone hardened.

"You sure?"

"Yep." The finality to the word told her Brody was gonna be as tight-lipped as a colicky horse.

It didn't matter. The morphine was fast taking her into a blissful, worry-free slumber. And except for Jericho's arms, that's the only place she wanted to be.

❧

Flames flew over her body. She thrashed in an attempt to put them out, but they surrounded her and wouldn't relent from roasting her.

Had she fallen in the middle of the forest fire? She tried to call out for help, but her throat was thick and wouldn't work.

"The fever's gettin' worse." Flynn's voice penetrated the smoke in her head.

Someone ran a cold rag up one arm and down the next, but it only soothed for a moment before the heat rushed back in.

"Seen this a hundred times in the war," Brody said gravely.

"There's gotta be more we can do."

"Not much'll help once the wound's infected."

"Thunderation." Flynn spoke softly but harshly. "If I get my hands on Jericho, I'm gonna string him up so fast he'll be seeing the pearly gates before he can blink."

"Doubt he'll be comin' anywhere near here again, not after making him dodge bullets yesterday."

Dodge bullets? Protest pushed for release. Had her brothers shot at Jericho?

"He never should've come back to Colorado," Flynn said.

Brody was silent for several heartbeats. "Reckon someone has to hunt down criminals."

"If he suspected Otis was an outlaw, why didn't he warn Ivy against going treasure hunting with the fella?"

Otis an outlaw? Ivy would have snorted at the prospect if she'd had an ounce of energy. But she couldn't manage a word, even though she wanted to chaw out her brothers and tell them to stop bullying Jericho. They had to know by now there was nothing they could do to keep her away from the man she loved.

Jericho cared about her too. That much was clear enough. He might even love her and had agreed to think about sticking together. Surely eventually they'd figure out a way to make things work.

"This is all Jericho's fault." Flynn's voice rumbled with frustration.

"The way Greta tells the story, you and Wyatt were the ones pushing him to marry Ivy."

"Had my reservations. But reckoned if anyone could make her happy, Bliss could."

Yes, he could make her mighty happy. But she wanted the chance to make him happy too. And she wouldn't get to if her brothers were forcing Jericho to stay away.

She pried her eyes open. She needed to give them a piece of her mind, tell them to stop interfering with Jericho and her. Things were already hard enough, and she didn't need her brothers making it worse.

Pushing up on her uninjured arm, she tried to focus on Brody sitting in a chair next to her bedside. But her eyes felt heavy and glassy. Her head ached. And she was as weak as a baby bird just hatched.

His dark brows furrowed, and he shifted a cup toward her mouth. "Hey, darlin'."

She shook her head and took in Flynn standing at the end of the bed. His thumbs were tucked into his belt, and his anxious eyes peered at her from within the shadows of his battered hat.

"I love Jericho," she croaked. She began to shake, and her head pounded harder. She wanted to say more, but she fell back onto the mattress, too weak to do anything but give way to oblivion.

⟢⟣

Jericho tugged on the handcuffs. The adjustable ratchet was tight against Otis's wrists.

"You must be getting quite a reward for turning me in." Otis reclined in the hay-filled wagon bed, claiming to be weak and in pain, even though the doctor had confirmed the gunshot wound was healing well.

Jericho reached for the manacles around Otis's ankles and rattled them, making sure they were still as secure as they'd been earlier when he'd put them on.

"What are they paying you?" Otis spoke casually, but the outlaw was once again trying to connive his way out of the situation, just as he'd been doing ever since Jericho had captured him.

Jericho had kept Otis manacled and locked up in Fairplay's makeshift jail for the past three days. And he'd paid a couple of trustworthy cowhands to stand guard while he'd ridden back up to Windy Peak and brought down Hance's dead body along with the other two accomplices. One of them probably wouldn't make it. But the other was recuperating.

From the information Jericho had gathered from the two, they were simply pawns in a bigger scheme to find the gold.

He'd been telegramming back and forth with Pinkerton ever since bringing Otis in, and the agency had sent two lawmen up from Denver to help him transport Otis to Chicago, where he would be held in prison until his trial.

"Listen, Bliss." Otis pushed himself up. "I can take you to another treasure down by Pueblo that Hance and I were going to after we located the one here."

"No thanks." Jericho stepped away from the wagon bed and reached for his horse, a trickle of perspiration making its way down his spine. The early morning sun was already hot and the air dry without a breath of wind. Except for a lone stagecoach rattling away, Main Street seemed as withered and lifeless as pale prairie grass.

"With the gold from Windy Peak along with the gold from the Pueblo hideout, you'll have at least ten times what the bounty is."

For a fellow who'd just spent three days in a shack, Otis still didn't have the hardened, crusty look of a criminal. Jericho suspected that's why he'd kept himself clean, asking for a change of garments every day along with water to wash up, so he could appear less threatening.

"In fact, the gold in Pueblo would be enough for a man to get a fresh start anywhere he wanted."

The lawman driving the wagon had pivoted on the bench and was watching Otis with new interest. The second escort paused in the process of saddling his horse. Maybe Otis's tactics would work—and had obviously worked in the past—on someone less principled, but the criminal wouldn't be able to move Jericho. Not even a fraction of an inch.

"No one in their right mind can turn down the offer of gold." Otis shifted his attention to the two lawmen, sizing up their interest. "Especially a large enough supply to keep a man from having to work another day in his life."

No wonder Otis always managed to get loose. He knew how to read people well and play on their weaknesses. If he rattled on long enough, he'd convince one of the lawmen to believe him and cut him loose in the middle of the night or when Jericho had his back turned.

Jericho unsheathed his knife, returned to the wagon bed, and grabbed Otis. "You're talking too much."

Otis shrank back as though instinctively trying to protect himself. No doubt the man had developed the habit as a child in warding off his father's blows. Whatever might have happened and no matter how horrible, that didn't excuse anyone from learning to make better choices and moving forward with honorable intentions.

Jericho pulled Otis's shirt taut and slit it at the hem, rending the linen until a long, loose strip formed. He cut it free, then dangled it in front of Otis. "I didn't keep the gold from Windy Peak. I'm returning it to the mine owner the Kingston Gang stole it from." Without waiting for a reply, Jericho wrapped the strip around Otis's mouth.

The outlaw's brows rose in surprise, whether from his news about the gold or the gagging, Jericho didn't know or care. All he cared about was making sure he got to Chicago before the man somehow finagled his way free.

Jericho hadn't returned the gold to its rightful owner yet. But he'd brought it into Fairplay and locked it away in a vault at the mayor's house for safekeeping until all the inquiries were completed. Now that he knew the Kingston Gang had been involved, tracking down the original mine owner would be a little easier.

Sheathing his knife, he glanced down the street toward Steele's house and envisioned the Independence Day celebration when he'd spoken to Wyatt at the dessert table and Wyatt had recognized how much Jericho loved Ivy even before he'd been willing to admit it.

"You love her. Reckon every cowhand this side of the Divide knows it but you. Best you work through whatever's holding you back before you end up losing her."

A sharp pain twisted at Jericho's heart. He hadn't been able to stop himself from going out to Healing Springs Ranch yesterday to check on Ivy and see her one last time.

As he'd ridden across the yard, Flynn had stepped out the front door of Brody's house. When Jericho started to dismount, Flynn shot right in front of his horse. The second Jericho's feet touched the ground, a bullet nearly pierced his boot.

"Go on, hightail it outta here!" Flynn wore his hat brim low but couldn't disguise the fierce love and loyalty in his eyes and tightening his features. "And don't come back."

Jericho returned to his saddle. "Just came to say good-bye to Ivy—"

"She ain't gonna say good-bye to you." Flynn aimed his revolver at Jericho with an unswerving hand.

Heaviness had fallen over Jericho as he'd taken in Flynn standing on the porch threatening to kill him. He never would have thought it possible six years ago when they'd traveled west together. Never would have imagined it when he and Nash had taken over watching Flynn's place back in '65. Never would have predicted it when he'd left with Dylan two years ago.

But Jericho had gone and done what he said he'd never do. He'd fallen in love with Ivy. And in the process, he made an enemy out of the McQuaid men.

All the more reason to leave. All the more reason never to come back, just like Flynn had instructed.

"Let's go." Jericho motioned to the two lawmen and then reached for his mount's lead line. He forced his feet to move to the northeast on the road that led toward Kenosha Pass and Denver, even though his entire body protested and tugged him south to the route that would take him toward Healing Springs Ranch.

The urge to ride out to Ivy again was overwhelming, tightening his muscles and pinching his stomach. His footsteps slowed, and he nearly stopped.

What good would it do? Even if he managed to get past her brothers, he was afraid that with one look he wouldn't be able to make himself ride away for good like he needed to. He'd only end up making her promises that ultimately he'd regret.

No, they were both better off if he just left now without complicating things.

Setting his face toward the northern mountains with the large areas of blackened, charred forest, somehow he made it down the street to Steele's house. As he halted, he patted his coat pocket.

He had one last thing to do. Once done, it would sever his ties with Ivy forever.

CHAPTER

25

Ivy hovered in and out of consciousness, always fighting the pain and heat. The torture was worse when the doctor came to administer the bromine. She couldn't keep from screaming at the burning in her wound, as if the fires from the very depths of hell were licking at her flesh.

Her family hovered near, there every time she awoke. Sometimes Wyatt or Flynn sat by her bed. Sometimes Greta or Linnea or Savannah. But usually whenever she woke, Brody was bathing her overheated skin and forcing her to sip bitter-tasting herbal brews.

After all Brody had gone through during the war, she guessed he had the most experience in handling a wounded and sick patient. Even so, she could see the fear etched into his face getting worse day by day.

The person she most wanted to come visit hadn't. Jericho. Surely she'd remember if he'd been here. But she hadn't seen his face once.

His name beckoned to her, drawing her to wakefulness.

The soft light of dawn permeated the room. The windows were open as wide as they could get, and the coolness of the high-country night lingered in the air so that she shivered.

At her movement, Brody stirred and lifted himself from where he'd been bent over, head on his arms on the edge of the bed. His black hair was mussed and his face haggard with dark circles under his eyes, just like the Brody she'd known before Savannah had chased away his nightmares and helped him find healing.

"Go on and get to bed, Brody," she whispered. "You look worse than a corpse in a coffin."

He straightened and pressed a hand against her forehead. After a second, a grin split his lips, and his eyes turned glossy. "Mornin' to you too, sunshine."

"Someone's gotta tell you like it is."

"Yep." He wiped at his eyes. "Reckon I gotta have you around for a while longer getting into my business."

A while longer? Had she been close to dying? She glanced at the room as if that could somehow give her the clues she needed to figure out what had happened while she'd been sick. The washbasin sat on the bedside table, along with an assortment of medicines and ointments. Rags and towels littered the floor next to drinking glasses and a pitcher.

She pushed up to her elbows, but at the sting in her wound, she lowered herself back down. "How long have I been in bed?"

"Near to a week today."

"A week?" This time she sat up, heedless of her wound. For several seconds the room spun, but just as quickly it came into focus.

Brody's gentle touch on her arm steadied her. "Go slow, darlin'. You've been mighty sick."

"How sick?"

Brody opened his mouth to respond but then closed it and swallowed hard while glancing out the window.

"That bad?"

He nodded.

She vaguely remembered having a fever. Had her wound become infected? She lifted a hand to her forehead. Her skin was clammy but cool. She arched her shoulder, and though the wound still pained her, the burning was gone.

She reached for his hand and grasped it tight. "Thank you, Brody. It couldn't have been easy for you to sit here by my side."

He met her gaze. She expected to see the hauntedness back in the depths of his eyes. But though wide with concern, peace radiated within them.

For as emotionally wounded as Brody had been when he'd first arrived in Colorado, he'd come a long way.

"I admit I did a whole lot of worrying." He squeezed her hand. "But also did a whole lot of praying."

"And a whole lot of nursing me back from the dead."

"That too."

She wanted to ask about Jericho, if he'd come, if he'd taken a turn sitting by her bed. But he'd probably been busy hauling down the men from the cave. Maybe even taking them to Denver to a secure prison.

From somewhere else in the house came the rattle of pots and pans, along with the babbling of a baby, probably Hartley. He was mighty cute but was also a tornado on two legs.

Brody cast a glance toward the closed door and then stood and stretched. "Think you can eat something?"

"Yep. Didn't think you'd ever ask." Ivy's stomach rumbled

with hunger pangs. After a week of going without any vittles, she was ready to try keeping something down.

Brody disappeared for a short while, his deep voice mingling with Savannah's and coming from the direction of the kitchen. Savannah always brought a servant with her every time she and Brody came up from the Double L Ranch on the Front Range. The servant cooked and cleaned and took care of Hartley while Savannah helped with the wild mustangs and offered her vet services to the Healing Springs livestock.

As Savannah and Hartley entered the room with Brody, Ivy welcomed them with a smile. Hartley had blond hair like Savannah but was stocky and tough like his pa. Though Savannah tried to corral Hartley and keep him from climbing up next to Ivy, she eventually gave in and let Hartley up on the bed while she brushed and braided Ivy's hair.

By the time Ivy finished a few bites of eggs and toast, she was tired again and pushed aside her plate. Before she could recline, Flynn rushed inside the room, bringing the familiar scent of the barn and cattle with him.

At the sight of her sitting in bed, he halted and hung his head. His shoulders heaved up and down several times before he pulled in a deep breath, swiping at his eyes.

"I'm fine and dandy, Flynn."

"You sure?"

"Sure as heaven above."

At her usual response, Flynn wiped at his eyes again.

"I never did see so many grown men blubbering all in one day." She couldn't keep from teasing her brothers. "Reckon I need to get you all real mad so you stop making such a fuss over me."

With a grin, Flynn crossed to her. When he reached her bedside, he bent and wrapped her into a hug, holding her tightly for several moments. She couldn't remember the last time Flynn had hugged her, probably not since she'd gotten the news of Ma's death. Even then, the hug had been brief, mainly because Ivy hadn't been all that sad.

"Thank the Lord Almighty." Flynn pulled back enough to see Ivy's face. "Don't you ever go doing something as stupid as getting stabbed again."

"I'll try not to."

"Good. Don't wanna have to give you a whupping."

She smiled at his attempt at teasing her back.

For several minutes, Flynn asked her how she was feeling, assessing her as best he could. "The doc's been coming every day. Been injecting the wound with bromine. But Brody's been working out his own remedies with a few concoctions he saw some of the Southern doctors use during the war to keep infection from spreading."

Brody had picked up the squirming Hartley and was busy tickling him and earning the sweet sound of giggles.

Ivy pictured Jericho doing the same to their young'un. Jericho was gonna make a fine pa. Just the thought of him again brought a swell of longing into her chest. She wanted to see him real soon but reckoned Flynn wasn't gonna be too happy about it.

"Better send word to Wyatt that I ain't dyin' anytime soon."

Flynn nodded. "Yep. Did right away."

She plucked at the coverlet. "I'd be obliged if someone could let Jericho know I'm doing fine."

The room fell silent. Even Hartley went quiet, as though he sensed a sudden tension in the air.

"He'll wanna come out and visit now that I don't have one foot in the grave."

Flynn and Brody stared at the coverlet as though it had suddenly turned into a mighty fine work of art. Savannah picked up Hartley, settled him on her hip, and then combed her fingers through the baby's fuzzy hair.

What weren't they telling her? "C'mon now. Might as well spit it out."

Flynn cleared his throat but didn't look up.

Savannah glanced from one man to the other before shaking her head and meeting Ivy's gaze. Her gentle blue eyes were filled with a sympathy that sent Ivy's pulse into a free fall.

"What happened?"

"He left earlier in the week."

Left. Ivy's mind spun to remember all the little things she'd picked up during her times of coherency. Someone had claimed Jericho was hunting down outlaws, that Otis was a criminal. If that was true, then of course he'd be gone. He had to take Otis—and the others who'd been in the cave—to prison, probably in Denver.

"Makes sense." She tried for an attitude of nonchalance, not wanting anyone to realize just how much she missed him. "Got any idea when he's coming back? If he's been gone all week, it oughta be real soon."

Flynn and Brody still didn't meet her gaze.

"He didn't say anything about when he's returning." Savannah's comment held a note of pity that set Ivy on edge even more.

Hadn't she overheard Brody and Flynn talking about shooting at Jericho? Had they kept Jericho away? Prevented them from being together? Her muscles tensed. "He came to see me, didn't he?"

When no one responded, she had the answer she needed. "Land sakes, Flynn! Thought I was dreaming, but I wasn't hearing things after all. You really did shoot at Jericho, didn't you?"

Flynn finally lifted his chin, and his eyes flashed with obstinacy. "I was making a point, plain and simple."

"And what point was that?" Ivy's ire was rising, but she didn't care.

"That I don't want him getting within a hundred miles of you, or next time I'll blast him to pieces."

"Flynn!" Ivy pushed up to her knees. "You had no right to interfere."

Flynn's expression remained stubborn, and she guessed she wouldn't get him to change his mind about anything.

Brody hadn't taken his gaze from the coverlet. Savannah was making her escape with Hartley, closing the door behind her.

"Brody?" Ivy asked. "You have any part in this?"

Brody bent forward, braced his elbows on his knees. His eyes were dark and serious. "He's a bounty hunter, Ivy."

She shrugged. In the cave, she'd guessed he had some kind of job hunting criminals. And it didn't matter.

"He's involved with the most dangerous outlaws alive." Brody seemed to be pleading with her, as though he hoped to make her understand why they didn't want her to be with Jericho. "He was here undercover, tracking down one of the worst war criminals, a man by the name of Rodney James."

Ivy sensed where Brody was going with the conversation before he finished, and her stomach knotted. "Otis."

"Yep."

"But Otis didn't seem like a bad fella. Not like Hance." She shuddered as she remembered the way he'd gone after her and hurt her so easily.

Brody's mouth took on a pinched quality. "Can't even begin to describe the crimes Rodney James committed. The details are too tragic to repeat."

If Jericho was with so dangerous a criminal, would he be safe? It was hard to imagine Otis being able to harm Jericho. But that didn't mean Otis's fellow outlaws wouldn't attempt to come to his rescue.

"Where is Jericho now? Did he take Otis to the prison in Denver?"

Brody shook his head and raised his brow at Flynn.

Flynn released a long sigh.

"What's wrong?" she asked.

"He didn't go to Denver, Ivy. He went to Chicago."

She had the terrible feeling Flynn was telling her Jericho had gone back to his job in Chicago and didn't have any plans to return to Colorado. After promising he'd take some time to think about their relationship, how could Jericho just leave her? Of course, if Flynn shot at him, he wouldn't have been able to explain anything or reassure her they'd find a way to be together.

She climbed to the edge of the bed. As she put her feet on the floor, Brody stood and took hold of her arm to assist her. She shook him off.

"Where do you think you're going?" Flynn asked.

"To Chicago. And you better not try to stop me." Even with both feet planted firmly on the floor, she swayed and had to grab the headboard to keep from falling.

Flynn stepped closer, his hand outstretched as though to catch her if she fell. "You can't just up and leave for Chicago."

"Watch me." She took a wobbly step, and when Brody reached for her again, she glared at him.

"Thunderation, Ivy!" Flynn growled. "Get back in bed before I hog-tie and toss you there."

"You drove him away!" She tottered and this time would have fallen except for Brody scooping her up. She slapped at his chest and tried to wiggle free. "Both of you drove Jericho away with all your shenanigans."

Even as she struggled, Brody carefully deposited her into bed. She wanted to crawl right back out, but she was too weak and her wound throbbed. Instead, she glared at her brothers. "I love him. And I'm aimin' to spend my life with him whether you want me to or not."

"We just want what's best for you." Brody palmed the back of his neck, his face lined with frustration. "Look at the heap of trouble you got into this time. It ain't ever gonna be safe with Jericho."

Those were almost the same words Jericho had used to describe why he'd kept pushing her away. He was haunted by the memories of all that had happened to his mom and didn't want that happening to anyone he cared about. Even so, she was different. "I don't need safe."

"Reckon Jericho felt like Brody and me." Flynn's tone took on a sadness Ivy didn't like. She'd much prefer the anger. "The kid was doing his blasted best to steer clear of you from the get-go. Probably had good intentions but couldn't stay away for the better half of a second."

"It don't matter. Whether you like it or not, I'm going to Chicago just as soon as I'm strong enough."

Flynn fished inside his trouser pocket. "He doesn't want you to follow him."

"You don't know that."

"I surefire do know." Flynn took out a paper and began unfolding it.

She raised herself so she was reclining against the headboard. "You're just trying to scare me. And it ain't gonna work this time. I'm old enough to know my mind and what I want. And I know that what me and Jericho feel for each other is just as real as what you feel for Linnea, what Brody feels for Savannah, and what Wyatt feels for Greta."

Flynn smoothed out the sheet but didn't meet her gaze.

"We're meant to be together, and we'll figure out a way to make things work in Chicago. That's all there is to it."

Flynn paused and then handed her the paper.

The top read, *Record of Deeds, know all men by these presents.* It went on to record Landry Steele's signature along with the words *do hereby sell and convey unto the said Ivy McQuaid the following described premises situated in the county of South Park and the Territory of Colorado.*

The handwritten paragraph underneath described in specific details the parcel she'd been wanting to purchase from Steele.

A thrill wound through her. She was holding the deed to her land. Her name was spelled out along with the amount Steele had been asking paid in full. How had this happened? And how had Flynn gotten a hold of it?

When she glanced up at Flynn, she waited for him to jerk the deed out of her hands and tell her there was no way— not in a hundred years—he was gonna let her go off and live on her own, that there was no way she could take the deed.

But he only pressed his lips together as if he was using every ounce of restraint not to say the words.

She looked to Brody, and his eyes said he knew something she didn't.

Her sights shifted to the sheet again, and her heart thudded a strangely uneven beat. What did all this mean? Clearly, Jericho wanted her to stay. That meant he intended to return to her after he delivered Otis to prison, didn't it?

"Jericho sent me a message." Flynn's voice dropped low, and Ivy's stomach dropped with it. "He said as long as we agree to letting you have your own place, he'll keep away."

"What?" The ache in her chest swelled.

Flynn removed another paper from his pocket and handed it to her.

She unfolded it and saw that Jericho's neat handwriting took up two brief lines: *We all agree she'll be safest if she's nowhere near me. Let her have the land for her own ranch, and I promise I won't come back.*

CHAPTER
26

Jericho didn't want her. Ivy crumpled his note, tossed it to the floor, then slumped against the mattress, the air squeezing from her lungs just as if she'd been thrown from her mount and grassed.

She oughta be thankful she had the deed to the land. And she oughta be thankful her brothers wouldn't be able to oppose her starting her own place. She'd known they'd give her a heap of trouble once she told them her plans, but she'd decided not to think about it until she actually had the land.

And now she did. Somehow Jericho had found a way to purchase it for her. Maybe he'd used part of the gold they'd found after all? Whatever the case, he'd sent her a message that was mighty loud. In fact, it was deafening.

He didn't want her chasing after him to Chicago. He wanted her to live here. And he wasn't aiming to come back. Ever. He'd made a promise he wouldn't.

He'd chosen his work over her. She knew that wasn't an

entirely fair accusation. He was doing something mighty fine with his hunting of criminals. But still . . . it hurt.

Flynn nodded at the deed on the bed beside her. "Can't say I'm real thrilled with the idea of you goin' off and havin' your own place."

Ivy wanted to argue with Flynn, tell him she'd be fine, that she'd already plotted out how to make a go of raising sheep. But the words stuck in her throat.

Brody stared at the floor, his shoulders slumped like he'd been whupped. She hoped he felt bad for chasing Jericho off. And she hoped Flynn did too. But deep down, she suspected that even if her brothers hadn't shot at Jericho, he would have gone anyway.

When he'd come back to Colorado, he'd been trying to steer clear of her, just like Flynn said. But she'd gone and thrown herself at him like she usually did.

She closed her eyes to hold back a sudden sting of tears. Jericho had never wanted to stay, never wanted to be with her. She'd been the one pushing for it, pushing him to change his plans so they could be together.

"Mighty sorry, Ivy." Brody's soft comment rammed into her like the sharp horns of a bull.

The pressure unleashed the gates so that her tears started to flow. She rolled over on her side until she was facing away from her brothers so they wouldn't see her crying. It had always been this way with Jericho—her wanting him more than he'd ever wanted her. And this time, even though Jericho had admitted he wanted her, it still hadn't been enough.

Hot trails trickled down her cheeks. She tried not to sniffle, but one came out anyway.

"Shoot, Ivy," Flynn said gently. "I always liked Jericho, but you've gotta see this is for the best."

The tears only flowed faster. "I don't wanna talk about it anymore."

Silence fell over the room.

She just longed to be left alone so she could cry without anyone seeing or hearing her. "I'm tired. Reckon I could use some privacy so I can sleep a spell."

The silence dragged out a few more heartbeats before footsteps crossed the room and the door opened and closed. She glanced over her shoulder to make sure no one was there before burying her face into a pillow. The sobs welled up so forcefully, her chest felt on fire.

Oh, Jericho. Why? Why did you have to leave? Why couldn't you care enough to try to make things work?

Her pillow captured her sobs and the tears. But it couldn't contain the pain that pressed for release. One that went deep inside. One that had festered long before she'd met Jericho. One that had started after her ma had married Rusty. Even though Ma had done it to save the farm, Ivy had always resented her for the decision. Rusty had demanded Ma's attention and affection all for himself, so she'd had none left for anyone else. Maybe Ma hadn't meant to reject Ivy, but she'd done it anyway. She'd rejected Ivy for Rusty.

Her brothers hadn't meant to push her to the sideline, but it had happened when they'd gotten busy with their own lives and families. Now Jericho had tossed her aside too. She'd offered herself and her future to him, but he'd thrown her love away without even a good-bye.

Her sobs into the pillow only swelled, but she hugged it tight to muffle the sound. Jericho hadn't said good-bye.

Even if her brothers had prevented him from it, he could've figured out a way to see her one last time.

What was wrong with her that everyone was always abandoning her? Why didn't anyone ever love her enough to stay?

With despair settling into all the cracks of her broken heart, she finally drifted to sleep.

⁓✦⁓

She only stayed at Brody's for one more day before moving back to the bedroom she shared with Astrid at Wyatt's. When Wyatt carried her up the stairs and deposited her on the bed, she climbed under the covers and decided she didn't ever want to get up.

But a few days later when Greta went into labor while everyone else was gone, Ivy had no choice but to emerge and help her sister-in-law. By the time Astrid returned with the other three children from a ride out to the inn to check on the progress of the building project, Ivy was holding a newborn babe, a little girl.

After helping to bring the tiny bundle into the world, somehow Ivy felt as though she had a connection with baby Willa. Though her chest wouldn't stop aching from the loss of Jericho, she found a measure of comfort in taking care of the newborn, holding and cuddling her every time Greta wasn't feeding her.

By the time July turned into August, they were all aware Willa wasn't thriving the way she should. The baby struggled to breathe, her skin remained a shade of blue, and she grew increasingly limp and lethargic. The doctor did everything he could to help the infant, but two weeks after her birth, Willa died.

Greta and Wyatt were devastated, and Ivy did her best to lend her comfort amidst their grieving. But the loss of the baby somehow felt like another rejection. The thought was irrational, she knew. But once again, she retreated to her bed and couldn't find the energy to get out, even though her stab wound was mostly healed.

Astrid nagged her to stop lying around. Flynn and Brody pestered her, trying to convince her to resume life. Linnea and Savannah both came to visit multiple times, soothing and bribing. All the nieces and nephews attempted to cheer her up. But Ivy couldn't shake the melancholy.

By mid-August, she guessed Jericho had long since made it to Chicago and completed his mission in delivering Otis to prison. He'd had plenty of time to write a letter to her if he'd chosen to. But with every passing day and no word from him, the finality of his leaving only added to her despair.

"It should've been me, God," she whispered as she stared at the log wall. "You should've taken me and not Willa." She didn't need to live. Her life had always been aimless, useless, restless.

At a clearing of a throat from the doorway of the bedroom, Ivy closed her eyes and pretended to be asleep, as she'd taken to doing whenever anyone came up to talk to her.

A moment later, the clearing throat sounded again, this time louder.

Ivy remained motionless.

At the uneven boot thump crossing to the bed, she guessed Flynn had come to plead with her for the hundredth time. And she didn't care. After his part in driving Jericho away, her brother could go drink pickle juice all day as far as she was concerned.

At a poke in her backside, she let out a yelp but lay motionless in her sagging mattress.

A beat of silence passed. Then the poke came again. This time harder and sharper. Enough that she cried out and shifted in a half-hearted effort to scoot beyond reach. "Cut it out and go away!"

Another jab was her only answer. And it was so painful that she growled out her frustration, tossed aside her cover, and sat up. As she turned, she found Judd—not Flynn—standing beside her bed, a cattle prod in his hand.

"What do you think you're doin'? Trying to give me another injury?" Her voice was harsh and loud. She was being disrespectful, but suddenly she was plain mad, though she didn't know exactly why.

Judd twirled the long stick that they sometimes used to round up cattle. "Reckon if you're acting like a lazy cow, you need to be treated like one." His bushy white eyebrows gathered in a scowl, and his lips pursed beneath his long, drooping white mustache.

For a second, Ivy couldn't gather her wits. She hadn't expected Judd, hadn't expected a cattle prod, and certainly hadn't expected to be called a lazy cow.

Before she could dodge the prod, he poked her again, this time in her stomach. "Past time for you to get on up and quit feeling sorry for yourself."

The end of the prod dug hard, giving her no choice but to jump up from the bed. "C'mon, Judd! This ain't funny."

"I ain't trying to be funny." His legs were spread as though to block her from getting around him. He wasn't a large man, but he was as wiry and tough as old leather. She'd watched him wrestle plenty of steers to the ground and knew she couldn't get past him even if she tried her hardest.

She locked gazes with him, putting on her fiercest glare. In her nightgown and with her hair hanging in tangled waves over her shoulder, she guessed she looked about as menacing as a pup growling at a coyote.

He held the prod out, and the glint in his eyes told her he aimed to use it again.

She tried to take a step back, but the bed was in her way. "What's got you all riled up?"

"I'm afeared we ain't gonna be ready for winter, that's what. Now let's go. We got a heap of work ahead of us."

Ready for winter? Heap of work? "What are you talkin' about? You're sounding as crazy as a bedbug."

"We're gettin' to work on that ranch of yours."

She started to shake her head, but he aimed the prod for her thigh. She jumped out of the way, but barely. "Stop! I ain't gotta ranch."

"You surefire do. And as your foreman, I'd rather live in a cabin come winter than in a tent."

"Foreman?"

"Yep. And I'll be skinned alive if I'm gonna sit back and suffer on account of you acting like a lazy cow."

This time when she met his gaze, his eyes brimmed with love and affection that brought an ache to her throat. And she finally understood what he was telling her. He was aiming to leave Wyatt and Greta and the home he'd made at Healing Springs so he could help her get a fresh start.

Tears sprang to her eyes, and she blinked them back. She'd shed too many blasted tears in recent weeks. And she didn't want to cry a single drop more. But Judd's offer was something that went beyond the ordinary. As generous and kind as it was, she couldn't accept it. "It's too much, Judd. I can't let you sacrifice like that—"

"Wyatt don't need me no more."

"You love being here. The kids. The family—"

"They ain't goin' nowhere."

It wouldn't be the same. But maybe with Wyatt and Greta's plans to eventually move to the new house by the inn, he was ready for a change. "Your garden?"

"Reckon a garden can grow on your land every bit as much as on Wyatt's."

She couldn't possibly take Judd up on his offer, could she? She hadn't given the land much more than a passing thought since the day Flynn had shown her the deed. In fact, she didn't even know where the deed was. Truth was, she didn't want it, not when it would be a forever reminder that Jericho had bought it for her with his reward money from catching Otis, a fact Steele had let slip at baby Willa's funeral.

"The land's not really mine." She rubbed at the sore spot on her backside. "It's Jericho's, and I ain't taking a handout from him. No how, no way." Especially knowing he'd used it to bribe her brothers into letting her have her own place without a fight.

Judd dug in his vest pocket and produced the deed. "Whose name is on this-here paper?"

She didn't have to glance at it to know her name was there. "Don't matter—"

"If that man's gonna give himself his own hangin', don't mean you have to join him."

What was Judd saying? That Jericho was hurting himself by leaving South Park? She wasn't so sure about that. After all, he had a good job and a new life carved out for himself in Chicago.

But Judd was right about one thing. Just because Jericho left, didn't mean she had to stop living.

"Fact is, we can't build on a bog 'cause the place would sink after the first storm." Judd held out the deed, but she had a feeling he wasn't talking about building in the real sense of the word. "We've got to build on somethin' solid if we want to make it past the rain and wind and snow."

Her mind spun, trying to make sense of Judd's advice. But she couldn't wrangle the wisdom from his proverb.

As if sensing her confusion, he continued. "You get on with building your life on the good Lord 'cause He's the only thing that ain't gonna crumble away when the going gets rough and people leave you behind. Believe me. I oughta know."

She had the feeling he was referring to losing his wife and kids long ago. If Judd hadn't given up when everyone he'd loved had been brutally murdered, then how could she give up when she hadn't lost nearly as much?

Yep, her losses and the rejection still stung something fierce. But maybe she'd been looking too much to people to make her life meaningful instead of looking to the Almighty first. Was it time to get her life squared away and solidly built upon the good Lord, who wasn't gonna leave her even when everyone else did?

Judd waggled the deed at her.

She reached for it but hesitated. Was she really ready for this next step?

And why not? Why not move on? Why let her feelings for Jericho dictate things?

A spark flared inside. She wasn't a weak woman. Nope, she was strong and determined and capable. She'd prove to Jericho and everyone else that she had exactly what it took to build a place and run her own ranch. And someday, if Jericho ever came back, she'd show him she'd gotten along just fine without him.

She let her fingers close around the deed. "When do we leave?"

Judd's lips and mustache curled up into a smile. "The sooner the better."

At the exhalation of a breath in the hallway, Ivy guessed one or more of her brothers had been listening to the entire exchange with Judd. No doubt they were relieved she was getting out of bed and living again.

It was time to forgive them for their part in sending Jericho packing. But that didn't mean she'd forget what they'd done. Maybe not ever.

CHAPTER
27

Jericho pushed open the door of the Little Blue Angel. The piano music, cigar smoke, and coarse laughter greeted him. Through the haze of the dimly lit interior, he searched the crowded saloon until his sights alighted on Dylan.

At a table in the center, Dylan leaned back in his chair and grinned as the woman on his lap wrapped her arms around his neck and planted a kiss on his cheek. Another woman hovered above him, her fingers combing his hair. With low necklines, tight bodices, and painted faces, the women were clearly of ill repute.

Didn't matter what kind of women they were. Dylan seemed to attract females the way spilled molasses attracted ants.

He picked up a shot glass and downed the dark liquid in one swallow before tilting his head and capturing a kiss from the woman on his lap. She happily obliged, letting her hands roam freely over his chest.

Jericho paused, and the swinging door slammed into his

backside. The sight of the kiss and the intimacy only stoked something inside him, something that reminded him of Ivy and that day in the cave when she'd knelt beside him, grabbed his shirt, and kissed him with a fervor that had set him on fire as easily as the flames did the mountain forest. He hadn't been able to resist drawing her onto his lap and kissing her until they'd both been breathless from their wanting.

As the same wanting stirred within him again, Jericho closed his eyes and tried to block out Dylan and his women. He'd blocked out his longings so far since his return to Chicago, and he'd kept the needs locked far away. But every once in a while, they escaped—like now—and tormented him with all he was missing.

With the growing darkness of the September evening, he'd planned to simply head home after leaving the main Pinkerton Agency office. But Dylan had sent word that he needed to see him right away. Usually that meant Dylan was in some kind of trouble and required bailing out.

Jericho shoved aside his wayward thoughts, opened his eyes, and surveyed the saloon. The typical crooks lounged around the dozen or so tables, including Black Jack and Dopey-Eye. More shady characters perched on stools along the mahogany counter, where the proprietor was busy pouring liquor.

As a police officer in the second precinct, Dylan claimed that he frequented the saloons in the area to keep abreast of trouble as well as to deter crime. While the strategy had worked to some degree, Dylan also used the opportunity to imbibe much too frequently. And to lust after women.

Even so, Jericho was thankful he hadn't needed to rescue his friend recently from any drunken brawls, hadn't needed to drag him home after he'd passed out, and hadn't needed to wake him up from a hangover to keep him from being fired.

Overall, Dylan seemed to be maturing. At the very least, he wasn't getting himself into trouble every other night. Maybe all the information Jericho had shared about his family had awakened the desire to do better. Except for the night Dylan had brought up the possibility of going back for a visit, and Jericho was left with no choice but to relay Bat's warning. That night Dylan had gone out and drunk himself to oblivion.

From all appearances, Dylan didn't need rescuing tonight. So why the urgent message?

Jericho started forward, winding through the revelers. He garnered a few raised brows since most of them knew he was a Pinkerton agent, especially now that he'd done the near impossible and brought in the infamous Rodney James.

It had taken him four grueling weeks to haul Otis to Chicago. He'd hardly slept in order to keep tabs on Otis day and night. Good thing he had, because one of the Denver lawmen had conspired to release Otis, lured by the promise of being taken to a hideout containing more gold.

When Jericho reached Chicago, he'd made sure Otis was safely locked in a prison cell before he'd dropped into bed and slept for two days straight. Over the few weeks since then, he'd been handling small assignments while waiting for the Department of Justice contract to come through. After that, he'd get his next big mission, rumored to be finding another war criminal hiding in Texas.

The problem was that Jericho's reputation as a bounty hunter had grown. And the next time he set out, he wouldn't be able to conceal his identity quite as well. The other problem was that the idea of traveling to Texas didn't excite him.

If he was completely honest, he'd lost the thrill for his job altogether when he carried Ivy off Windy Peak. In fact, he'd lost the thrill for just about everything when he'd ridden away from Fairplay.

Maybe he'd once been able to push his feelings for Ivy out of reach, even from himself. But not anymore. He couldn't stop thinking about her. She was on his mind every day and night. Rather than time lessening his ache for her, the pain of missing her stabbed him harder with each passing day.

"Bliss." Dylan locked in on Jericho, his roguish smile falling away.

"What's so urgent?" Jericho shouldered a man out of the way as he neared Dylan's table.

Dylan lifted the woman off his lap and then stood. Immediately each of the women latched on to one of his arms, sidling close and pressing up against him, as if he needed reminding of the pleasure they had to offer.

But Dylan wasn't paying them attention anymore. Instead, he narrowed his brows, his green-blue eyes flashing with something dangerous, something that set Jericho on edge. He stopped several feet from his friend, sensing that if he got any closer, Dylan might come at him with both fists flying.

For a few long seconds Dylan glowered and Jericho waited.

"What's wrong?" Jericho finally asked.

"You know."

"No, clearly I don't."

Dylan extricated his arm from one of the women, reached into his pocket, and pulled out a letter. He tossed it onto the table.

Jericho studied the neat, slanted cursive but didn't recognize it. "Who's it from?"

"Flynn." The one word was loaded with enough accusation to fuel a steam engine.

Apparently Flynn had told Dylan about everything that had transpired between Ivy and him over the summer. Now Dylan intended to make him pay for breaking his promise not to get involved with her.

Jericho straightened his shoulders, puffed out his chest, and let his arms hang at his sides. "Go on. Hit me. I deserve it."

Dylan tensed. His nostrils flared. And in the next instant, his fist connected with Jericho's jaw. The blow knocked his head back and sent him off-balance into the table behind him. Glasses clinked, chairs scraped on the floor, and curses filled the air.

As he righted himself, he rubbed his jaw to ease the sting. The music and chatter faded, and silence descended throughout the saloon. All eyes were upon him, including Dylan's. "You broke her heart."

Jericho didn't need to ask Dylan to clarify who he was referring to. He knew as plain as daylight. "I didn't mean for anything to happen—"

"Well, it did, you lowlife rat." Dylan's voice rang out in the stillness. "That's exactly why I made you promise to stay away from her. So you wouldn't hurt her."

"I'm sorry. I won't do it again."

"You're blamed right you ain't gonna do it again!"

Jericho glanced around at the curious faces and wide eyes all peering at the two of them. He cocked his head toward the door. "Can we take this outside?"

"Reckon the only thing I have left to say to you is get back there to Colorado and make her happy."

Jericho's mouth stalled around his response. Dylan was giving him permission to be with Ivy?

"Flynn says she loves you and that she's in a real bad way without you there."

"What?" Jericho's pulse stuttered at the news. What did "real bad" mean? He thought she'd be pleased to have the land, that it would distract her, give her purpose. Hadn't it been enough?

"He wants me to convince you to return and marry her."

"Flynn said that?" Jericho itched to swipe up the letter and devour every word so he could hear more about Ivy. "Flynn hates me and would rather see me die a long and painful death than get anywhere near Ivy."

"I would too." Dylan spat the words and balled his fists again. "But since she cares about you and needs you to be there for her, then we'll have to put up with a scalawag like you." The hard clench of Dylan's jaw told Jericho his friend wouldn't be moved.

The trouble was, Jericho couldn't go back, could he?

He shook his head, but Dylan cut him short with a shove. "Did you sleep with her?"

Heat slapped Jericho in the face. He glanced around again at the crowd hanging on to every word of Dylan's and his conversation. With Dylan's newest question, the place grew so quiet he could hear a coin twirling on a table nearby.

"Aw, man!" Dylan's shoulders slumped and his expression fell for just a second. Then he turned into a raging bear and plowed into Jericho. "I'm gonna kill you."

Jericho slid back but bumped into the table again. "Hold

on!" He held up his hands to ward Dylan off. "I didn't sleep with her. I vow it."

Dylan kept coming. "Your promise means nothin', Bliss. Nothin'!"

"I kissed her a couple of times. That's all."

Dylan grabbed at Jericho's shirt and twisted it hard so the collar began to choke him. He could overpower Dylan if he needed to. But suddenly he didn't want to. He didn't want to do anything. Without Ivy he had no motivation to go on. He hadn't since he'd arrived in Chicago.

As if sensing Jericho's unwillingness to fight, Dylan loosened his grip and whacked one of his shoulders. "Do you love her?"

Jericho wasn't sure whether to tell Dylan the truth. But what difference did it make if Dylan knew?

Dylan shook Jericho. "Tell me! Do you love her?"

"Yes." Jericho could only hang his head, avoiding his friend's eyes and the disappointment sure to be there.

Dylan was quiet for several exhalations. "Then go back and marry her."

Did he dare? Could he really drop everything—his work, his next assignment, his future at Pinkerton—and return to Colorado to be with Ivy? How could he live with himself knowing how much she was hurting on account of him? He wanted more than anything to make her happy.

At the same time, maybe they both just needed more time to get back to their lives the way they were before the summer came and disrupted everything.

As if sensing the direction of Jericho's thoughts, Dylan slapped at his chest. "You're nothin' but a coward, Bliss. A big coward."

Jericho staggered backward. And this time nothing got in his way to halt him.

"Go on. Get out of here!" Dylan waved a hand at him in dismissal. "You messed things up, and now you don't have the guts to go and fix them. You make me sick."

Jericho somehow managed to find the door and push his way out into the night. The chill of autumn hung in the air along with the dampness from Lake Michigan. A crowded horsecar rattled past, leaving the waft of manure in its wake. In spite of the evening hour, the sidewalk and street were congested by pedestrians, and he allowed the swell to carry him along past cheap eating establishments, barrooms, pawn shops, and hotels.

He stumbled the three blocks until he reached his dad's town house. He made it up the front flight of steps and into the dark foyer. As the door closed behind him, he leaned back against it and rested his head, only to find himself staring at his dad's prostrate form sprawled across the settee in the parlor. The light from a lone lantern illuminated the flask on the floor.

His dad being inebriated was nothing new. It happened almost every evening. He started drinking in the morning, and by the time he got home from the office it didn't take long to pass out. At least he'd taken to passing out at home in recent years instead of at a saloon.

With a sigh, Jericho pushed away from the door and crossed to his dad. With his arm draped across his eyes, his mouth hung open and emitted a rattling snore. Jericho was reminded of Nash every time he looked at his dad's face and wished again, as he had over and over, that Nash was still around to try to talk some sense into their dad.

As it was, Jericho could only grab the afghan from the back of the settee and drape it across his dad. Once he finished tucking the blanket, Jericho bent and picked up the flask. If only he could find a place to hide it where his dad wouldn't find it.

The liquid inside sloshed around. There was enough left in the bottle for another long sip. . . .

Jericho lifted it to his nose and sniffed. Scotch whiskey.

His throat and mouth dried up. He tipped the bottle higher. Did he dare take a drink? Maybe finish what was left?

He put his lips onto the rim and tasted the bitter residue. For just tonight he wanted to lose himself in the drink. Seeing Flynn's letter, hearing Dylan's accusations, and learning about Ivy's pain was too much to bear. It only opened the wound he hadn't wanted to acknowledge, a wound that had been tearing him apart inside since the day he'd let her brothers take her away from him on the trip down from Windy Peak.

He was so tired of the ache of missing Ivy, so tired of the heaviness that resided inside him and had since his mom's death, so tired of the endless search for justice.

What if it wasn't possible to ever find peace? What if drowning himself in drink was the best way to get relief? Maybe that's why his dad did it.

The truth was, Jericho hadn't found peace yet any other way. He'd thought by focusing on his work and keeping people at arm's length, he'd eventually gain satisfaction. But leaving Ivy behind hadn't worked, had only made him more discontented.

He started to pour the whiskey into his mouth, but at a loud snore from his dad, Jericho halted. What was he doing?

A furious panic rushed through him. He'd been one sip away from becoming his dad totally and completely, something he'd vowed would never happen.

With a cry of self-disgust, he threw the flask against the brick wall above the fireplace.

The bottle shattered. Glass and whiskey sprayed everywhere.

He sank to his knees and watched the alcohol drip from the mantel onto the tile floor. "Oh, Lord Almighty." His desperate plea echoed in the silence of the lonely town house. He bowed his head and tried to breathe past the bitterness rising in his throat.

What was wrong with him? The drinking hadn't brought his dad relief. Maybe it worked in the short run to make him forget his problems. But it had turned him into a deserted wasteland.

Was that what pushing people away would do too? Bring only emptiness and pain? Jericho had used the excuse that he was leaving Ivy to keep her safe. But maybe all along he'd been trying to keep himself safe.

Dylan was right. He was a coward.

"God. Tell me what to do." The truth was, he couldn't find relief in drinking or in isolating himself from those he loved or even in chasing after elusive happiness like Dylan. Ultimately the only One who could give him freedom from his emptiness was the Almighty.

The verse Judd had read to him in the summer sifted through his mind: *"The steps of a good man are ordered by the* LORD. *. . . Though he fall, he shall not be utterly cast down: for the* LORD *upholdeth him with his hand."*

The verse assumed they would fall. It wasn't a matter of *if* but *when*. And God was promising that *when* Jericho hit his knees—just like he had at that moment—the Almighty's hand would be there to hold him up. All Jericho needed to do was reach out and grasp it.

Could he do it?

His labored breathing filled the silence. His chest tightened. And then before anything could work to stop him, he held out his hand. "I've fallen down, God. I need you to hold me up and walk alongside me."

He waited and prayed, letting God's presence and peace settle around him. Although he might stumble many more times in his life, he wanted to move forward as a good man whose steps were ordered by the Lord. And to do that, he knew exactly where he needed to go.

CHAPTER
28

"How much longer do I need to wear this blasted thing?" Ivy tugged at the neckerchief covering her eyes.

Judd guided her toward the door of the cabin they'd built last month. "Quit your bellyachin', or you're gonna ruin the surprise."

"I've got too much work to do today for surprises." Even as the words left her mouth, she couldn't contain her smile.

So much had happened over the past two months since she and Judd had moved out to her ranch. They'd lived in tents during September and part of October while they'd labored on the cabin, outhouse, and smokehouse. For the last couple of weeks, they'd been busy getting the interior of the cabin fixed up, installing a stove, and furnishing it by using the stash of money she'd saved up.

They didn't have fresh produce of their own, but Greta had been more than willing to share the bounty from her garden since Judd was the one who'd done most of the hard work on it. Ivy had spent long hours preserving vegetables with Greta, while Judd had done some hunting and had started smoking meat for the winter.

Now the shelves Judd had constructed were full to the brim with canned goods. Even though Ivy knew she could always call on her brothers over the winter if she ever got in a bind, it felt real good to have everything stored up.

She'd had just enough money left to make her first sheep purchase from Utah, and the seller had promised to deliver them before winter set in. With the end of October drawing near, snow had already started to fall in the higher elevations. They didn't have too many more days left before additional snow would make the mountain passes difficult for traveling—if not impossible.

Even if she didn't get her sheep before winter, she was still mighty happy with all she'd accomplished.

As Judd opened the door and the cold air swirled through her skirt and sent a chill over her bare feet, she was guessing somehow the sheep had come in and Judd had kept them over at Flynn's or Brody's and was hoping to surprise her with them.

Her heart swelled with affection for this man who'd become a father and mentor over the past weeks. He was crusty on the outside, but deep down he was the softest man she'd ever known.

"Come on now," he said testily. "Quit dragging your feet, or you'll force me to get the cattle prod back out."

Her smile only widened at the thought of the summer day when he'd climbed up to her room and prodded her out of bed. He hadn't coddled her like everyone else. He'd been downright rough. But it had worked. He'd woken her up to her need to stop trying to build her life on a crumbling foundation and instead to find her acceptance in God's unfailing love, in the One who would never leave or forsake her.

She still missed Jericho something fierce. And at times her heart and arms ached for baby Willa. She'd always miss them, especially Jericho. But she was learning to take her aches to the Lord instead of trying to bear them all herself.

As she stepped outside, the cool dew on the grass settled between her toes. "What is it?" she pestered Judd again. "You gonna make me wear this thing all day?"

He harrumphed and led her a dozen paces away from the cabin. The morning sun bathed her skin with warmth even if the air was chilly.

She breathed in deeply, relishing the scent of the juniper and spruce that bordered the cabin. She was finally home. Not just because she had a place of her own, but because the restlessness she'd felt for so many years was drifting out of her life. A new peace had come in to take its place. Even her resentment toward her ma didn't seem quite as important anymore. Or maybe now that she'd experienced such deep heartache at losing Jericho, she could sympathize better with the losses her ma had faced.

"Alright." Judd brought her to a stop. "Now hold still."

She remained motionless as he tugged the knot in the neckerchief free at the back of her head. When the cloth fell down, she blinked against the brightness of the sunshine. As she took in the sight that met her, she gasped.

There in the middle of the clearing stood what appeared to be half the town of Fairplay—men, women, even children. "Surprise!" came a chorus of happy shouts.

"Holy Saint Peter!" Where had they all come from? And when had they arrived? No wonder Judd had kept her busy inside the cabin for the past hour, helping him dry and sort seeds for next year's planting.

Judd was grinning like a little tike who'd just roped his first livestock. "They're here for a barn raisin'."

"Barn raisin'? You said we'd have to make do with a lean-to for the winter."

"That ain't what your brothers said." He nodded to the forefront of the crowd where Flynn and Wyatt and Brody stood, hammers and saws in hand, watching her expectantly. "They insisted we needed a barn before winter, and they organized this whole thing."

Behind them sat half a dozen wagons overflowing with mill-cut lumber.

She couldn't pay for the supplies. Not yet. But someday, when she started not only shearing her sheep but breeding and selling her lambs, she'd pay them back.

"It's a gift," Flynn said, as if reading her mind.

"I appreciate the offer. But I gotta pay you back. Hope you can understand."

He hesitated, then nodded. "Reckon I'd do the same." He held her gaze for a second, and in that statement she knew he was offering her more than just a barn. He was offering her respect as an equal.

Though they hadn't spoken much since she'd left with Judd to live on her own land, she'd sensed a slow change in her relationship with her brothers, that they were learning to let go of her.

"Thank you, Flynn."

"Once we get the barn done later today, the womenfolk brought the fixings for a meal."

The barn raisings she'd been to while growing up had always ended with eating and dancing. With so few socials, they had to make the most of every minute.

Flynn jerked his head toward a couple of steers someone had brought along. "Also figured while we're all together, we oughta have a cowhand competition."

"Won't object to that." She hadn't participated in any more since Independence Day. While a part of her missed the thrill, she'd been too busy to think on it much.

"Good." Flynn glanced at Wyatt and Brody, who both nodded as though to encourage him. He sighed and then plunged ahead. "Reckon, then, that you won't object to joining in the competition. This time as yourself."

Her pulse trickled to a halt. Had she just heard Flynn correctly? Was he giving her permission to join in the competition?

As if seeing the confusion in her expression, Wyatt stepped in. "Yep. We discussed the issue with the organizers. And they agreed. If a woman's good enough, then she oughta be given a fair chance, same as the fellas."

"Well, howdy-doody." She stared from Wyatt to Brody to Flynn and back. Clearly her brothers had worked some kind of magic with Mack Custer and the other competition organizers to get them to agree on women participating. Maybe now that they'd already watched her compete as Buster Bliss and knew she was skilled, they were more willing. Whatever the case, she couldn't believe her brothers were not only supporting her competing, but were making sure she wouldn't be shut out.

"You gonna stand there all day catchin' flies?" Judd's question was laced with mirth. "Or are we gonna build a barn?"

Only then did she realize her mouth was hanging open. She snapped it closed. What could she say to her brothers?

She wanted at the very least to thank them, but her throat clogged with a sudden swell of emotion.

Brody and Wyatt had already turned to the wagon beds and were starting to unload the lumber alongside the other men and boys. But for a second longer, Flynn watched her. His eyes spoke what his words didn't—that he was sorry for everything that had happened over the summer with Jericho and hoped she'd forgive him.

Her heart welled with love for this man who'd taken care of her and raised her through the years. He'd loved her the best he'd known how. He hadn't been perfect. Nobody was. But he'd stuck with her through thick and thin, and she was grateful for that.

She nodded at him, hoping her eyes conveyed her forgiveness. It wasn't the first time and wouldn't be the last time they'd have issues. But they were a family. And that meant they'd keep on forgiving and loving and sticking it out for the long haul.

Flynn nodded back. Then he glanced around among the groups now organizing into teams. He seemed to be searching for someone. But apparently not finding who he was looking for, his shoulders slumped, and he limped off to join the others.

She watched the buzz of activity a moment longer, joy swirling inside. "C'mon." She slipped her arm into the crook of Judd's. "Let's go build us a barn."

◦◦◦

Ivy leaned against the new zigzag rail fence that jutted out from the completed barn. The sky overhead was lavender with the coming of night. A few lanterns had already been lit, chasing away the lengthening shadows. And the scent of roasted pig lingered in the air.

After a day of grueling work, they'd raised the frame, sided the building, and completed the roof. The interior was an empty shell, but the hard work was done. Ivy could only stare at it in utter amazement.

The structure rose two stories to a gabled roof, allowing for a loft. Doors on both ends would provide cross ventilation and keep moisture under control. A row of empty window squares on both sides of the ground floor would give plenty of natural light. She and Judd would likely put shutters on since they wouldn't be able to afford any glass panes this year. And they'd have to paint the wood to protect it from the harsh winter elements.

Everyone had feasted not only on pig but roasted chicken, recently harvested corn and beans and squash, freshly baked rolls, honey-sweetened applesauce, and more.

Now the cowhand competition was underway. With the shorter autumn days, they could only get in three events. They'd started with the bronc riding and steer wrestling, and they were finishing up with the roping contest. She'd already gone, and so far none of the other fellas had beat her time. But not for lack of trying. Even Brody had given it a shot and hadn't come close.

For her, the winning came as easy as a horsefly riding a mule's ear. Even if she wanted to bust out a smile that would let everyone know just how happy she was about coming out on top for her first contest as herself, she'd kept her smile locked away. She might not be pretending to be Buster Bliss anymore, but that didn't mean she had to get carried away.

As the final contestant stood from where he'd roped the

steer, she waited for the time announcement. At the shout of seven seconds, she let her shoulders relax. She'd done it. Fair and square.

"Looks like you won, Aunt Ivy." Sitting on the rail next to her, Wyatt's oldest son, Ty, swung his legs. Astrid had already headed home with Wyatt's two youngest children. She and Astrid weren't sore at each other anymore, and Astrid was no longer pining after Jericho, thank goodness. She'd finally started paying attention to other young men. But their friendship had changed. They had changed. And maybe that was okay too.

Ty twisted a long piece of grass in his mouth. "Reckon ain't nobody ever gonna beat you. Leastways until I grow up and do it."

"Maybe you will. But you're gonna have to be real good if you have any hope of winnin' against me." She took in the view with a deep sense of contentment. They'd built at the bottom of a hill, the forest behind the cabin with the barn positioned in the clearing to the southeast in a level area so that when the north wind blew, it'd take the barn stench away from the cabin and not to it.

The rolling hills to the east sloped to the plains that dominated South Park. But her land to the west, though grassy, was more rugged and suited for sheep.

"And that's it folks!" Mack Custer strode out into the middle of the paddock, his pocket bulging from the coins he'd managed to collect. "Sorry we can't keep goin'—"

"Hold up! We've got one more contestant!" Flynn shouted excitedly as he shouldered through the bystanders. When he reached the rail, he glanced in the direction he'd come, as though waiting for someone to follow him.

"Who is it?" Mack lifted on his toes to see behind Flynn.

Before Flynn could answer, a man with a strong, lean frame stepped up to the fence, a man with a determined, proud bearing in his shoulders and an assured way of holding himself.

Ivy's stomach bottomed out. Jericho.

As if she'd spoken his name aloud, his attention darted to her. His face was covered in a scruffy layer of stubble, a sign he hadn't shaved in days. His garments were dusty, as if he'd ridden hard and hadn't changed. And the light brown hair showing beneath the brim of his hat was curled up and overlong.

But he'd never looked better or more handsome.

"Well, I'll be. It's Jericho Bliss himself." Mack Custer's scowl disappeared, replaced by a gleam that said he was busy tallying how much more money he could make by letting Jericho compete.

As the level of enthusiasm in the crowd escalated, Jericho climbed the fence and hopped down into the main area. He did so with such ease, Ivy's heart sped with an undeniable attraction, one that hadn't lessened with time. His strong jaw, the determined set of his lips, and the proud jut of his chin still made him one of God's finest specimens of manhood.

Ivy gave herself a mental shake and focused on the steer. Nope. No how. No way. She wasn't gonna give Jericho the satisfaction of even looking at him.

What was he doing back in South Park anyway? Did he have another outlaw he was hunting down? Someone else like Otis pretending to be an ordinary citizen? Even as the questions pushed forward like a bloodhound hot on a trail, she shoved away the thoughts. She didn't want to think about

Jericho Bliss again, didn't want to care, didn't even want to watch him compete.

But she couldn't just walk away, could she? She had to stay at the fence and at least pretend to observe.

She tried for a nonchalant pose and expression, sitting on the railing as casually as possible, even though her insides had knotted as tight as a stake rope. She kept up a steady stream of conversation with Ty, mighty glad for the kid's presence at her side and his ability to jabber on about everything and nothing at the same time.

When the steer was unleashed, Jericho was on its trail in the better half of a second, had his rope looped around its horns, and was dragging it down to the ground before she could take a full breath. In the next instant, he dismounted and landed so near the creature, he was grabbing the steer's front legs and tying the hooey knot all in one motion. As he jumped to his feet and raised his arms, the crowd went wild with cheering.

Nobody needed to hear the official time to know Jericho Bliss had won the contest. He was amazing. Although she didn't want to think about Jericho or admire him, she gave herself permission to appreciate his skills for just a few seconds. He deserved the accolades.

But even as she watched him tip his hat to the crowd, somehow his beautiful eyes found her. His gaze locked in on her, a gaze filled with such longing, it sent her heart tumbling in an avalanche to the bottom of her chest. The pain of the hard landing jarred the breath from her lungs, and she ripped her sights from him.

A sudden urgency jabbed at her. She had to get away. She couldn't be around him and act like she didn't care. Because the fact was, she still cared. Way too much. Just the sight of him was unleashing things she didn't want to feel, things she'd thought she'd been able to put behind her . . . all the hurt, disappointment, and heartache.

Now that the emotions were welling up, she'd never be able to hide her feelings. He'd come over, talk with her, give her one of his crooked grins, and she'd be helplessly in love with him all over again, unable to stop herself from throwing herself at him just like she had every other time.

She couldn't do it. She couldn't humiliate herself again. She had to get away.

With a frantic glance around, she hopped down and started weaving through the crowd, putting as much distance as she could between herself and the corral. Once out of the thick of onlookers, she picked up her pace and raced toward the cabin. As much as she wanted to go inside, slam the door, and bar it shut, it was one of the first places people would come searching for her once they realized she'd run off.

Yep. She was being a big coward. But she aimed to hide until Jericho left for the night. In fact, if she had to, she'd hide from him until he left South Park, which hopefully would be real soon.

CHAPTER
29

Jericho pushed past the people slapping his back and congratulating him. His heart thudded hard with the need to find Ivy. She'd been there on the fence watching the competition. And then in the next instant she'd disappeared.

Had she run off to get away from him? If so, he wouldn't blame her. He didn't deserve to see her again, didn't deserve to be anywhere near her. But even if the sun and moon conspired against him, he had to talk to her at least one more time.

He made his way to the middle of the yard filled with teams, wagons, and young children running around playing. He caught sight of Flora, Linnea and Flynn's redheaded little girl, and almost grabbed her to ask if she'd seen Ivy. But at the flash of something in the woods behind the cabin, he stopped.

Ivy *was* hiding.

His chest pinched painfully. He'd made a mistake in coming back. He shouldn't have done it.

After putting his affairs in order in Chicago, he'd tele-grammed Flynn with his plans to head to Denver. A return telegram from Flynn had been waiting for him when he'd arrived after daybreak this morning at the Pinkerton office in Denver. It had informed him of the date of the surprise barn raising and asked him to be there. At first Jericho hadn't planned to come, hadn't felt worthy to be there on the special day. But when the morning had ticked away, an urgency had seized him and hadn't let go until finally he'd headed on out.

Didn't matter that Flynn had seen him riding up to Ivy's place and was the first to approach him when he dismounted. Didn't matter that Flynn stretched out his hand to greet him warmly—and that neither his gun nor his fist made an ap-pearance. Didn't matter that Flynn invited him to participate in the roping contest.

All that mattered was what Ivy thought. And clearly she had no desire to see him.

He closed his eyes to fight against the despair that had ridden with him the past weeks as he'd journeyed back to Colorado. He'd guessed this was how things would go, had tried to prepare himself. But he'd been hoping Ivy would at least give him a chance to explain himself and plead with her.

And he'd rehearsed what he had to say at least a hundred times.

Drawing in a fortifying breath, he opened his eyes and scanned the area. He couldn't give up. He'd have to figure out a way to talk to her without allowing her another op-portunity to run off.

He grabbed the coil of rope on his saddle. Using a stealthy and silent tread he'd perfected over the years, he circled round the cabin and climbed beyond the spot where he'd glimpsed her. Then he sidled in, keeping low and concealing himself as best he could behind the smattering of pines.

With the deepening of the evening, the forest was shadowed, but he had no trouble finding her. She'd hunkered down behind a boulder and leaned back, her legs stretched out in front of her. Her split skirt fell away revealing the trousers underneath that clung to her endlessly long legs.

She rested her head against the boulder, her hat on her lap. She'd let her hair down, likely when she swiped off her hat. And now the long dark waves tumbled over her shoulders in a glorious thick curtain, framing her beautiful face, highlighting the darkness of her eyes and lashes.

At the crack of a stick somewhere in the forest, she stiffened and glanced over her shoulder, peeking around her hiding place, clearly expecting him to approach from the front.

Little did she know that, from his perch in the hill above her, he had full view and access to her. Crouching, he began to unwind the rope. As he formed a knot and widened the loop, he slowly rose. "Told you I'd beat you in no time."

At his bold statement, she sat forward and homed in on him, her eyes widening in surprise.

"Your roping skills are good but still no match against mine." He fingered the rope, tucking it out of sight behind his thigh.

She watched him a few seconds, as though she might actually be glad to see him. Then her brows bent into a scowl. "Go away, Jericho. I don't wanna talk to you."

"I realize you probably don't want to speak to me ever again, but I've traveled over a thousand miles to tell you—"

"Don't say it." She hopped up, as quick and nimble as always, and started walking away. "I ain't listening."

"Please, Ivy. Give me a chance—"

"Your chance already came and went."

She was right. She'd already given him more than his fair share of opportunities to have her. But he had to try again, had to let her know he was done running. He lifted his rope and acted on instinct. He wound it in a sharp circle, twirling it in the air. Then, before she could get too far away, he flicked his wrist and let the rope fly.

He'd left the loop wide enough that it fell over her head and shoulders. By the time she realized what was happening, the rope was already skimming her torso. With a cry of surprise, she spun back around. But he'd already yanked at the slip knot, cinching it tight, pinning her arms to her side.

"Jericho Bliss! Let me go before I string you up and give you the whupping you deserve."

"When I'm done talking, I promise you can string me up . . . if you still want to."

She wrenched against the rope worse than a belligerent calf. "I will."

"I'll even lend you the rope when I'm done with it." He tugged the loop tighter, not enough to hurt her, but enough to keep her from getting loose.

"Fine." She struggled anyway, her eyes flashing with anger and hurt and frustration.

Her attention dropped to his neck, then skimmed the length of him. For a second she seemed to be admiring his body. And the very thought spilled heat low in his gut.

When her gaze lifted to his, the desire in her eyes sparked the air. She ducked her head, as if she didn't want him to see her reaction. But it was too late. Her spark ignited his hope.

He started toward her, coiling the rope as he made his

way down the hill, keeping his hold on her taut and secure. When he was only a few feet away, he stopped. "I've had plenty of time to think on us, and I've made my decision." Would she remember the conversation they'd had about their relationship that day they'd been trapped in the cave during the fire? The one when she'd asked him to think about their future together?

"It's too late, Jericho."

"You told me that in the end, you'd accept my final choice."

"That was before you left." She wiggled against the rope.

"I love you, and I want to spend forever with you."

She froze.

"That's my answer. It always has been. I was just too scared to admit it."

She didn't seem to be breathing.

"I was a fool for leaving you the way I did the first time two years ago. And I was an even bigger fool for leaving you this past summer. If you'll forgive me and let me prove how much I love you, I promise I'll never leave again."

There, he'd said it. The words he'd been rehearsing for weeks. They wouldn't be enough to fix everything he'd broken between them, but he hoped it would be a start.

"What happens next time you get scared?" Her voice radiated with pain—pain he'd put there.

He loathed that he'd caused her so much distress, and he had to make it up to her.

"I can't keep on lettin' you break my heart."

"I can't promise I won't hurt you again." He'd still have struggles. They both would. "But when I do hurt you, I promise to make things right just as soon as I can."

She watched him warily.

"There's one other thing I can promise." Still holding the rope tight, he lowered himself onto one knee. With his free hand, he dug in his trouser pocket. His fingers closed around the delicate object that had once belonged to his mother. When he pulled it out, he held it up between them. "I can promise to love and cherish you until my dying breath."

She dropped her gaze to his outstretched hand and then gasped.

"Will you marry me, Ivy?"

CHAPTER
30

Ivy stared at the beautiful ring. The diamonds encrusted into the gold band sparkled in the dusk.

Was Jericho really down on one knee proposing to her, or was she dreaming?

She pinched her arm. At the pain, she flinched.

One of his brows cocked.

"Just checking to see if I'm awake."

"This is me being about as real as I've ever been." His blue eyes remained full of expectation and love and honesty. He wasn't promising things would always be easy. It hadn't been yet. But he was promising to love her forever. And really, that's all she needed.

"Prove it." She tugged on the rope.

"Prove what?"

"That I ain't dreaming."

He stood, still holding out the ring. She couldn't believe he'd not only told her he wouldn't ever leave her again but was asking her to marry him.

Slowly she finished coiling the rope, drawing him nearer inch by inch. She didn't stop until his chest brushed up against hers. Then she lifted her face. Her arms were still tied down, preventing her from pulling him into a kiss. Which was a good thing. Because she'd told him she wouldn't kiss him again until he asked for it. And she aimed to keep her word.

He leaned closer so his breath brushed against her cheek. In the next instant, his lips grazed her ear. "This isn't a dream, Ivy. I want to marry you more than anything."

She brushed her cheek against his scruffy one, relishing the coarseness against her skin. Then she rose on her toes and let her lips caress his ear in return. "I said you have to prove it."

As she returned to her heels and leaned back, she waited breathlessly.

His gaze dropped to her mouth, just as she hoped it would. Then his lips curved up into a lazy smile. "You sure know how to drive a hard bargain."

"Yep. Reckon I do."

He snaked an arm around her. "Kiss me."

Every nerve tingled with sweet delight. "You ordering or asking?"

"Both."

"I'll do it, but only if you promise to let me kiss you whenever I want from now on."

"Only if you promise the same to me—"

She pressed into him, silencing him with a kiss that contained all the love she'd ever felt for him—which was nearly a lifetime of it.

His palm flattened against her lower back as if he'd never be sated until he had all of her. She sure as heaven knew she'd never be satisfied until she had all of him.

He started to deepen the kiss, but before he could, she broke away. He chased after her lips, but she turned her head and leaned into the crook of his neck. "Yes."

"Yes?" His question was laden with longing.

"Yes, I'll marry you."

He was silent for a heartbeat. Then his arms tightened around her. "Does that mean what I think it does?" He bent in and nuzzled her neck.

She closed her eyes, her body singing, her heart racing. "I'll go anywhere and do anything so I can be with you, Jericho. Even if that means I have to travel to the ends of the earth."

He paused then and broke away, holding her at arm's length, his eyes turning suddenly serious.

Her heartbeat stuttered. Were they gonna have this conversation already? Him telling her she couldn't live in Chicago because she wouldn't be safe? She jutted her chin. "I'm going with you this time. Ain't no way you're leaving me behind."

"I'm not going anywhere, and I'm not leaving you behind."

Her defenses rapidly crumbled. "You're not?"

"I'm staying here. Pinkerton needs another agent in Colorado to do ongoing detective work. And they want someone to help protect the transport of money and gold between the mining towns and Denver."

"Really and truly?"

"Really and truly."

"Speaking of gold." He lifted a hand into her hair, plunging it in as though he'd been waiting a long while to do it. "Finally got confirmation that the gold we found in the cave on Windy Peak had been stolen by the Kingston Gang from the Old Boston Mine up by Leadville."

"I'm getting along just fine without gold—thanks to you."

"Think you could handle taking a reward?" He dug his fingers into her hair deeper. "The mine owner's offering us a hefty sum for returning the gold."

She could certainly use it to get more sheep, add fencing, buy a wagon, and Lord knew what else. But there was only one thing she wanted—the thing that mattered most. "The reward's ours to split evenly. I know exactly what I'd like to use my half for."

As she told him, Jericho's gaze softened, and he nodded. "That's a fine idea. We'll use the whole reward for that if we have to."

She couldn't contain her smile. It felt like it would bust her right open. Jericho's grin slid up too, making him so fine looking that she wanted to throw her arms around him and kiss him senseless.

As she tried to lift her arms, his lasso stopped her. "You ever gonna let me loose?" She glanced pointedly at the rope.

"Only after you let me put my ring on your finger." He glanced pointedly at the ring he still held in his hand.

"So you're planning to keep me tied up until our wedding day?"

"I'm planning to use this rope to drag you to the preacher tonight."

Her heartbeat turned over itself in a wild tumble. "Tonight?"

He tugged at the rope, and she toppled against him—right where she wanted to be. "You got a problem with me marrying you tonight?" His voice rumbled low and did crazy things to her insides.

"Reckon I can oblige you."

"Good, because I've waited long enough to be with you. And I don't want to have to leave you again, not for one second more than I have to."

Holy Saint Peter, this man could talk sweet. And she was eating it up, every single word. As he dropped his mouth against hers, he captured her with hunger that told her he'd never get enough, not tonight, not next week, not next year, maybe not ever. But that he sure wanted a lifetime to try.

Good thing she did too.

⁂

"I pronounce that they be man and wife together, in the name of the Father, and of the Son, and of the Holy Ghost. Amen." Father Zieber's declaration rose into the night air.

"Amen," Jericho whispered. As Ivy peered up at him, joy swelled within his chest. She was his wife. He couldn't have asked for a better ending to his journey than to not only win back her affection but to end up married to her.

Dylan's words from the saloon that last night together had haunted him—that he needed to go back, marry Ivy, and see to her happiness, otherwise he'd be making the biggest mistake of his life. Silently Jericho lifted a prayer of thanksgiving that God had gotten through to him, shaken him up, and started him down a different path. If only Dylan would start walking the straight and narrow too.

Father Zieber closed his prayer book and beamed at them. Several lanterns hung around the outside of Ivy's little cabin shedding light on their ceremony. Most of the crowd from the barn raising was still present and had gathered around when Jericho had called out to announce the wedding.

"Young man"—Father Zieber clasped his shoulder—"you may kiss your bride."

Jericho was already reaching much too eagerly for Ivy. He drew her into his arms, and fused his mouth to hers in a kiss that contained all the months of wanting that had led him back to her. Part of him still couldn't believe he was here, with her, and that she'd forgiven him and taken him back so willingly. He was struck again as before by how he didn't deserve her, but he wanted to make a lifetime of trying to be worthy.

Cheers and whistles filled the mountain air around them.

Ivy pulled back first. Her cheeks were flushed, and her eyes sparkled. She'd never looked more beautiful than she did at that moment. He wanted to envelop her in his arms for another kiss, but he forced himself to release her.

"What is it with you McQuaids and hasty weddings?" The middle-aged minister quirked a brow at Ivy's brothers, who were standing nearby with their wives and children.

Wyatt grinned and wrapped his arm around Greta and pressed a kiss to her cheek. "Reckon when we McQuaids see a good thing and know what we want, we don't waste any time in going after it."

Flynn tugged Linnea closer into the crook of his arm. "Reckon when we realize God's given us a partner who can make us into a better person, we aim to make the most of the time."

Brody eyed Savannah with a hungry look. The man didn't have to speak for everyone to know what he was thinking. As Wyatt punched his arm, Brody managed a half grin amidst the teasing and laughter that wafted around them.

Ivy slipped her hand into Jericho's and laced her fingers

through his. The simplest touch set him on fire just as it always had. And he was relieved he didn't have to hold himself back any longer, that she was his in the sight of God and man.

"This wedding might seem hasty," Jericho said. "But let me tell you, it's been a long time coming."

"Amen to that." Judd's words drew laughter. "Guess it's a good thing we got the barn built, 'cause I know where I'll be sleepin' tonight."

As more laughter and chatter filled the air, Jericho peered down at Ivy's upturned face, her beauty taking his breath away.

"I love you," she whispered, her eyes radiating it.

She hadn't yet spoken those words to him, and it hadn't mattered. But now with her declaration out there, he had all he needed to make his life complete—the love of the good Lord and the love of a good woman.

He bent down and brushed his lips against hers. "I love you too, Mrs. Bliss. Now and forever."

CHAPTER
31

DYLAN MCQUAID
CHICAGO, ILLINOIS
JUNE 1870

Dylan McQuaid rubbed a hand across his eyes and then blinked them open to daylight and a cracked ceiling overhead. At the throbbing in his temples, he let out a low moan, which could hardly escape past the dryness of his mouth. He was hungover.

At a caress across his chest, he sat up abruptly, finding himself in a strange bed with a strange woman.

"You're awake, finally." The woman ran her fingers up his bare back.

"Where am I?" He glanced around the tiny room with a dingy set of drawers with chipped blue paint, a scuffed wooden chair where he'd tossed his clothes, a lone window without any curtains, and a rusty metal bedframe.

"Remember, we're at my sister's place." The woman

wrapped both hands around his bicep and tugged at him, trying to draw him back down to the mattress beside her. "When I told her we were engaged, she said we could stay."

Engaged? What in the blazes had he said to this woman last night? No doubt he'd gone and made her promises about marriage and love and a future together. And no doubt she'd gone and believed every blasted word he'd uttered.

Shucks.

Dylan shoved off the covers and stood. In the same motion, he swiped up his clothes and began to don them, heedless of the fact that the woman on the bed behind him was watching him.

"Where you going?" Her voice contained a note of worry.

He hopped into one pant leg, then the other, trying to get the wheels inside his brain rolling, even if sluggishly. That slow motion was all it took for shame to well up and nearly strangle him. He'd done it again. After he'd promised himself he wouldn't, he'd somehow ended up with another woman. "I've got to get to work this mornin', darlin'."

"It's Sunday, the Lord's Day."

As he slid a suspender over his shoulder, he paused. The Lord's Day? He released a scoffing breath. The Lord wouldn't want anything to do with the sorry likes of him. Not after the complete mess he'd made of his life.

"Stay with me for a little while, Dylan." The woman's beckon was low and sultry.

He slapped his other suspender up. She knew his name, but he didn't remember hers. In fact, he didn't remember much of anything about the previous evening, and now all he wanted to do was hightail it out of wherever he was and try to forget about the night and this woman.

That made him the worst kind of lowlife scum. He wouldn't deny it. And he wouldn't deny how much he loathed himself either.

"Wish Chicago criminals took Sundays off." He snatched up his gun belt. "But seems they have a hankerin' for getting into trouble every day of the week. Course now, somebody's got to go out—even on the Lord's Day—and make sure pretty ladies like yourself are kept safe."

"That's true."

At the resignation in her tone, he released a notch of tension in his back. He hated when the parting with a woman got ugly. It was one of the reasons why he'd tried to do better since Bliss left last autumn and went back to Colorado with the intention of marrying Ivy.

Dylan could admit he wasn't real happy Bliss had betrayed his word not to view Ivy as anything but a sister. He didn't care that he'd forced the promise from Bliss when they'd both been tenderfoots. He didn't care that Bliss had obliged him for years even though he'd been sweet on Ivy since the day he met her. He didn't care that Bliss was a grown man and Ivy a grown woman and the two were perfectly capable of making up their own minds. Dylan didn't like the union one bit.

While he tried to tell himself it was because Bliss had shared affections with Ivy, Dylan knew he wasn't fooling anybody, not even himself. The simple fact was, Dylan hadn't wanted his friend to leave him behind. Stuck in Chicago. Stuck in a life he'd never planned. Stuck in the downward spiral of destruction and deprivation.

"Can I see you after you're done with work tonight?" the woman asked, her tone hopeful.

Dylan buckled on his revolvers, refusing to turn and see

the expectation sure to be radiating from her eyes. Had he been out with her before? Or had last night been the first time? And where in the blazes had he met this woman?

Yep. He was a lowlife piece of scum twice over.

"You could come by the store again."

The store. His mind began to clear, and memories sauntered back. This was Katherine, the young woman from Olson's Grocery Store. Mostly so far he'd indulged in harmless flirting and stolen kisses. How had the sorry likes of him gotten carried away with a good girl like her when he barely knew her?

Katherine. But her sister had called her Kit.

"I've told Papa all about you," Kit said. "He wants to meet you. Now that we're engaged, I can introduce you to him and Mama and the rest of the family."

Distant shouting filtered from somewhere in the building along with the echo of pedestrians already about on the summer morning. He glanced out the window, noting familiar businesses and signs. Kit's tenement—or her sister's—wasn't far from the boardinghouse he'd lived in since he'd moved out of Bliss's dad's home. And it wasn't far from the police station where he worked.

He buttoned up his shirt, his fingers moving faster. He needed to get out of the tenement before Kit wrangled another promise from him. Even though he had the day off, he'd head over to the station like he did most days.

As he shoved his arms into his oversized sack coat, she chattered about how her family wanted to meet him, how she'd told them about him, and how they already liked him.

He had to say something, tell her that if he'd proposed—which apparently he had—he'd been drunk and hadn't meant a word. But how could he let her down? Especially when she was so excited?

He'd have to figure out a way to tell her later. . . .

"Tonight, then?" she asked. "You'll come have dinner with my family and me tonight?"

"Maybe. I'll see how work goes today." He stuck his feet into his boots, not bothering to tie them before starting toward the door.

"Please, Dylan?" The thread of almost panic in her question stilled his hand on the doorknob.

He braced his shoulders. "I'll try."

"Thank you."

There was a slight chance he'd go. *Very* slight. Which meant he wasn't entirely lying to her, was he?

"And Dylan? Please don't say anything to Papa or Mama or anyone else about—well, about us staying the night together. Papa will disown me if he finds out."

"Don't worry, darlin'." He made himself glance back at her with a wink and a smile, even as he hated himself for acting so cavalier. "No one will ever have to know about it."

Sitting in the middle of the sagging mattress, a sheet draped around her, with her long, dark hair cascading down her bare shoulders, she was a beautiful young woman. He was reminded of why he'd been attracted to her.

But no how, no way was he getting married to her. Not now. And not anytime soon. He wasn't dragging a wife into the mess he'd made of his life.

As he left her and the tenement behind and started toward the police headquarters, he rubbed at the familiar ache in his head. All he really wanted to do was sleep for a few more hours. But he hated being alone in his little apartment and avoided going there whenever possible. He reckoned that's part of why he seemed to find himself in trouble with women.

If only he could have left Chicago with Bliss . . .

He blew out a breath filled with frustration. For a Sunday morning, the streets were quiet, the usual hubbub reduced to a few homeless youth out peddling papers and a group of transient workers who slept on the sidewalks conversing over coffee.

From the church one block over, he could hear the piano strains of a hymn. Most good folk were attending a Sunday morning service . . . no doubt his brothers and their wives were all sitting in pews, maybe even singing the same hymn.

He passed by the closed storefronts, the usual vendors and peddlers absent. The advertisements, however, were always present, covering the wooden buildings with promises of products that could produce a brighter future. From what he'd learned, a brighter future wasn't that easy to come by.

His steps slowed as he reached a brick building with the words *Police Station* painted in black on the sign that hung beneath the arched second-story windows. He wasn't wearing his uniform, but since he wasn't officially on duty, it wouldn't matter too much.

He was getting close to completing his list for the superintendent. A little more sniffing around, and he'd figure out the last few officers involved in taking bribes from Rocky Roger Kenna, an alderman in the First Ward who owned numerous saloons and brothels and who regularly paid police officers to turn a blind eye toward his crimes.

Dylan clomped up the few stone steps. Of course with his own drinking and womanizing, no one suspected he was collaborating with the general superintendent of police to put an end to the corruption within the police department. That's why the superintendent had picked him. Because he blended in with the riffraff easily enough. He wasn't proud of that fact, but at least he was using his downfall for some good.

Straightening his back, Dylan yanked open the door. He might have sunk low, but there was a line he wouldn't cross. He had to hang on to a measure of his integrity, or he wouldn't be able to live with himself—a feat that was already hard enough.

As he entered the building, a waft of pastrami and rye met him. Constable Tipton, sitting behind his desk, paused with an overflowing sandwich in his mouth. He nodded at Dylan and hurried to finish his bite, his eyes rounding as though he wanted to speak.

With his head still throbbing, Dylan wasn't in the mood for small talk and tipped his hat at the constable before he bypassed him, weaving through the maze of desks and chairs and cabinets. Without any lanterns lit, the place was dismal, the only light filtering through the front window.

"Hold on, McQuaid." Tipton's muffled call came around the mouthful of sandwich.

"Don't mind me." Dylan waved off the man.

"Got a letter for you."

Dylan paused and glanced back at the constable. In his custodian helmet and tight navy-blue tunic with gleaming buttons, Tipton represented all that was good and worthy within the police department, one of the few untouched by the tendrils of vice woven all throughout the fabric of Chicago police and politics.

Tipton swallowed the pastrami and wiped the back of his hand across his mouth. "From Bliss."

Dylan's insides lurched. A letter from Bliss? Dylan hadn't heard from his friend once over the past months. Yep, the mail was slow, especially when winter isolated the high country of the Rockies from the rest of the world. But Bliss could've written to him before now, instead of abandoning him so thoroughly.

"Bliss's old man delivered the letter himself." Tipton held out an envelope. "Said it was sitting around his house for months."

"Months?" Dylan started back through the maze of desks toward Tipton. "And he's just now bothering to let me know?" Dylan tamped down his rising irritation. Elijah Bliss was a drunk and had been for years. Getting angry at the man wouldn't do any good. In fact, Dylan was mighty lucky Mr. Bliss had the wherewithal to bring it to the police station at all, much less late.

As Dylan took it, his heart gave an extra beat at the sight of his friend's handwriting. The envelope was open—no doubt Mr. Bliss had read the letter from his son. Tipton poked at the pastrami before he took a big bite, avoiding Dylan's gaze. No doubt Tipton had read the contents too.

Dylan made it to his desk, flipped open the flap, retrieved the sheet within, and unfolded it to reveal more of Jericho's handwriting. Dylan had no right to pray or hope Bliss wasn't giving him bad news, but what other reason did family have for writing except to tell of deaths?

He scanned the date from November of last year—over six months ago. He closed his eyes and took a deep, painful breath. When he began reading again, he couldn't keep his hands from shaking. There was no denying it. He missed his family and had since the day he'd arrived in Chicago.

Flynn had sent a few letters directly to the police station a couple of times after Bliss had told the family about their life in Chicago. But he hadn't known what to say in reply to his brother's letters and so hadn't responded at all. What was the use in communicating with family? He wouldn't be able to return to South Park and see them again. Not with the death warrant hanging over his head for unpaid gambling debts.

Dylan focused on the words penned on the paper telling of Bliss and Ivy getting married on his first night back, Ivy's small ranch, and her venture in raising sheep. Bliss was still working for Pinkerton and searching for outlaws, but his traveling didn't take him far from home for long.

Dylan's muscles tightened. When was the bad news coming? It was just a matter of time before it would. Bliss probably saved it for the end of the letter.

His attention skipped to the final paragraph. *"Ivy and I both agreed on what to do with the reward money. We took the gold to Bat and paid off your gambling debts and ended the death warrant. That means you're free. You can come back to Colorado. We want you to come home. Everyone does. . . ."*

Dylan's pulse tapered to a halt. Ivy and Bliss had paid off his gambling debt to Bat and his gang? The amount had been inordinate, too much for a working man to ever repay honestly. He'd long ago given up hope that he'd be free of the debt. But he vaguely remembered Bliss's tale of finding stolen gold last year with Ivy. Apparently, they'd been rewarded for returning the treasure.

And they'd used their reward to help a scoundrel like him.

Hot tears stung the backs of his eyes. He lowered himself into his chair. Why would they use the gold on him? He didn't deserve a single nugget. Not after the way he'd lived. Not after the mistakes he'd made. Not after the trouble he'd brought to his family. Not after the angry way he'd parted with Bliss, making all kinds of accusations against his friend.

Surely Ivy and Bliss needed the gold to build up Ivy's ranch and purchase sheep. They could use it to invest in more land. They didn't have to erase a debt he'd brought upon himself by his own foolishness and stupidity. He never should have been gambling in the first place. Or drinking.

He read the last paragraph again. *We want you to come home. Everyone does.* They'd not only paid off the money he owed, but they were inviting him to come home.

His throat pinched, and tears clouded his vision.

Home. Was it really possible he could return? Without the debt and the death warrant, nothing was stopping him. He would be free. *Free.* For the first time in years.

Dylan dropped his head and let the tears flow. Hot moisture dripped onto his palms. Ivy and Bliss were forgiving him and giving him a new chance at life. What if that was what God was offering him too? The opportunity to accept His forgiveness and move forward with a new life?

A tremor shimmied through Dylan. He wasn't worthy of a second chance from his family or from God. But what if he accepted this gift? What if he left today and never looked back at his old life? What if he allowed God to work in him to clean him up and change him? Was that even possible?

Even as doubts assailed him, Dylan knew deep in his bones that he could do nothing less than give it a try. He was so tired of living in misery and being such a failure. He wanted to become the kind of man who would make his family proud. Maybe he'd never been able to live up to his brothers' reputations. But somehow, now, with this gift of God's grace and mercy, Dylan wanted to try—really try—to live rightly before God and man.

He sucked in a deep breath, wiped his eyes, and smiled.

He was finally going home.

Jody Hedlund is the bestselling author of over thirty historicals for both adults and teens and is the winner of numerous awards including the Christy, Carol, and Christian Book Award. Mother of five, she lives in central Michigan with her husband and busy family. Visit her at jodyhedlund.com.

Sign Up for Jody's Newsletter

Keep up to date with Jody's news on book releases and events by signing up for her email list at jodyhedlund.com.

More from Jody Hedlund

While Brody McQuaid's body survived the war, his soul did not. He finds his purpose saving wild horses from ranchers intent on killing them. Veterinarian Savannah Marshall joins Brody in rescuing the wild creatures, but when her family and the ranchers catch up with them both, they will have to tame their fears if they have any hope of letting love run free.

To Tame a Cowboy
Colorado Cowboys #3

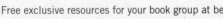

You May Also Like . . .

Traveling the Santa Fe Trail on a botanical exploration, Linnea Newberry longs to be taken seriously by the other members of the expedition. When she is rescued from an accident by Flynn McQuaid, her grandfather hires him to act as Linnea's bodyguard, and Flynn soon finds himself in the greatest danger of all—falling for a woman he's determined not to love.

The Heart of a Cowboy by Jody Hedlund
COLORADO COWBOYS #2
jodyhedlund.com

On a trip west to save her ailing sister, Greta Nilsson is robbed, leaving her homeless and penniless. Wyatt McQuaid is struggling to get his new ranch running, so the mayor offers him a bargain: He will invest in a herd of cattle if Wyatt agrees to help the town become more respectable by marrying . . . and the mayor has the perfect woman in mind.

A Cowboy for Keeps by Jody Hedlund
COLORADO COWBOYS #1
jodyhedlund.com

After the disappearance of her father and sister, Ellen Creighton wants nothing to do with the holy water they were seeking, even if it would cure her deadly genetic disease—until a friend helps her recognize its true power in this suspenseful, time-crossing romantic adventure.

Never Leave Me by Jody Hedlund
WATERS OF TIME #2
jodyhedlund.com

BETHANYHOUSE

More from Bethany House

Scientist Marian Creighton is skeptical of her father's lifelong research of ancient holy water—until she ingests some of it and finds herself transported back to the Middle Ages. With the help of an emotionally wounded nobleman, can she make her way back home? Or will she be trapped in the past forever?

Come Back to Me by Jody Hedlund
WATERS OF TIME #1
jodyhedlund.com

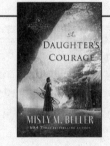

Charlotte Durand sets out on an expedition in search of a skilled artisan who can repair a treasured chalice—but her hike becomes much more daunting when a treacherous snowstorm sets in. When Damien Levette finds Charlotte stranded, they must work together to survive the peril of the mountains against all odds.

A Daughter's Courage by Misty M. Beller
BRIDES OF LAURENT #3
mistymbeller.com

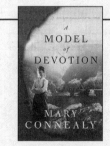

A brilliant engineer, Jilly Stiles sets her focus on fulfilling her dream of building a mountaintop railroad—and remaining independent. But when a cruel and powerful man goes to dangerous lengths to try to make Jilly his own, marrying her friend Nick may be the only way to save herself and her dreams.

A Model of Devotion by Mary Connealy
THE LUMBER BARON'S DAUGHTERS #3
maryconnealy.com

BETHANYHOUSE